LOST IN A KISS

Cade took the dress from Tess's hands and set it on the trunk. "You know what I've been thinking, Tess?" he said quietly. "I've been thinking that I made a mistake when we were kids," he murmured, his palms sweeping across her shoulders and down her arms until their hands were linked. "And I'm not going to make another one. This time around, I'm not going to miss what's right in front of my face."

"Cade—"

He brushed her lips with a kiss so light she barely felt it, but her heart thundered, her pulse racing so fast, she felt breathless.

"I'll stop if you want me to," he murmured, but she didn't want him to, and she dragged his head down for a kiss that she hoped would leave him as breathless as she was . . .

BOOK YOUR PLACE ON OUR WEBSITE
AND MAKE THE
READING CONNECTION!

We've created a customized website just for our very
special readers, where you can get the inside scoop on
everything that's going on with Zebra, Pinnacle and
Kensington books.

When you come online, you'll have the exciting
opportunity to:

• View covers of upcoming books

• Read sample chapters

• Learn about our future publishing schedule
  (listed by publication month and author)

• Find out when your favorite authors will be visiting
  a city near you

• Search for and order backlist books from our
  online catalog

• Check out author bios and background information

• Send e-mail to your favorite authors

• Meet the Kensington staff online

• Join us in weekly chats with authors, readers and
  other guests

• Get writing guidelines

• AND MUCH MORE!

Visit our website at
http://www.kensingtonbooks.com

THE HOUSE
ON MAIN STREET

SHIRLEE
McCOY

ZEBRA BOOKS
KENSINGTON PUBLISHING CORP.
http://www.kensingtonbooks.com

ZEBRA BOOKS are published by

Kensington Publishing Corp.
119 West 40th Street
New York, NY 10018

All Kensington titles, imprints, and distributed lines are
available at special quantity discounts for bulk purchases
for sales promotion, premiums, fund-raising, educational,
or institutional use.

Special book excerpts or customized printings can also
be created to fit specific needs. For details, write or
phone the office of the Kensington Special Sales Man-
ager: Attn.: Special Sales Department. Kensington Publishing Corp., 119 West 40th Street, New York, NY 10018.
Phone: 1-800-221-2647.

Zebra and the Z logo Reg. U.S. Pat. & TM Off.

ISBN-13: 978-1-4201-3235-9
ISBN-10: 1-4201-3235-0
First Printing: November 2013

eISBN-13: 978-1-4201-3236-6
eISBN-10: 1-4201-3236-9
First Electronic Edition: November 2013

10 9 8 7 6 5 4 3 2 1

Printed in the United States of America

Chapter One

Some days are just meant to be crappy. Obviously, this *is one of them.*

Tess McKenzie grabbed a pile of wrinkled magazines from a dusty shelf and tossed them in a garbage bag. Three weeks before Christmas and this was how she was spending her time. Not strolling through the mall or window-shopping in downtown Annapolis, but standing in an old house in Apple Valley, Washington, sorting through her sister's collection of trash and fighting back tears.

She hated crying.

She hated *this*.

Emily gone. Dave gone.

Life completely turned upside down.

"Are you planning to throw everything away?" Aunt Gertrude griped. Perched on a rickety stool a couple of feet away, a cigarette dangling from between her fingers and a Santa hat on her head, she looked like an ancient Christmas elf with an attitude.

Tess lifted an ugly porcelain dog with a crack

down its middle and dropped it into the bag. "If it's all as junky as this, yes."

"One man's trash is another man's treasure," Gertrude said, taking a puff of the cigarette and blowing smoke into the musty air.

"Sometimes it's just another man's trash."

"Emily and Dave did the best they could with what they had. You just tossing it all away is a travesty. They deserve more than that." At seventy-two, Gertrude had lived enough life to say what she liked and what she didn't, and she didn't like Tess's plans to clean the place out and sell it.

Tough.

It had to be done.

If the massive pile of outstanding bills Tessa had found in her sister's desk drawer was any indication, it should have *been* done eons ago.

She didn't say that to Gertrude, because she'd said it a thousand times since the funeral. Set in her ways and stubborn as old Ms. Peach's mule, Gertie refused to see reason. She wanted life to go on the way it had been. Same crumbling Victorian house. Same little junk shop on its lower level. Same town. But things had changed, and changed in a big way. There was nothing either of them could do about that.

"Are you planning to wear that hat all day?" Tess changed the subject.

"It's tradition. The kids love it."

"What kids? We haven't had a customer all day."

"We will. This time of year, we always get kids looking for stuff to buy for their moms and grandmas for Christmas. Emily hung all the best ornaments, just like she does every year." She gestured to the Christmas tree that stood in the corner of the room, its synthetic branches bowed under a hodgepodge of grimy Christmas decorations. "It looks dang pretty, if you ask me. But you won't."

"I never need to ask. You're always more than willing to share your opinion," Tess muttered, her throat tight. She could picture her sister standing near the tree, completely ignoring the mess and clutter of the room as she hung those ornaments. That's the way Emily had been. Eager to see what she wanted to see rather than what she needed to.

"Humph." Gertrude puffed on her cigarette again. "That's like the pot calling the kettle black."

"You're right," Tess agreed. She was trying, really *really* trying to be reasonable, but dealing with Gertrude wasn't easy. "The tree is . . . nice," she lied. "We just need to clean the ornaments."

"Why? They're clean enough."

"To hang in this shop? Sure. To sell? Not even close."

"Whatever you say, Tessa Louise."

"Anyone with eyes in her head would say the same. The whole place is a junk pit. I don't know what Emily and Dave were thinking." There. She'd said what she was really thinking, and she didn't regret it. Much.

She carried the trash bag into the foyer, the hard, hot lump in her throat nearly choking her.

This was hard.

Harder than she'd thought it would be.

In for the funeral and back home. That's what she'd planned, but Emily and Dave had left the house to her.

The house and Alex.

She blinked back tears as she opened the front

door. Cold air streamed in, the crisp, hard bite of winter cooling her hot cheeks. Sunlight dappled the wide front porch and fell on the piles of garbage bags she'd already thrown there. She tossed the new one on top.

Her arms ached, her back hurt, and her heart?

It throbbed hot with a sickening mix of grief and anxiety.

She should be in downtown Annapolis making the presentation she'd been preparing for two months. Ten apartments designed for comfort and ease of living, no expense spared on materials. Everything top-notch and high-end. She'd slaved over the presentation because winning the contract would have brought her a step closer to becoming a partner in Master's Design Incorporated. Something she'd wanted from the day she'd joined the interior design firm seven years ago. She wouldn't get there now. Not with her boss stepping in and making the presentation. Not when she wasn't sure how long she'd be in Apple Valley, or how soon she'd be back at work.

"Close the door. You're letting all the warm air out," Gertrude called from the bowels of the house. Probably still perched on the stool, smoking that damn cigarette.

"What warm air? This place is freezing." Tess walked back inside and grabbed a new trash bag, ignoring Gertrude's narrow-eyed glare as she shoved an armful of stained-beyond-salvation linen napkins and something that looked like an overcoat and smelled like sweat and urine into the bag.

Where had Emily and Dave gotten this stuff?

The dump?

A glossy ceramic clown lay on the floor, its cracked and smiling face mocking her. She tossed it in with the rest of the garbage.

"Hey! I liked that clown." Gertrude finally managed to move her skinny behind from the stool.

"It's broken."

"Barely. All it needs is a little glue." Gertrude pulled the clown out of the bag, frowning at its cracked head.

"All it needs is a decent burial."

"I'll fix it tonight and add it to my collection." Gertie completely ignored her.

"Your room is already filled with more trash than the Apple Valley dump. You need to clean it out. Not add more to it."

"There's no reason for me to clean anything out."

"The house will sell more quickly if—"

"I don't want it to sell."

"Do you have to be so difficult, Gert?" Tess snagged the clown from her aunt's hand and shoved it deep into the bag.

"Who's being difficult depends on which side of the argument you're on," Gertrude responded sagely, wiggling her drawn-on eyebrows, the Santa hat bobbing on her orange hair.

Tess gave up.

Facts were facts. A huge Victorian on three prime acres in the middle of town was money in the bank. Which was a whole lot better than junk on shelves.

She shoved an armload of *Reader's Digest* magazines into the bag, her fingers nearly numb with cold. She needed to buy gloves, a hat, maybe a scarf. Things she had at home but hadn't had the presence of mind to pack.

"Did you hear me, girl? I don't want to sell this place."

"Yeah. I heard you, Gertie. I've heard you every single one of the five million times you've said it," Tessa muttered as she dragged the overstuffed bag out the front door.

Out with the bad. In with the good.

Bull crap.

There was no good in this situation.

Just a truckload of bad and a porch so burdened by bags of garbage it might collapse at any moment.

She tossed the bag into the yard, enjoying the satisfying crack and thud as it hit sparse dry grass.

"You pick that bag up. You pick it up! Hear me?" a skinny little man called from the yard next door, his white hair standing up in a halo around his wrinkled face.

She wanted to ignore him. She really did. "I'll have everything out of the yard by the end of the month, Mr—?"

"Beck. Zimmerman Beck, and the end of the month isn't good enough. You think I want to look out my front door and see a dump every morning for the next three weeks?"

"You don't want to see it, just don't look out your door, old man!" Gertrude chose that moment to step outside, an old blanket around her shoulders, the Santa hat flopping to the left side of her head.

"I'm two years younger than you, Gertrude, so if I'm old, you're ancient and looking every minute of it."

"Why, you—"

"Mr. Beck, I assure you, I'll have this mess cleaned

up as soon as humanly possible." Tess stepped in front of Gertrude, half-near tempted to toss a bag over her aunt's head and throw her out with the rest of the trash.

"Not good enough," Beck said, his hands on his hips, his body vibrating with the force of his indignation.

"It's going to have to be." She bit back a sharper reply. No sense arguing with the guy. She'd do what she could as quickly as she could because she wanted out of Apple Valley just as desperately as Zimmerman Beck wanted the yard cleaned up.

"You can tell that to the sheriff. I've already called him, and he'll tell *you* that there are bylaws. *Bylaws.*"

"You called the sheriff?" she said, her heart rate upping a notch or two.

The sheriff? was what she wanted to say.

As in Cade Cunningham?

The one man she absolutely did not want to see, no matter how long she had to stay in Apple Valley?

"Be glad I didn't call the health department. Place is a dump. Has been a dump for too many years to count."

"I'll show you a dump, you little weasel." Gertrude moved surprisingly fast for a woman in the eighth decade of her life, down the porch steps and across the yard, the blanket flying behind her like a cape.

"Calm down, Gertrude." Tess snagged her arm, pulling her up short before she could jump the rickety white picket fence between the yards.

"Not until I teach this horse's behind a lesson in manners."

"I'd like to see you try, you old battle-ax!" Zim hollered, his face mottled purple with rage.

Dear God! Was the guy going to have a heart attack while he stood at the edge of their bedraggled yard?

"How about you both just calm down?" Tess stepped between the two as a woman walked out of the bungalow across the street.

Wonderful.

Having her sister and brother-in-law die hadn't been sucky enough. Being left a junk-pit in the middle of a town she'd sworn she'd never come back to hadn't been enough punishment for whatever wrongs she'd done. She was now going to have to stop a street brawl between two septuagenarians while the neighbor watched.

"Zim! I've been calling your house for a half hour," the woman called as she crossed the street. Pretty, with raven hair and deep circles beneath her dark eyes, she didn't fit the demographics of the neighborhood: Over fifty. Retired. *Nosy.*

"I've been hanging lights. Trying to get into the Christmas spirit. Tough to do when I'm living next door to a dump," Zim griped.

"Does that mean you're too busy to eat some of the gingerbread I just took out of the oven?" The woman ignored Zim's comment about the dump, which put her right at the top of Tess's favorite-person list for the day.

"Gingerbread, huh?"

"Yes. Homemade whipped cream, too," she said as she met Tessa's eyes. "I'm Charlotte Garrison. Charlie to my friends."

"Charlie. Humph! A boy's name," Zim muttered, but his anger had fizzled out, his face pasty white once again.

"Tess McKenzie." Tess offered her hand. "Sorry about the mess. As I told Mr. Beck—"

"There's no need to explain. Your family is going through a lot right now. We understand that. Don't we, Zim?" she asked.

Beck had the decency to blush. "Now, I never said I didn't have sympathy for their loss."

"At times like this, it's good to extend a little grace," Charlotte continued. "If you need any help cleaning things up, Tess, just give me a call. You have my number, don't you, Gertrude?"

"You know I do," Gertrude snapped, but even she had lost her steam, her hat wilted, the blanket limp around her shoulders.

"Why don't you two take a break from your work, too? Maybe after Alex gets home? We can have hot chocolate and gingerbread together."

Alex.

The mention of her nephew made Tessa's heart trip and her stomach churn. The house was easy. Start in one room, work her way through until it was empty. Alex she had no plan for, no idea how to begin connecting with him.

Just thinking about it made her head ache and her chest hurt. She cleared her throat, trying to remove the giant-sized lump suddenly lodged in it. "Maybe another day. I have a lot to do, and—"

"You don't have to explain. I understand." Charlotte smiled, hooked her elbow through Zim's. "Come on. Let's go inside before we turn to icicles," she said, leading him away from the fence.

"Hope she mixed some arsenic in that whipped cream," Gertie said, loudly enough to scare a couple of starlings out of the old pine tree at the edge of the yard.

"Shhhhh! Do you want to start the feud all over again?"

"As a matter of fact, I do. Zimmerman Beck is a pain in the ass. A little arsenic in his afternoon snack will make the world a better place."

"Will you please just *shut up*, Gertie!" Tess hissed, as Zim paused at Charlotte's door and shot a hot glare in their direction. Charlotte nudged him inside, offering a quick wave as she closed the door.

Crisis averted.

Thank God.

"*Shut up?* Is that what you just said to me? I raised you from the time you were knee-high to a peanut, and you're talking to me like that?"

"If you're going to act like a spoiled child, I'm going to speak to you like you're one."

"Let me tell you something, little miss. Zimmerman Beck has been hounding us for months, trying to get Emily and Dave to close down and sell this place. The man is a wretched old fart with no sense of humor and an ice-cold heart. So, when it comes to him, I'll say what I want, when I want, how I want, and you'll just have to deal with it!"

Gertrude turned on the heels of her sturdy white sneakers and stalked back in the house, slamming the door for good measure. The mound of garbage bags on the porch listed and fell, spilling trash onto packed earth and brown grass.

The crappy day just kept getting better.

Tess dragged one of the bags from the porch and started refilling it, absolutely refusing the tears that burned behind her eyes. They wouldn't bring Emily back and wouldn't clean up the mess that she'd left.

A cold breeze tickled the leaves that still clung to an ancient birch in the center of the yard and pushed an old swing that hung from one of its thick branches. Rusted metal chains creaked, and for a moment, Tessa was sure she heard her sister's laughter drifting on the air.

Emily.

Always happy and laughing and carefree.

Gone.

It didn't seem possible. Shouldn't *be* possible.

Tess cinched the bag and set it against the side of the house, the rumble of a car engine breaking the afternoon silence.

Please, don't let it be Cade. Please, don't let it be him. Please . . .

A black-and-white cruiser pulled up to the curb, SHERIFF emblazoned on the side.

It was Cade. Of course. Because that was the way her day had been going.

He got out of the car, all lithe hard muscle and re-strained power. Ten years hadn't put any paunch on his gut, taken any fullness from his dark brown hair. Hadn't done one thing to make him less attractive.

He met her eyes across the hood of his car.

"Tess," he said.

Just that, and she was back thirteen years, hoping and praying and wishing that he'd invite her to his senior prom. He'd invited Emily, of course. A year older than Tess, a year younger than Cade, and the most beautiful girl at Apple Valley High. There'd never been any doubt that the best-looking guy in school would ask the best-looking girl. Tessa had still dreamed, though, because she'd been just young enough and foolish enough to believe that dreaming could make something true.

She smiled, extended a hand, proud and relieved that it wasn't shaking. "Cade. It's been a long time."

"It sure has." He dragged her into his arms.

His shoulders had filled out.

His chest had broadened.

And his thighs . . .

Man! His thighs!

They were like rocks. Only warmer, and a heck of a lot sexier.

"I've missed you, Tess," he murmured against her hair, and she felt the warmth of his breath trickling down her spine and straight into a place she'd locked up tight. There was nothing she could do about that, but she *could* sound as cool and unruffled as she wanted to feel.

This was Cade, after all. Her best childhood friend a*nd* her deepest adolescent crush. She knew how to put on an act when she was around him. She'd perfected it during the years he'd dated Emily.

"I guess you're here about the mess," she said. Cool as a cucumber. Absolutely unruffled.

"Your neighbor called. He thinks the house and property are eyesores. I can't say I disagree." He glanced at the house, shoved his hands into his coat pockets. His hair was just a little long, the ends brushing his collar. Soft looking. The kind of hair a woman would love to run her fingers through.

She noticed, because she was a woman. *Not* because she still harbored feelings for the guy.

"I already assured Mr. Beck that I'd get the place

cleaned up as soon as possible. Things have been . . . difficult."

"I know. I'm not going to issue you a citation or a warning. But Zim called in the complaint, and I had to honor that. Besides, I wanted to see how your family was holding up."

"We're fine."

"You sure?" He touched her hand, his fingers skimming along her knuckles. He'd done the same thing a hundred times when they were kids, but they weren't kids anymore. There were ten years between what used to be and what was, and she didn't want either of them to forget it.

"Yes." She stepped over a dried-out rosebush, desperate for a little space. "Thanks for stopping by, Cade. I need to get back to work."

"You need a place to put all that garbage. I have a pickup. I can come by tonight, throw everything in the back, and drive it to the dump tomorrow morning."

"That's not—"

"A bad idea," Gertrude called out from the front doorway. "Why don't you come by for dinner? I'm making pot roast. After you eat, you'll have plenty of energy for the job."

"No need to bribe me. I already offered to help." Cade grinned, flashing his dimple. The one that had always made Tessa's heart sigh.

"It's not a bribe. It's dinner. Unless you have other plans?" Gertrude sashayed onto the porch, the Santa hat still on her head, glossy red lipstick smeared across her mouth. She must have primped before making her appearance. Cade had that effect on women.

"None that I can't change for you, Gertrude," Cade drawled, and Tess wanted to smack him.

"You always were a flirt, Cade." Gertrude returned his smile. "Come here. Give me a hug, damn it!" she barked, opening her arms.

He walked right into them. Not even a second of hesitation. That's the way it had always been between him and Gertrude.

"Sorry that I couldn't be at the funeral, Gert. By the time I got word of the accident, it was too late."

"I know you would have been here if you could have." Gertrude kept an arm around Cade's waist. "Your grandmother said you were in Japan, training search-and-rescue teams. Not my idea of a vacation. If I had two weeks off, I'd be in Hawaii."

"I enjoyed it. I'm glad to be back, though." His dark blue gaze settled on Tessa again. Fine lines radiated from the corners of his eyes, hinting at passing time and dusty dreams. Tessa's throat tightened with memories she'd shoved so far down, she'd thought they'd never find their way up again.

"Well, the town is happy to have you back. That deputy sheriff of yours is okay, but he's not you. Come on inside. I have something for you." Gertrude tugged him up the porch steps and into the house.

Next thing Tessa knew, she was standing in the sparse and dried-out yard alone.

No more Cade.

No more Gertrude.

Just the pile of trash that Emily had left her and the hard, hot lump in her throat.

Across the street, Charlotte's front door opened, and Zimmerman walked outside, his white hair smoothed down, a road map of wrinkles lining his aged face. He caught sight of Tessa and stopped short, scowling in her direction.

"Get that junk cleaned up, girl. 'Cause I'm getting tired of looking at it," he called.

Tessa offered a smile and a quick wave, then walked toward Emily and Dave's old Victorian, leaving every bit of *junk* exactly where it was.

Chapter Two

Cade picked his way through the cluttered parlor of the old Riley house, following Gertrude into what used to be a large dining room. Now it was so stuffed with dusty junk that it should have burst at the seams years ago. This-N-That Antiques is what Emily and Dave had called the place. Public Dump would have been more appropriate.

The front door opened and closed.

Tessa. Deep red hair. Freckles. Violet eyes. Cade had been shocked at her beauty, surprised at how happy he'd been to see her again.

Footsteps sounded on the stairs that led to the upstairs apartment. Floorboards creaked. A door closed.

Apparently, Tess wasn't quite as happy to see him.

"Hold on just a minute, Cade. I have to get this door open." Gertrude grunted as she shoved a few dusty items to the side and wrestled with the pocket doors that closed off the antique shop portion of the house from the old kitchen.

"Need some help?" He reached over her Santa hat and shoved the doors apart. The room beyond smelled like mildew and dust, the dank air heavy and still. Like every other room in the house, the old kitchen was filled to overflowing.

"Must have been awhile since you've been in here, Gertrude."

"Dave was planning to clean it out, make it a working kitchen again. We were thinking of selling coffee and cookies. Little stuff like that, you know?" Gertrude sidled past an old pinewood table and skirted by a stack of cast-iron pans. "Too bad he never got around to it. It would have made us a little money to fix this place up."

"Yeah. Too bad," Cade responded, hoping she couldn't hear the sarcasm in his voice. Dave Riley had had a million plans. What he hadn't had was the ability to work hard enough to make a go of them.

"You standing in judgment of the dead?" Gertrude asked, her sharp green eyes narrowed.

"Just agreeing with you."

"Right." She turned away, her bright red Santa's hat sliding backward as she walked to an old china cabinet. A layer of grime coated the wood, and Gertrude swiped a hand over the dusty glass. "Should be in here."

"What?" Cade glanced at his watch. His first day back at work since his training trip to Japan, and he had a lot to catch up on. Even in a town the size of Apple Valley, crime happened. Stolen livestock. Missing pets. The occasional drunk and disorderly or domestic violence call. Not big-city stuff, but enough to keep busy.

"Miriam's angel." Gertrude opened the cabinet door and pulled out a small angel. "Here it is." She held it up triumphantly.

Maybe six inches tall, its hands cupped around a red heart, face serene and eyes closed, the angel sported a layer of dust that couldn't hide its beauty.

"It's nice."

"Nice? It's more than that. It's *history*. Made by Miriam Riley herself and finished on Christmas Eve, the very night she passed away. You bring this to your grandma Ida and tell her it should be displayed in the town hall."

She thrust the figure toward him, and he took it, the ceramic oddly warm in his hands. The angel's face was crackled, the white glaze yellowed from age. It *looked* old enough to have been made by the first mayor of Apple Valley's wife, that's for sure.

"Are you sure you want to donate this, Gertrude?"

"As sure as I am about anything right now."

"Why don't you wait, then? See if you still want to donate it in a few weeks?" He tried to hand the angel back, but she shook her head, nearly knocking the Santa hat from her bright orange hair.

"If Tess has her way, we won't be here in a few weeks. You'd better take it now before she tosses it into one of those damn trash bags."

"If it's trash, that's where it should be." Tessa appeared on the threshold of the kitchen, her face pale, her odd-colored eyes deeply shadowed. She'd thrown on an oversized gray sweater—a guy's sweater, unless Cade missed his guess—and it fell right to the middle of her long, lean thighs, skimming over slender curves that he didn't remember her having when they were kids.

"See?" Gertrude spit out, jabbing her finger in Tessa's direction. "She's like a one-man trash removal army."

"If the place wasn't such a dump—"

"It's not a dump!" Gertrude cut Tess off. "It's an antique store. It's supposed to have antiques in it. You take the angel to Ida, Cade. I'm sure she'll appreciate it more than my niece does."

Ida *would* appreciate it. As mayor of Apple Valley and president of the town's historical society, Cade's grandmother appreciated everything that had to do with Apple Valley's past. "I'll bring it to her. You know where to find it, though, if you change your mind."

"I won't unless Tess does. I don't know what I did wrong while I was raising her that she can't be content to stay here where she belongs. But, *no*, she's got to move all the way across the country, and now she wants to take me and Alex with her," Gertrude griped.

"I'm standing right here, Gertrude." Tessa rubbed her forehead, her fingers long, the nails short and unpainted. Last Cade had heard, she worked for some fancy interior design firm on the East Coast. A small-town girl who'd made good. That's what people said when they talked about Tess. Which they did. People in Apple Valley talked about everyone.

"And I'm ignoring you," Gertrude retorted. "Wait right here, Cade. I'll get something to wrap the angel in."

Gertrude stomped from the room, her orange hair nearly vibrating with indignation.

Obviously, she and Tess were back to their old habits. Arguing. Fighting. Butting heads. Nothing new there. They'd done the same almost every day for as long as Tessa had lived in Apple Valley.

Tess didn't look like she was up to the fight. There

were dark circles under her eyes and the freckles that dotted her cheeks and nose were the only color on her face. She'd lost her sister, inherited Emily and Dave's mess of a house, and, if rumors were true, she'd become guardian to Alex. Any one of those things would be a lot to deal with. All of them together . . .

Cade wasn't surprised that she looked like she was struggling.

"Gertrude is a piece of work." Tess sighed, offering a half smile.

"Want me to talk to her?" he asked, touching her arm like he had a million times before. *This* time, heat shot through him. He wasn't sure what to do with that.

This was *Tess*, after all.

His friend. His buddy.

Not someone that he would ever have imagined feeling more than friendship and affection for.

"We'll work it out, but thanks." She ran a hand over the old table, frowning at the dirt on her palm. "I really need to get back to work. I have a lot to do."

"I'll be back this evening to help out. In the meantime, don't work too hard."

"You don't have to—"

"We're friends, Tess, and you've just lost part of your family."

"We *were* friends. That was a long time ago."

True, but with Tessa standing just a few feet away, it didn't feel like a long time. It felt like yesterday.

Gertrude burst back into the room, waving a white box and several sheets of colored tissue paper. "Let's pack that angel up and get you out of here!"

She worked quickly, wrapping the angel in paper and then setting it in the box.

Cade took it. "Thanks. I know Ida will appreciate the donation."

"No need for thanks. Just tell her to make sure it's taken good care of. Come on, I'll walk you out."

Gertrude grabbed his arm, and he let her pull him from the room. He had work to do. Plenty of it. But there was a part of him that was tempted to stay. Just to spend a few more minutes talking to Tessa. Somewhere beneath the beautiful woman was the tomboy he used to hang out with. Once he found her, there'd be no spark, no quicksilver fire racing through his blood.

"We'll be expecting you at six thirty. Don't forget," Gertrude called as he picked his way across the cluttered yard.

"I'm not one to forget a home-cooked meal, Gertrude," he responded, and she laughed, closing the door as he reached his cruiser.

Silence settled deep, the neighbors going about their business the way they had for more decades than Cade had been alive—quietly and without any fuss or muss. Charlotte Garrison was the only young person on the street. A transplant from the East Coast who'd inherited her grandmother's house, she'd come to town with nothing but an old Chevy station wagon, a suitcase, and an air of mystery that seemed to feed the town gossips.

He glanced at her bungalow as he set the angel in the cruiser. She waved from the window, holding a hand up for him to wait.

Too bad they hadn't quite clicked.

She hadn't seemed to mind his hectic schedule

the way Darla had. Then again, Cade and Charlotte had only been out twice. He and Darla had been married for six years. More than enough time for her to find things to complain about.

He met Charlotte halfway across her yard and stood under the barren branches of a giant birch, watching her hips sway as she walked toward him. She'd lost weight, her gorgeous curves hidden beneath too-baggy jeans, a sweatshirt, and an apron.

"What's up, Charlie?"

"Thought you might like some gingerbread." She held up a tinfoil-wrapped loaf, and he could smell the spicy sweetness of the cake.

"Did you keep any for yourself?" he asked, worried about her pallor and the way her clothes hung. They might not have hit it off romantically, but they'd become friends, and that counted for a lot in Cade's book.

"Enough to feed an army." She handed him the loaf.

"Does that mean you ate some?"

"You need to stop worrying about my eating habits, Cade." She smiled and patted his cheek, her palm cool and dry and just rough enough to let him know she worked hard.

"You lose any more weight and a stiff wind will blow you away."

"I don't think there's any worry about that," she said, glancing away the same way she did every time they got close to something personal. "Looks like they're cleaning things out over at This-N-That Antiques."

"Looks that way."

"Zim isn't happy about the mess." She brushed

thick dark hair from her forehead, revealing the scar at her temple. He'd asked her about it once, but she hadn't had much to say. An accident when she was a kid. Must have been some accident. The scar was thick and ragged, disappearing into her dark hair.

"Is Zim ever happy about anything?"

"You've got a point there. I don't think I've seen the man smile more than a dozen times in the seven months that I've been in town."

"A dozen smiles is more than most of us have seen from Zim in a lifetime. Guess he's got a soft spot for you."

"Only because I feed him," Charlotte said with a smile.

"So that's the key to making Zim happy, huh? I'll have to spread the word. Did you hear the fight going on over at the Rileys' a little while ago?"

"How could I not? Zim and Gertrude were going at it like alley cats. Tessa looked like she wanted to kill them both."

"She has a lot on her plate," he said, jumping to Tessa's defense, the knee-jerk response as familiar as sunrise.

"That's for sure. I heard she's planning on selling the property."

"It sounds that way."

"It'll be a shame if she does, don't you think? There's still a Riley in town. It seems like the house should always belong to one of them."

"Tess inherited the house. It's her decision to make." Though he had to admit, it did seem strange to think of the place belonging to someone who wasn't related to the first mayor of Apple Valley. The Rileys were legends in town, and seeing the house belong to another family would be like seeing an era end.

"You're right, but I'm still hoping she doesn't sell. I'd better get back inside. I'm making tea for the women's social club tomorrow. Three different kinds of finger sandwiches and two different kinds of scones."

"Makes me wish I was a woman."

"There are a lot of single women in town who would be devastated if you were." She blew a kiss and walked off.

He couldn't fault himself for watching her go. She'd lost weight, but she still had curves, and he was a man who appreciated them.

A short yellow school bus rumbled down the road and pulled up behind Cade's cruiser. He waited, watching as the door opened. Seconds later, Alex Riley appeared, skinny shoulders hunched, head bobbing to some silent tune.

Poor little Alex Riley. That's what the blue-haired ladies at the diner always whispered when the Riley family walked in for the Friday-night special. They'd be whispering more now that Alex had lost both his parents.

"Hey, Alex. How's it going, buddy?" Cade asked.

Alex shuffled past, humming under his breath, his hair golden red, his eyes the same clear blue as his mother's had been.

"Home," Alex whispered as he opened the gate and walked into the neglected yard. If Alex were his son, Cade would have walked with him, put a hand on his shoulder, led him up the crumbling cement walk to the overburdened front porch.

The thought wasn't as bitter as it used to be.

Cade waited until the bus pulled away, then climbed into his cruiser and headed back to the station, the box with Miriam's angel gleaming white on the passenger seat.

Tessa stepped away from the window as Cade's car disappeared from view. Thank God, he hadn't seen her when she'd ducked behind the dusty drapes. Not that she'd been standing in the window watching him talk to Charlotte. She'd been waiting for Alex's school bus. It just so happened that Cade and Charlotte had been right in her line of sight. It also just so happened that she hadn't turned away when she'd realized that they were.

"You're an idiot, Tess," she hissed as the front door opened and closed and footsteps tapped on wood stairs.

Alex. Going straight to his room just like he had every day for the past week.

Her heart thudded painfully as she opened a trash bag, grabbed a bunch of old clothes from a decorative box, and threw them away.

"You going up there to check on him?" Gertrude asked, perched on the stool again and tapping a cigarette on her scrawny thigh.

"Don't smoke in the house, Gertie. It's bad for Alex." Tess ignored the question, because she didn't *want* to go upstairs and she didn't feel right *not* going.

Gertie frowned at the cigarette as if it had jumped into her hand and was about to light itself. "You know, up until last week I hadn't had a cigarette since he was born."

"Smoking isn't going to bring Emily back."

"Neither is avoiding Alex. Are you going up there or not?"

"He's happier by himself."

"You wouldn't be saying that if you'd spent any time around him."

"I've spent every Christmas of his life with him."

"So, what's that? A hundred hours in ten years? You want the 'Aunt of the Year' award for that?" She broke the cigarette in half and tossed it out the door.

"What I want is my life back."

"I bet Emily does, too. Bet Dave does. At least you're alive and breathing. I've got to get out of here. I've got a hair appointment with Adele in ten minutes. If I'm late, she won't be happy. See you in an hour."

"But—"

Too late.

The front door closed. The house fell silent. She was alone with her nephew, and she had no idea what to do about it. She loved Alex. She *did*. Had loved him from the moment she'd seen his fuzzy reddish hair and startling blue eyes. *Emily's eyes.* Tess would give anything to look in them one more time.

Music flowed from the upstairs apartment, the sound like a thousand raindrops falling on tender new grass. Soft and sweet and heartbreaking. Tess followed it through the dingy overstuffed store and up the stairs into the apartment.

This, Emily had done right. Large bright rooms and dark woodwork. The integrity of the Victorian maintained in patterned wood floors and Queen Anne furniture. Nothing fussy or cluttered or overdone. A large kitchen and living room had been carved out of several small rooms, and a wide hall led to the apartment's bedrooms.

Alex's door was closed.

Tess could take it as a sign that he wanted to be left alone.

That's what she *wanted* to do, but Alex was Tessa's responsibility, and she could hear his heartbreak in the song that poured from his room.

She knocked.

Waited a minute and opened the door.

Music swirled around her, sucking her into the world Alex created, his head bent over an upright piano, his fingers flying over yellowed ivory keys.

A twin bed stood against the far wall, blue blankets and sheets and pillowcase neat and tidy. Everything in the room was neat, tidy, and blue. Walls. Curtains. Throw rug on the dark wood floor. Even the old upright piano had been stripped and then painted glossy sapphire blue. Light from the window reflected off its gleaming surface and splashed across Alex's face, glinting on his tearstained cheeks.

Tessa had never seen him cry.

Not the day he was born. Not in the hundred hours of time Gertrude had thrown in her face. Not at the funeral.

"Alex?" She touched his arm.

He just kept playing, his knobby shoulders hunched, his eyes closed.

If only she didn't love him so much, she could leave him to his music and his world. But she did, and that was so much harder than she'd ever thought it would be.

"What is it, Alex? Do you miss your parents? Is that why you're crying?"

The sad, seeping music continued, and her heart broke more with every keystroke, with every tear that dropped onto ivory keys.

"You're going to make yourself sick, buddy." She gently lifted his hands and closed the piano lid, the silence deafening, her heart thundering with uncertainty.

Right?

Wrong?

She didn't know, because she didn't know this boy with his copper hair and distant eyes.

"Home," Alex said so quietly she wasn't sure he'd actually spoken.

"What?" She touched his cheek, her heart shattering as she looked into his eyes. *Emily's eyes.*

God, she wanted to do this right.

"My home." Alex's words were raw and rusty and soft.

She heard them clearly, though.

Just be finished with it, Tess thought. *Walk away. Pretend you don't know that he wants to stay.*

Alex's fingers tapped against the piano lid, his gaze darting her way, tears still dripping down his face.

"I get it," she forced out past the lump in her throat. "This *is* your home. We'll stay in it, okay? We will. I promise." She lifted the piano lid so that his fingers fell against the keys. Just a moment of hesitation and he was playing the same sad melody.

She wanted to cry for him and for Emily and for

Dave. Maybe even for herself, because there was no way she could go back to Annapolis now. She'd have to sell her brownstone, put in her resignation and . . .

What?

Find a job as an interior designer in Apple Valley, Washington?

That wasn't going to happen.

She'd have to think of something, though. Emily and Dave hadn't been the kind of people to invest in life insurance. All they'd owned was the house and the stuff in it. Alex's therapy had been expensive. There hadn't been money for anything else.

So, maybe they *had* done the best they could with what they had, and maybe Tessa had let frustration color her perspective.

But she had a life she'd worked hard for.

She'd *had* a life.

Now she had Alex and Gertrude and an old Victorian filled with junk that no one wanted.

Things'll work out just fine, she could swear she heard Emily say as she walked out of the room and left Alex to his music.

Chapter Three

"Hey, boss, you heading out soon?" Max Stanford walked into Cade's office like he owned the place, his uniform perfectly tailored, his shoes polished, every blond hair in place. Guy looked like he spent hours in front of the mirror. If Cade hadn't liked him so much, he'd have despised him on principle.

"In a minute."

"Your shift ended a half hour ago." Max leaned against the doorjamb, his arms crossed. A transplant from Los Angeles, he'd patrolled some of the toughest beats in the country and had worked his way up to homicide detective with the LAPD before following his girlfriend to eastern Washington five years ago. They'd broken up two years ago, but Max had stuck around.

"Since when do you keep track of my work schedule?" Cade saved the file he was working on and closed down his computer.

"Since I heard you were going to have dinner with Gertrude McKenzie and her niece."

A dinner he would be late for, Cade thought as he

glanced at the clock ticking away the time. "You've been talking to Ida."

"I rent her garage apartment. Talking to her isn't unusual," Max responded dryly.

"You discussing it with me is. So, what's up?"

"Ida asked me to make a display case for that angel you gave her. I blame you for that."

"Blame yourself. You should never have let my grandmother know you were more than a pretty face," Cade said, and Max smiled.

"My pretty face did a hell of a better job at the gun range this morning than your ugly one. Or have you forgotten that?"

"First time in five years you've out-marked me. I'm not sure that's something I'd be bragging about."

"What? You're not going to throw jet lag in my face and ask me to buy that as your excuse?"

"I don't make excuses, Stanford." He stood and stretched out the kinks in his neck and back. "But if you're offering one . . ."

"Forget it. I'll take bragging rights where I can, but that's not what I wanted to discuss. The way I see things, if I hadn't agreed to make that display case for Ida, you'd be stuck doing it."

"And?"

"I want a date with that gorgeous redhead I saw coming out of This-N-That Antiques the other day."

"Tess?"

"If Tess is Gertrude's niece, then, yes. Since you're going to Gertrude's for dinner tonight, I thought you could put in a good word for me."

"Forget it." Cade stood and grabbed his coat from a hook near the door.

"You're saying she's off-limits?"

Was he? Cade thought of the quick shot of heat that he'd felt when he'd touched her arm. A fluke. Some strange by-product of jet lag. It hadn't meant anything, but old friendship did. "I'm saying she's an old friend, and I'm not going to set her up with a guy who's broken every female heart between here and the Cascades."

"Painful, Cunningham."

"Exactly. I need to head out. See you tomorrow." Cade walked down the narrow hall and into what had once been three holding cells but was now a lobby. Old brickwork and high windows with bars gave the feel of a bygone era, the modernized building retaining its turn-of-the-century charm.

A large Christmas tree stood in the corner of the room, decorated with silver tinsel and colorful gift cards that the townspeople were donating to a homeless shelter in downtown Spokane. Emma Bradley's idea, and a good one. She'd had quite a few of them since being hired as full-time dispatcher in the spring, including the fancy coffeemaker on the corner of her desk and the plate of cookies sitting beside it.

He snagged one as he walked by.

"Heading out, Sheriff?" Emma asked without looking up from her computer. Fresh out of college with a degree in criminal justice, she'd planned to go to law school but had come home from Seattle to care for her ailing father.

"Yeah. You should be, too."

"Should be, but the last thing I feel like doing is going home. Dad's on a rant about the new medication the doctor has him on. Thinks he's being poisoned." She rubbed the bridge of her nose, her gray eyes deeply shadowed.

"How's the new caregiver working out?"

"Dad thinks he's a Mafia hit man. Fortunately, Jake doesn't seem to mind. Hopefully, he'll stick around for a while. I'm about out of leave." She tugged at a strand of straight brown hair. Mousy and sweet, she was the youngest of ten children, and the only one who'd cared enough to return home when Rick was diagnosed with Alzheimer's.

"If you need time off, take it."

"Unpaid leave won't pay the bills, Cade."

"We'll work something out," he offered, but she shook her head.

"I wouldn't feel right if I didn't earn what I was paid. Besides, being here is a lot easier than . . ." She shook her head. "Things are going fine for now. That's what matters."

"Like I said, if that changes, we'll work things out."

"Meaning you'll try to pay me for work I'm not doing. That's not how I do things."

"You can repay me in cookies." He grabbed another one from the plate and left. No need to give her time to respond. The people he worked with were like family, and he'd been raised to take care of his own.

Cold air whipped through his coat, the noisy hubbub of the town center enveloping him. A few people called greetings as he climbed into his Ford F-1. He smiled and waved, but he wasn't much in the mood for stopping to chat. Offering to help the McKenzie women had seemed like the right thing to do at the time, but he wasn't all that excited about heading back to the old Riley place.

He'd spent plenty of time there as a kid, hanging with his buddy Dave, sneaking through the old rooms, whispering so they wouldn't disturb old man Riley. The patriarch of the family, he'd been the great-grandson of the town's founder, but Dean Riley hadn't had the work ethic or community mindedness that had made Daniel Riley the beloved first mayor of Apple Valley. As a matter of fact, for as long as Cade could remember, Dean had been known for being a grumpy old miser.

He'd become a legend in his own right after he'd died.

Not the kind of legend Cade wanted to be, but he guessed the old guy would be laughing his ass off if he knew that people in Apple Valley were still talking about the fortune that Dean had supposedly stashed away somewhere in town.

Cade didn't buy into the story, but he sure spent a lot of his time busting grave robbers and treasure hunters who did.

He put the truck in gear and drove down Main Street. Christmas lights hung from the eaves of every building. More lights sparkled in the trees and reflected off the smooth surface of the pond that sat in the middle of Riley Park, a perfect winter wonderland that still hinted at the gardens that had once been there. Even the little white church that stood on a knoll overlooking the pond sparkled, its simple nativity scene spotlighted in a halo of golden light.

The place was as familiar to Cade as an old friend, and he loved every bit of it. Sure, he'd wandered over the years, gone overseas and served in the military, but no matter where he'd wandered, Apple Valley was home.

He followed Main Street away from the town center, continuing on the two-lane road until it narrowed. Here, the houses were old and stately, the lots larger. The largest of all was the Riley property. Three acres just a mile from the hubbub of the town center.

He pulled over, parking his truck at the curb. Lights shown from nearly every window, splashing onto the dried-out yard. A CLOSED sign hung from the front door, and the large store flag that Emily had hung five years ago drooped from one of the porch support beams, its letters and colors faded by hot summer sun and harsh winter weather.

He rang the doorbell and the door opened immediately.

"You're late. My pot roast is drying out," Gertrude griped, the silly Santa hat still perched on her head. It didn't cover her hair. Hair that had gone from vivid orange to faded pink.

"New look, Gertrude?"

"You want to see a new look? Go to Adele's Hair Emporium tomorrow after I've rearranged her face."

"You know I can't condone that, right?"

"And you condone this?" She touched her hair and glared.

"What happened?"

"I pissed her off, that's what happened. Five minutes late for my appointment. Of course, she *says* it was an accident. Old hair dye or something. Says she'll fix it in the morning. As if I would let her touch my hair again. Come on. If we're going to eat, we better do it before my roast turns to jerky."

Cade followed her up the wide, curving staircase. Flowered wallpaper peeled away from the plaster wall. Dingy carpet treads curled up at the edges. As far as Cade could tell, nothing had changed in the years since he'd been there. Not for the better anyway. Everything was just a little older, a little dustier, a little worse for wear.

A cluttered landing held a boatload of old things. Three doors used to open off the landing. Now an archway led into a large living room–kitchen combo. No clutter here. Just comfortable furniture and clean but outdated appliances.

A small round table stood near the kitchen area, and Gertrude gestured toward it. "Go ahead and have a seat. Tess! Alex! Time to eat."

She slammed a pot of something that smelled really good onto the table and huffed to the refrigerator.

"You're not taking your mood out on Cade, are you?" Tess asked as she walked into the room with Alex.

"Who says I'm in a mood?" Gertrude dropped a bowl of salad onto the table and glared at her niece.

"Me. You've been griping since you got home from your hair appointment." Tess pulled out a chair for Alex, the curve of her hip a half foot from Cade's face.

The very nice curve of her hip.

That little zing of heat shot through him again, and he looked away.

"If I want to gripe, I'll gripe. At my age, I've earned the right." Gertrude settled into the chair next to Alex. "It's pot roast tonight, honey. You know how you love my pot roast."

Alex tapped his free hand on the tabletop, his fingers dancing along the scratched Formica. He made no move to eat the pot roast Gertrude scooped onto his plate, just hummed quietly while Tess buttered a roll and set it on a napkin next to his hand.

"Come on, buddy, you have to eat," she said, her face taut with worry, her eyes red rimmed and hollow. She pressed a fork into Alex's hand, and he took a small bite of carrot, chewing absently, his gaze distant and unfocused.

Poor kid. Cade had tried not to listen to the murmurs about little Alex Riley, but it was difficult to ignore Ida and her cronies. Ever since Darla left, they'd converged on his house every Monday, bearing a week's worth of casseroles and decades' worth of gossip. Cade had about six dozen foil-wrapped meals in his freezer and a bucket-load of information about Apple Valley residents.

He dug into his pot roast, the soft tick of a clock and the clink of silverware against plates the only sounds. The house felt heavy and dark, the silence something Cade wasn't used to. He had five siblings, and there hadn't been a moment of quiet in his life until he'd grown up and moved away from his parents' home. Even now, he preferred noise to quiet.

"So," he said to break the silence. "You like baseball, Alex?"

Alex paused with a carrot halfway to his mouth, his gaze skittering to Cade and then away again. "Piano," he answered quietly, his voice like rusty wind chimes.

"Yeah? I used to play piano." A million years ago, but if mentioning it kept Alex talking, Cade would bring it up. According to Ida, Alex almost never spoke, didn't have friends. Didn't have much but two empty-headed parents, a wiseass aunt, and the Riley house. Even that wouldn't be his much longer.

"You bring that angel to Ida?" Gertrude asked through a mouthful of potato.

"I did. She's already lined up interviews with a few Riley relatives. She wants to see if she can corroborate the story before she displays the angel." Ida was like that. A stickler for the details.

"All she has to do is talk to me," Gertrude huffed. "I heard the story straight from Dave. He said Miriam made that angel, and I have no reason to doubt him. Seeing as how the Riley house is going to be sold for scrap and razed to the ground—"

"Gertrude!" Tess cut in, her gaze on Alex. "This isn't the time."

"You say that every time I bring it up," Gertrude muttered, but she glanced at Alex, too, her face softening as she looked at the silent boy.

"Done. May I be excused?" Alex asked so softly Cade barely heard him.

"You hardly ate anything, Alex," Tessa said, but she didn't try to stop him when he got up. He walked into the hall, scrawny and small for a ten-year-old, his narrow shoulders hunched as he disappeared into a room.

"Next time, think before you speak, Gertie," Tessa hissed as soon as the door closed.

"You think he doesn't know that you're planning on dragging him all the way across this country? You think he doesn't understand that you're going to take away everything he loves? The boy may be autistic, but he's not stupid!"

"I'm not taking him anywhere." Tess stood abruptly, grabbing Alex's plate and her own and walking into the small kitchen. She dumped the contents into a trash can, her shoulders tight, her back rigid.

"What do you mean, you're not taking him?" Gertrude snapped. "You're cleaning out the house. You're putting it on the market. What are you going to do? Buy a hovel for me and the kid and go off to your fancy life?"

"Let's discuss this later."

Tessa responded with a lot less anger than Cade expected. She and Gertrude used to go at it like a couple of alley cats when Tess was a teenager. Usually because of some big dream that Tessa had. Some plan for leaving Apple Valley and her family behind. Not something Cade had ever wanted to do, but he'd admired her for standing up to her aunt—encouraged her to do it, actually.

This time, he'd just sit back and listen. Too much time had passed for him to jump into the fray. Besides, like Tessa, he'd learned the power of patience and the strength of silence.

"What is that supposed to mean?" Gertrude stood, her frizzy fried hair nearly vibrating. "This is my life, too. If you have some big plan for tearing me away from it, you'd better damn well let me know."

"If I recall"—Tess responded calmly, but there was fire in her eyes and a hint of the old Tess in her voice—"you wanted nothing to do with my plans for this house or for Alex this morning when I wanted to discuss a time frame for listing the property with a real estate agent. As a matter of fact, you threatened to disown me if I set foot in your room or touched one of your precious pieces of ju—one of your *collectibles.*"

"Listen here, you—" Gertrude sputtered.

"I don't have time for this, Gert. I have work to do. Emily and Dave's mess isn't going to clean itself. You go ahead and enjoy the meal, Cade. I'll be outside when you're done."

Tess stalked away, and, damn, if he didn't find himself watching the sway of her hips as she went.

"Get your mind out of the gutter, Cade," Gertrude growled.

"Get your mood out of it, Ms. Gertrude."

"I'm *not* in a mood."

"Then why did you just chase your niece away?" he asked mildly. Gertrude had a sharp tongue and no filter. Emily had been the same. Not that he'd spent much time worrying about that when he was a teen. Living next door to the hottest girl in school had been all he'd really thought about.

Young. Hormonal. Stupid.

That about covered the years from twelve to eighteen.

"I didn't chase. She ran. Just like she always does."

"She didn't run until you started in on her about selling the house and moving."

"Eat your pot roast before it gets cold," Gertrude commanded, every wrinkle in her face pulled into a scowl. The scowl couldn't hide the worry in her eyes, the tremor in her hand as she adjusted her Santa hat and sat down. She might be a tough old lady, but she loved her family.

"Stop worrying, Gertrude." He patted her bony shoulder and was rewarded with a deeper scowl.

"I'm not worrying. I just don't like having my life turned upside down."

"Tess is just doing what she thinks is right."

"She's trying to kick me out of the only home I have. That's what she's doing."

"I thought you didn't like dramatics," he responded mildly as he carried his empty plate to the sink and washed it.

"Just stating the facts."

"The facts as I see them are this. Tess inherited a mess. She's got to clean it up before the town comes down on her and hands her a boatload of fines. Much as Zimmerm—"

"I'll thank you not to mention his name while I'm eating. A woman likes to enjoy her meal."

"Much as your *neighbor* may annoy the hell out of me, he has the right to complain, and as sheriff I've got to respond. I looked into things back at the office, and the law is clear. You don't get the property cleaned up, and the town can hire a crew to come in and do it. That'll cost a lot more money than the estate probably has. If you can't repay the cost, a lien will be placed against the house. You want to lose the house and land, Gertrude?"

"You know that I don't."

"Then give Tessa a break and let her do what needs to be done." He set the plate in the drainer. "I'm going to give her a hand."

He ignored Gertrude's hot glare and left the kitchen, the wooden stairs creaking under his feet as he descended. Bitter cold air wafted in, newspaper skittering across the floor as Cade walked through the foyer. According to Ida, Emily and Dave had been proud of This-N-That, attending commerce meetings and talking the place up to anyone who would listen. Cade had worked really hard at ignoring the Rileys, so he hadn't heard either of them praising the neglected house and the junk shop it contained. Probably a good thing. He'd likely have told them they were delusional.

Cade shoved his hands deep into the pockets of his coat as he walked outside. A few trash bags were lined up near the porch stairs. Two had been abandoned near his truck. Tessa sat on the old swing beneath the white-barked birch, the rusted chains creaking as she twisted to the left and then to the right. She looked as lonely as the house felt.

"You okay?" he asked as he lifted a couple of bags and walked across the yard.

"Fine. I just wasn't sure you really wanted a bunch of trash in the back of your truck." She stood, brushing a hand down her firm, round behind. "It's a sweet ride."

"Yeah. Sweet," he murmured, dragging his gaze away from her ass and tossing trash into the back of the pickup. "But it's also practical. No sense having a truck that I can't use."

"A Ford F-1. Right?" She grabbed the two bags that were sitting beside the truck and tossed them in.

"You know your cars, Tess." That had been one of the things that he'd liked about her when they were kids. She'd been funny, tough, and eager to learn about anything and everything that Cade and his friends had been into. From the time she and her sister had been dropped off at Gertrude's until the hot summer day when Cade had discovered girls, he and Tess had been thick as thieves.

"I was taught by the best." She hurried back across the yard, grabbed several more trash bags.

"You were the only girl I knew who'd listen to me talk about the rusted-out car carcasses at the dump. That's a heady feeling for an eight-year-old boy."

"Yeah?" She heaved three bags into the truck. They were making quick work of the mess on the porch. Too quick, because Cade was enjoying the trip down memory lane. It had been awhile since he'd thought of Tess. Now he wasn't sure why.

Tess hurried back to the porch, and he leaned against the truck and watched her. She'd changed, but she was still the same, too. Fast, strong, eager.

"It wasn't such a difficult thing to listen to you talk about old cars," she said, panting as she jogged back with more trash. "I've always appreciated old things. I also appreciate warmth. Let's get this done, so you can go home and I can go inside and wrap up in a dozen blankets."

"Is that a hint?" He laughed, and she grinned.

"If it is, it's not a very subtle one, is it? I'm freezing. Get your he-man muscles moving, before I succumb to the cold."

He laughed again, but did what she wanted, grabbing up the last few bags and piling them in with the rest.

"The East Coast has made you soft, Red," he said, using the pet name he'd coined the day they'd met. "What are you going to do when it gets *really* cold?"

"If I start thinking about that, I may change my mind about staying."

"So, you were serious about not taking Alex to Annapolis?"

"He has enough challenges without me adding to them."

"It would have saved you some grief if you'd told Gertrude that."

"You know Gertrude. She likes to fight. Even when there's nothing to fight about."

"True, but she might have been too shocked to fight if you'd let her know your plans."

Tessa shrugged, moving through the yard with a garbage bag and picking up scraps of paper. Cade followed, grabbing a few broken plastic buckets and a length of hose. The yard already looked better.

Tessa tossed the bag into the back of the truck. "I think that's probably good enough for tonight. I'll finish the rest tomorrow. Thanks for your help, Cade."

"No problem," he said. "We've always been a good team."

He thought the comment would make her smile, but she just eyed him silently. Then walked away.

He caught up to her in two steps, snagging the back of her coat and pulling her to a stop. "There's no need to run away, Tess."

"I'm not running. I'm going inside before I freeze to death."

It was a lie. Cade knew it, but he wasn't sure why she'd tell it or what her real reason was for wanting to rush away. "You sure?"

Was she?

Tess wasn't sure how to answer that. On the one hand, she really was freezing. On the other hand, she was more worried about getting away from Cade than she was about dying of hypothermia. "It's been a long week, Cade. I'm exhausted."

He nodded, watching her solemnly. "You've been through a lot."

"The whole family has, and if I'm going to be any good to anyone, I need to get some sleep." That sounded reasonable. It even sounded true. It *was* true. Tess hadn't slept more than a couple of hours since she'd arrived.

"You do look tired." He traced the sensitive skin beneath her eye, his finger warm and calloused. It felt good, and it was all she could do not to throw her arms around his waist and hold on tight.

God, she needed someone. Desperately.

But not him.

Been down that road before. Knew where it led. Didn't want to make a return trip.

"Thanks," she responded wryly, because hearing that she looked tired was exactly what every woman wanted.

"That doesn't mean you don't also look beautiful." He smiled, flashing his dimple.

Her traitorous heart jumped in response.

That probably made her the biggest fool west of the Mississippi. She was almost too tired to care.

"Too little too late," she responded, keeping her voice light.

"Then I guess I need to apologize and find a way to make it up to you." His knuckles skimmed her cheek, and she shivered, taking a quick step back.

"No need. Good night, Cade." She threw the words over her shoulder as she ran across the yard.

He said something that she couldn't quite hear. She didn't ask him to repeat it, because tears were burning the back of her eyes, and she'd given up crying the night her mother had brought her and Emily to Gertrude's and left them there. She'd been five. Emily had been six. They'd been told they were going to finally spend Christmas as a family. Emily had believed it, bubbling with enthusiasm and joy at the thought of Christmas gifts and food.

Tessa had been suspicious, barely sleeping Christmas Eve night. She wasn't waiting to hear Santa's sleigh bells. She was waiting to hear the coughing rumble of her mother's old station wagon. The room had been dark as pitch, Gertrude's little ranch-style house silent and unfamiliar. Emily had been breathing deeply, completely trusting in their mother's promise that they'd finally spend Christmas in a house with a tree and presents.

Tessa still remembered hearing the old engine grumble and gasp. Still remembered creeping to the window and watching her mother drive away. Still remembered the hot tears that had spilled down her cheeks. She'd known Gretchen was never coming back, and she'd hated her for it.

She stepped into the house, the sounds of pots and pans clanging from the apartment above. She didn't have the energy to go upstairs. Didn't want to fight with Gertrude anymore.

What she wanted was to be back home, decorating her little Christmas tree, listening to Christmas carols and planning for Emily and Dave's yearly visit. Two days entertaining her family, and she'd always felt like she'd done her duty.

She'd loved them.

She *had*.

But she'd spent her childhood cleaning up Emily's

messes. She hadn't wanted to spend the rest of her life doing the same. No worries about that now. Emily was gone. Just one more mess to clean up and all those years would be behind her.

But, God, she wished she could have them back.

"I know you're down there, Tessa Louise," Gertrude hollered. "You may as well come up here and face the music."

Fingernails on chalkboard, but Tessa couldn't ignore it. No matter how much she wanted to.

Her family.

She'd always loved them.

Now, all she had to do was figure out how to live with them.

Chapter Four

Bang!
Scrape!
Squeal!
The sounds drilled their way into Tessa's brain.
She squinted at the alarm clock.

Five in the morning, and someone was making enough noise to wake the dead.

She pressed the pillow to her ears, but nothing could block the racket. It had to be Gertrude. *Had* to be.

She shoved aside the thick down quilt, shivering as her bare feet met cold wood floor. She had kinks in her neck, back, and shoulders. From tension and from sleeping on the old Victorian chaise lounge in Emily and Dave's room. She couldn't stomach the thought of climbing into the bed they'd shared. Couldn't imagine that her dreams would be sweet if she did.

She stumbled over the damn porcelain cat that had been sitting on the floor since she arrived. She should have cleaned the overstuffed room, but she hadn't had the heart to change anything. It had been her sister's space, and there was a tiny part of Emily that still seemed to live in the things she'd collected.

And cleaning out the room?

It felt too much like saying a final good-bye.

She crept into the hall, afraid of waking Alex. He slept fitfully and, according to Gertrude, had been known to wander. It hadn't happened in the ten days since Tessa had arrived, but she was terrified that it would.

Bang!

Tess followed the sound through the apartment and down the stairs, inhaling the acrid scent of burnt coffee. A light shone from the old kitchen, its glow splashing across the nicked and stained floor. The place had good bones. Really good ones. As a matter of fact, Tess had decorated quite a few Victorian mansions during her career. She'd seen some in worse shape than this one, turned into beautiful showpieces.

There was no reason why she couldn't do the same. Except that she didn't want to pour her energy and money into a house in a town she despised.

She walked into the kitchen, stopping cold when she saw the source of the noise.

Gertrude. Of course.

Shoving the china cabinet across the floor, her housecoat flapping as she moved, her face red from effort.

The china cabinet wasn't moving. The old vinyl floor was. The grimy black-and-white pattern buckling and ripping.

"What in the heck are you doing, Gertrude?"

"What does it look like I'm doing?" Gertie snapped, her off-colored hair standing up like she'd stuck her finger in a light socket. "I'm putting this in the mudroom."

"There's a mudroom?" Tess put her hand on the scarred wood to keep Gertrude from doing any more damage.

"What do you think *that* is?" Gertrude gestured to an open door at the far side of the room. Tessa hadn't noticed it before. But then, she'd been trying really hard to not notice much about her sister's place. It was too depressing. Too discouraging to think of Emily and Dave pinning their dreams on a pile of junk.

"A door?"

"Don't be a smart-ass, Tess. It doesn't suit you."

"Neither does being woken up at five in the morning."

"You were the one who spent yesterday complaining that we weren't getting any work done. I'm just trying to get a head start on today."

"You couldn't have waited until seven?" Tess walked to an old coffeemaker that sat on the counter. The dregs were burning on the bottom. In another couple of minutes the whole machine would probably go up in flames. She pulled the plug.

"Stop fiddling with the coffeemaker and help me move this!" Gertrude grunted as she set her shoulder against the back of the cabinet and pushed.

"Is there a reason you want to move it?"

"I'm donating it. The truck will be here at eight, and I have a lot of other things to move before then."

"This is one of the few nice pieces in the house."

Tess ran her hand over the cool wood. A little polish and elbow grease, and it would be a showpiece.

"So?" Gertrude scowled, every line in her face deepening. "You said we need to get rid of everything."

"I said we need to get rid of the junk." As a matter of fact, she'd spent two hours explaining everything in excruciating detail. If they were going to stay, they had to make This-N-That profitable. Get rid of the junk. Bring in some good antiques. Start selling things.

Pray to God that it worked, because Tessa's savings were limited, and at some point they were going to need more than Gertrude's social security check.

"Yesterday you said everything was junk."

"No, I . . ." She stopped before they could go back down the path they'd taken the day before. Gertrude could fight tooth and nail about nothing when she wanted to, and Tess wasn't in the mood. "Anything that belonged to the original Riley family needs to stay. For Alex."

At the mention of their nephew, Gertrude seemed to lose some of her steam. She sagged beneath her old yellow housecoat, her face sinking in. Suddenly she looked every bit of her seventy-two years. "I'm worried about that boy, Tess. I'm going to tell you that right now. He's not eating. Isn't talking. If we're not careful, we're going to lose him."

"I know." It was all she could say. All she knew to say, but she felt a lot more. Frustration. Worry. Fear. "Let's move this china cabinet back and clean off the table. I want to see if the surface is restorable."

"What if it is? Are you going to pay for it to be

done?" Gertrude grunted as they shoved the cabinet back against the wall.

"No, *I'm* going to restore it."

"The table is over a hundred and fifty years old. Made by Alex's great-great-great-grandfather Riley. You go fooling around with it—"

"Give me some credit, Gertrude. I've restored a few antiques in my time." More than a few. Hundreds. She'd built her reputation and her career on it, repurposing old pieces and using them as key design elements in houses and businesses. If Gertrude had ever shown any interest in the life she'd lived in Annapolis, she'd have known it, but Gertrude had only ever been interested in telling Tessa how wrong she'd been for leaving town.

"You think that makes you an expert?" Gertrude snapped. "You think because you went to some fancy design school and lived in some posh house on the East Coast that you know everything?"

"I'm giving you what you want, Gertrude." Tess rubbed the bridge of her nose, a headache pulsing behind her eyes. She hadn't had a day without one in a week and a half, thanks to Gertrude. "So why do you feel the need to keep arguing with me?"

"Because you're good at it."

"What is that supposed to mean?" Tess grabbed a box of old silverware from the table, her temper rising.

"Your sister never argued. She was so—"

"I know. Sweet and gentle and easy to get along with." She was also sneaky and prone to lying, but bringing that up seemed pointless.

"I was going to say insipid, but she was those

things, too." Gertrude lifted the carafe of burnt coffee dregs and ran cold water into it. "You, on the other hand, have never been sweet or gentle or *insipid*. You're just stubborn as an old mule and twice as ornery."

"Thanks." Tessa couldn't quite keep the sarcasm from her voice.

Gertrude frowned. "I don't like your tone."

"Yeah? Well, I don't like being compared to my sister and coming up short every time." Tessa grabbed a couple of old pans from the table. Cast iron, but not worth any money. She carried them to the mudroom door, pulling it open and walking into a nearly solid wall of stuff.

Something jabbed her cheek.

Something else poked her stomach.

"What the he—?"

"Oh. Yeah. Forgot about that," Gertrude said as she shuffled up beside Tess. "When I moved in, Emily and Dave took the stuff that was in my room and put it in here."

"Wonderful," Tess muttered, setting the pans down with a clank and turning on her heels. She couldn't take one more minute of the craziness. Not one more!

"Where are you going?"

"For a run."

"In your pajamas?"

"Yes!" she nearly shouted.

But she couldn't.

Even if she wanted every single person in Apple Valley to be talking about Tessa McKenzie running through town in her pj's—which she did *not*—Tess didn't want to freeze her butt off.

She retreated up the stairs, trying to put an invisible wall up behind her as she went, because she couldn't handle Gertrude following her into Emily's room. Did not even dare look into her aunt's green eyes. She might try to claw them out. She was that mad.

She yanked off her pajamas, tugged on leggings and a tank. Layered a long-sleeved cotton T over it. She had a down vest in her luggage. She pulled it out.

Still no Gertrude.

Thank God.

A floorboard creaked.

Feet tapped on wood.

She braced herself, sure that she was about to go another round with her aunt.

Something moved in the hall, a shadowy form that seemed to float rather than walk and that scared every bit of anger out of Tessa.

Until she realized who it was.

Alex.

"Hey, bud," she said quietly as she walked into the hall. "Where are you going?"

He just kept moving through the apartment, a heavy coat covering his thin body, snow boots on his feet.

"Alex?" She touched his shoulder before he could walk down the stairs. "It's too early for school."

He finally looked into her face, his hair falling over his forehead, his cornflower-blue eyes hollow.

His cheeks were gaunt. Had they been when she'd arrived?

She'd been too grief stricken to notice.

Now she couldn't stop noticing, assessing. Wondering if he were going to fade away into nothing before she could find a way to help him.

"I'm going to find her," he finally said. Clear as day, his voice gritty and rough.

Going to find her?

Outside? While it was still dark?

Tess couldn't get any of the words out. Her throat was clogged with fear, her heart beating rapidly. If she hadn't been awake, would he have slipped down the stairs and out the door?

"Going to find who? Gertrude?" *Please let it be Gertrude.*

He shook his head, his hands tapping a quick frantic beat on his thigh.

As far as Tess knew, there was only one other woman that he might have been looking for, and she was way too far away to ever be found. "Do you mean your mother, Alex? Is that who you want to find? She's gone, sweetie. In heaven, and you can't go there yet."

Wasn't that what you were supposed to say to little kids when someone they loved died?

She hoped so. God, she did.

Alex didn't speak. He just kept tapping his fingers on his thigh, his head nodding a little to the rhythm. Lost to her, and she felt sick with the knowledge.

"Alex?" She touched his shoulder.

"What's going on?" Gertrude called from the

bottom of the stairs, and Tessa was ashamed of the amount of relief she felt.

"Alex is awake. He wants to go look for Emily."

"You're kidding me, right?" Gertrude stomped up the stairs. "The boy isn't stupid. He knows he can't find his mother."

"He said—"

"Alex, you take off that coat and come in the kitchen. I'll make you some oatmeal. That sound good to you?" She took Alex's hand, tugging him away from the stairs and tossing a hot glare in Tessa's direction.

Obviously, Tess hadn't handled things the right way.

And, just as obviously, she wasn't needed or wanted at that moment. She shouldn't have cared. She hadn't wanted the job of guardian to her nephew. She wasn't mother material, and she knew it. She'd told Emily and Dave that a few years ago when they'd asked if she'd be willing to raise Alex if something happened to them.

She'd laughed and replied with some light-hearted quip about the two of them not being allowed to die together. If they did, Gertrude would be more suited to the job of guardian.

Obviously they hadn't listened, because they'd gone and died together. Tears stung the back of her eyes as she opened a closet at the top of the stairs and pulled out her running shoes. Emily and Dave hadn't ever cared to plan for the future, so the will they'd left with a lawyer friend had shocked and surprised her. Two stipulations. Clear as could be. If they both died, Tessa inherited everything, and she was named guardian to Alex.

She'd been speechless when she'd heard that.

Shocked. Horrified.

Angry.

Was it any surprise that she was already screwing up royally?

She jogged down the stairs, unlocked the front door, and ran into the frigid morning.

The sun hadn't even begun to rise, and the sky was black as pitch, a million stars twinkling against the inky darkness. Cold air speared through her T-shirt and the down vest. She'd forgotten how cold Washington winters were. She needed more layers, but she wasn't going back to the house.

Not yet.

Her breath puffed out in a white cloud as she raced up Main Street. At first, the houses were spread apart, the windows dark, the streetlights barely lighting the pavement. Eventually, the lot sizes grew smaller, the streetlights closer together. As she neared the town center, houses gave way to 1920s brick buildings standing shoulder to shoulder. Christmas lights shone from windows and wreaths hung from doors. Old signs and new ones announced businesses. Most were closed, but Tess remembered a small coffee shop from her years in town. The place had opened at five and closed at noon. As a teen, she'd felt sophisticated going there before school to get a cup of coffee.

Now she was just desperate for a little heat.

Murphy's Coffee House was exactly where she remembered, lights glowing from the display windows in the front of the whitewashed brick building. It hadn't changed much. Someone had painted the window trim blue instead of the puke green it used to be. The once-brown door gleamed glossy blue, but the chipped and scratched OPEN sign still hung from the doorknob.

The bell above the door rang as Tess walked inside, every cell in her body rejoicing as she was wrapped in warmth and the homey scents of fresh brewed coffee and pastries.

"Good morning!" Larry Murphy walked out of the back room, wiping his hands on his apron. Aside from a few more strands of gray hair and a few extra pounds around his waist, he looked just like he had ten years ago.

"Hi, Larry," Tessa responded with a smile.

His grin broadened, his ruddy face melting into a hundred smile lines. "Well! Tessa McKenzie! I was wondering how long it would take for you to come in and say hello!"

He wrapped her in a bear hug that nearly squeezed the breath out of her lungs. "How you holding up, kid?"

"Okay."

"Yeah? You don't look okay. You look half frozen and in need of a strong cup of black coffee. Am I right?" he asked, his New York accent growing thicker with every word.

He poured coffee into a white mug, set it on the counter. "And how about a couple of my pumpkin doughnuts? They're still hot."

"I'd love one."

"One? A girl your size needs two." He pulled them from the display case and set them on a plate.

"Who is it, Larry?" Kristen Murphy appeared in the kitchen doorway, her once plump figure thin and fragile, her head barely covered by gray peach fuzz.

Tessa's happiness fled, her heart squeezing tight as she looked into Kristen's green eyes.

Don't pity me, they seemed to say.

So she smiled, reached for the hug she knew Kristen would want. "Hi, Kristen."

"Tess! I'm so glad you finally came in." Kristen returned the hug, her body skeletal beneath jeans and a thick sweater. "I've been wanting to visit, but Larry has been worried I'll catch the flu that's going around."

"You're just getting better, hon. We don't want you sick again." Larry put an arm around Kristen's waist, his gaze tender as he looked at his wife. "I thought you were doing paperwork in the office."

"I'm sick of paperwork." Kristen met Tessa's gaze, her smile just as bright as it had always been. "He likes me to hide out in the office. He's afraid I'll get sick and end up in the hospital."

"The doctor said—"

"That I was fine," Kristen interrupted. "He gave me a clean bill of health last week."

"For now," Larry muttered.

"Breast cancer." Kristen offered the information to Tess. "Stage two, but the doctor thinks I'm going to be just fine. Finished my last round of chemo Thursday."

"I'm glad." Tess touched her frail arm, sorry that she'd let so many years go by without visiting the couple. She'd been back in Apple Valley a few times over the years, but only to see her family and only for a few days at a time. She hadn't bothered walking down Main Street or visiting the town center. She hadn't wanted to see anyone who had known her when she was a kid. Mostly because she'd wanted to put that part of her life behind her.

"Me too, but I can't complain. Things could be a lot worse. You go take your coffee and doughnuts to a booth and sit for a while. Come on, Larry." She grabbed her husband's arm and pulled him toward the kitchen. "Mrs. Simpson is picking up those pies at nine, and you're only halfway done."

"Such a taskmaster," Larry said, his eyes twinkling as he leaned down and whispered something that made Kristen giggle like a schoolgirl.

They disappeared through the open door, and Tessa carried her coffee and doughnuts to a high-backed corner booth. She tried to block out the sound of Larry and Kristen's quiet laughter, but it was impossible. She seriously considered grabbing a to-go cup from behind the counter and leaving, because the last thing she felt like doing was listening to the proof that some people really did achieve happily-ever-after.

Dang! She hated that she hated other people's happiness.

Okay. She didn't exactly hate their happiness.

She just didn't want to be witness to it. That happily-ever-after every girl dreams of? The lovey-dovey, finish-each-other's-sentences kind of relationship that made other people gag and go green with envy all at the same time? She'd seen it a time or two, but she'd never experienced it. All she'd managed was a string of bad relationships that had culminated in Kent.

Yeah . . . she didn't really want to think too much

about him. Why ruin a perfectly good cup of coffee and perfectly great doughnuts with indigestion-inducing memories?

She shivered and took a sip of hot coffee and let the warmth slide down her throat, hoping to chase away the chill. Only the chill wasn't just skin-deep. It was more like a soul-deep ice that had wrapped itself around her heart the day Gertrude had called to say Emily and Dave were dead. No matter how much hot coffee she drank, no matter how many blankets she wrapped up in at night, she couldn't ever seem to shake it.

The bell above the door rang as someone stepped into the coffee shop.

Tess scrunched down in the booth. She wasn't in the mood for talking, and if it was anyone she knew, that's what they'd want to do. Whoever it was crossed the room, the sound of heavy boots on tile echoing through the shop.

"Hey there, Sheriff!" Larry boomed. "What can I get for you this morning?"

Sheriff?

As in Cade?

Of course, Cade. There was only one sheriff in town. He was it.

"I'll take a cup of coffee and some information, if you have it." Cade had a voice as smooth and rich as milk chocolate.

Tess loved chocolate.

She slid lower in the booth.

She wasn't in the mood to face anyone, and she especially wasn't in the mood to face the guy she'd mooned over in high school. The guy who still seemed to have the ability to make her insides melt.

"One coffee. On the house," Larry responded. "What kind of information are you looking for?"

"Gertrude McKenzie says her niece is missing. I thought maybe you'd seen her."

Oh no!

No, no, no, no. No!

"Tessa, missing?" Larry sounded as incredulous as Tessa felt. "She's right—"

"Here." She stood and showed herself because, short of crawling under booths and tables and high-tailing it out the door, there was nothing else she could do.

"Hey," Cade responded, with an easy smile that flashed his dimple and made her legs go weak. "I was hoping I'd find you here."

"Does that mean you didn't put out an APB yet?" *Please, God . . . anything but that.* In a community the size of Apple Valley, she'd never live it down.

"Gertrude sounded more pissed off than worried." He crossed the room in two quick steps and slid into the booth across from her, a carryout cup of coffee in his hand. "I figured it was more likely you'd run away than gone missing, and there's only one place open this time of morning." He smelled like crisp winter air and pine needles, the scent reminding her of home.

Or what she'd always wanted home to be.

Wood-burning fires on chilly evenings. Hot coffee and good conversation. Gertrude's house had always smelled like cigarette smoke and stale perfume. Tess couldn't remember what Gretchen's place had smelled of. Probably pot and alcohol.

"They do have the best coffee in town." She took a sip and smiled, because talking to Cade had always been easy and comfortable. When so many other things in her life had seemed to chafe, he'd fit. Nothing had changed about that.

"And the best pumpkin doughnuts." He snagged one of hers and bit into it.

"Hey!" He'd also always annoyed the hell out of her. Apparently that hadn't changed, either. "That's mine!"

"You were going to eat both?"

"Maybe."

"Liar." He polished off the rest of the doughnut and wiped his hands on a napkin. "So, why did you run away from home?"

"I didn't run away. I went for a jog."

"It's kind of early for a jog, isn't it?"

"Not when Gertrude's around," she muttered, biting into the second doughnut before Cade could. The guy had always loved sweets. Apparently time hadn't changed that. It hadn't made his eyes any less blue, either.

They were like a dusky summer sky, clear and deep all at the same time.

"What were you two arguing about this time?" Cade took a long sip of coffee, eyeing Tessa over the rim. She'd pulled her hair into a messy ponytail, and curly strands stuck to her temple and forehead. Obviously, she had been jogging, her long-sleeved T-shirt clinging to toned biceps and pert breasts that he knew she hadn't had when they were kids.

Damn! She really *had* grown up.

"Alex. The house. My existence." She picked a chunk off the top of her doughnut and popped it into her mouth. "I finally decided that I needed a little air before I did something that would get me thrown in jail. And, for the record, I told Gertrude that I was going for a jog."

"She mentioned that."

"Then why did you come looking for me?"

Good question. He hadn't even been on duty when Gertrude called his home phone. As a matter of fact, he'd barely been awake. He'd headed over to the Riley place anyway. "Curiosity, maybe."

"Now that your curiosity has been satisfied, feel free to leave." She polished off the rest of her doughnut and took a gulp of coffee. A small crumb stuck to the corner of her mouth. Right at the edge where it curved into a smile.

He brushed it away, his fingers trailing over lips that had never looked kissable when she'd been Emily's kid sister.

They looked it now.

"You've changed, Tess," he said, because he couldn't quite wrap his mind around it.

"It would be weird if I hadn't." She brushed a few crumbs from the table, her cheeks pink. She'd left town without as much as a good-bye. Just packed her old Mustang and drove away before dawn the day after Christmas.

The day that he'd planned to propose to Emily.

He never had.

He regretted not saying good-bye to Tessa more than he regretted not marrying her sister.

"You still play hockey in the street when it snows?" he asked.

He wanted to see her smile again, see that quick curve of her lips and catch a glimpse of the kid she'd been. Remind himself that she wasn't a gorgeous woman who just happened to have walked into his life.

She was Tessa, and he'd missed her more than he'd thought. More than he'd ever acknowledged.

"I gave that up when I moved to the East Coast. Not enough ice and snow." She tucked a strand of deep red hair behind her ear. "I'm sure you don't spend your winter afternoons passing a hockey puck to your buddies."

"Not to my buddies." He'd spent plenty of afternoons passing them to local kids, though. The town didn't have much for teenagers to do during the winter months. Running a local kids' club kept the teens out of trouble and him from having to haul their butts into jail.

"Let me guess. You spend every Saturday afternoon shooting hoops or pucks with a group of juvenile delinquents. Isn't that what your father always called the boys' club crowd?" She finally smiled, her eyes sparkling the way they had when they were kids and shared a joke at someone else's expense. "And didn't you swear that you'd never waste your Saturdays working with a group of thankless kids?"

"Yeah. Well, Dad retired and decided to move Mom to Florida. Someone had to take over. It was either going to be me or Hannah Miller."

"The cheerleading coach?"

"She retired five years ago."

"And wanted to coach boys' basketball and ice hockey?" Tessa laughed. "She was ancient when we were in school."

"Now you see the problem. Ms. Miller would have turned the boys' club into a knitting club, and then

I would have had a dozen teenage boys out on the streets looking for trouble."

"So you had purely selfish motives, huh?"

"Absolutely."

"There goes your bad-boy reputation."

She plucked invisible lint from her down vest, slid her hand over the tabletop. No ring on her finger. He'd heard that she was in a serious relationship and that it had ended badly. Couldn't remember who he'd heard it from. Probably Ida.

"And my Saturday afternoons," he responded.

"I'm sure every blue-haired lady in town worships the ground you walk on because of it."

She flashed a smile and stood, stretching her lean arms and rolling her neck. She wore black leggings that showed off the long, lean muscles of her thighs and calves, and he couldn't quite stop himself from noticing.

"They're not the ones I'm hoping to impress," he joked.

"So, you're doing it to impress the ladies, huh? Clever."

"Not *ladies*. Just one beautiful redhead who could never quite keep up with my athleticism."

She laughed and shook her head. "I really doubt you spent more than a half a second thinking of me during the past ten years."

"What's that supposed to mean?" He stood and followed her out of the coffee shop, not quite ready to let her go.

"Nothing." She shivered and rubbed her arms. "It's freezing out here!"

"I think we already determined that you're a weather wimp."

"I'm not a wimp. I'm just—"

"Shaking violently from the cold?" He took off his coat, wrapping it snugly around her. She smelled like a spring day. Flowery and warm with just a hint of rain.

His gut tightened in response, his hand itching to reach for her. He almost gave in to the temptation. He and Tess had been about as close as two people could be without being family or lovers. That was a long time ago. She'd changed. So had he.

But, damn, if he couldn't shake the image of her in his arms, nestled close to his chest, her fingers grazing his abdomen.

She watched him through narrowed eyes. As if she could read his thoughts, knew exactly where his mind had just gone.

"I'd love to stay and chat awhile, Cade, but I have to get back. Alex almost went looking for Emily this morning. I caught him walking down the hall in his coat and snow boots. I want to make sure he's okay before he heads off to school."

Cade's heart rate upped a notch at the thought of the ten-year-old wandering around Apple Valley in the dark. The crime rate in town was about as low as it could get, but that didn't mean predators didn't lurk in the shadows. "He knows he's not going to find her, right?"

"Yes. Maybe." She sighed and rubbed the bridge of her nose. "I don't know. He's smart, but he doesn't communicate much."

"I've heard that."

"I guess people around here don't have much to talk about if they've turned to gossiping about a ten-year-old boy." She pulled her hair from its pony-tail, scraped it back up again.

"You sound bitter."

"Not bitter. Just . . . resigned to spending the rest of my life in a tiny little town in the-middle-of-nowhere Washington."

"Ouch," he said without heat. He loved Apple Valley, but not everyone was made for small-town living. Darla certainly hadn't been.

"I didn't mean that quite the way it sounded."

"Then how did you mean it?"

"I didn't plan to be here, Cade. I have a job and a life in Annapolis. This"—she gestured toward the businesses, all of them glittering with Christmas lights and tinsel—"is beautiful and quaint, and maybe I even missed it a little, but it's not going to pay the bills."

"What bills?" he asked, but she took off his coat and handed it back to him.

"I really do have to get going. You buy the dough-nuts next time!" she called as she sprinted east on Main.

He could have followed. He even wanted to. He didn't, because he'd tried the relationship thing with Darla. It hadn't worked out. If he'd learned one thing from his marriage to her, it was that women complicated things, and he didn't need complica-tions.

Right now, all he needed was a refill on his coffee before he headed into the office. Once he got there, he'd forget all about Tessa and her long, lean legs and sweet, sweet smile. He'd forget that he'd spent the night alone in bed. *Again.* He'd forget how empty his house had felt after he'd been with Tessa's little family.

Yeah. Coffee. Work. That's what he needed.

But maybe he needed a little bit of Tessa, too. Reconnecting with an old friend didn't have to be complicated. He was pretty sure he could keep it from being anything but what it was—fun and easy.

Sure you can, Cunningham. Just like you can keep the sun from rising and old Zim from complaining, he thought wryly as he walked back into Murphy's and got ready for the day.

Chapter Five

"So, what kind of bills do you think Emily and Dave Riley had?" Cade asked Ida as he poked at the mystery meat that lay like gray-brown mush in the center of the plate she'd just handed him. Ida liked to think of herself as Apple Valley's version of Mayberry's Aunt Bee, the benevolent housekeeper and cook and caretaker who delivered meals to the sheriff at the local prison. Only she couldn't cook worth shit, and if Cade ate what she'd just brought, he'd probably be puking his guts out for the rest of the day.

"Now, how would I know a thing like that?" She settled into the chair across from his, resting her elbows on the glossy surface of his desk.

She knew something.

Of course.

Ida knew just about everything about everyone in Apple Valley. Mostly she kept her mouth shut. Which is how she'd gotten the title of mayor fifteen years ago. She'd kept the title by holding her tongue when other people didn't. Cade respected that, but sometimes he wanted to shake the truth out of his grandmother.

This was one of those times.

"The same way you knew that Sandra Anderson was going to leave her husband before she did. The same way you knew that Ham Perkins was beating that little boy of his. The same way—"

"I knew that you and Darla weren't meant for each other?"

"That, too." He put down his fork and looked straight into Ida's dark brown eyes. There were more wrinkles around them than when he'd been a kid. A little more droop to the lids, but they hadn't lost any of their sharpness. "What do you know, Gran?"

"Why do you want to know?" she responded. "I think that's the better question. You haven't said one word about that family in a decade. Now, suddenly, you're interested. Why?"

"Because it's my responsibility to know what's happening in this town. If people are struggling—"

"You're the sheriff. Not the local Red Cross." She tapped her fingers on the desktop and gave him the look she'd perfected long before he was born. The one that said spill it.

"No, but Zimmerman Beck is up in arms about the property again."

"What Zim needs is a woman in his life. Ever since Elizabeth died, he's been impossible." Ida tugged at the edges of her bright red sweater and fluffed her white curls. "And what you need is to just tell me the real reason why you're suddenly so interested in the Riley family."

"I'm not." True. Very, very true. He was interested in the McKenzies. One McKenzie in particular.

"You're interested in Tess, then. Not surprising. You two were inseparable in grade school and middle school. I never could figure out what you saw in Emily when little Tess—"

"How about we just stick to the problem at hand, Gran? Zim wants the place cleaned up or he wants Tessa cited and fined."

"Makes sense."

"What's that supposed to mean?"

"The place is a pigsty, and it has been for years. I'm surprised you haven't done anything about it before now."

"There hasn't been a complaint until now." Cade tried to keep a lid on his temper. "Do you think Tessa and Gertrude have the money to pay a cleanup fee and fine?"

"That's a good question. One that, as mayor, I should probably get an answer to." She stood, smoothing wrinkles from her black skirt. "I think I'll go over and have a little chat with Tessa. I saw her at the funeral, but it wasn't the time to really discuss her plans."

"Gran—"

"Relax, Cade. I won't mention your name. I'm just going to feel them out a little, try to see if they need any help without stepping on Gertrude's toes. It's possible that the Rileys had enough insurance to cover all the therapy bills—"

"What therapy bills?" Cade followed Ida to his office door.

"Raising a child like Alex is expensive, Cade. Anyone with a brain in his head would realize it." She took her green wool coat from the hook on the wall and handed it to him. "You know what I've noticed?"

"What?" he muttered as he helped her into the coat.

"People have a lot to say about the mistakes Emily and Dave made, but no one seems to talk about what they did right. When it comes to Alex, they did everything they could, everything possible." She patted his cheek, her palm dry and warm. "Now, I'm sure you want to enjoy that nice meal I brought you, so I'll leave you to it."

He had no plans for the meal except to dump it, but he didn't say that to Ida. "You didn't just come to bring me mystery meatloaf, did you?"

"No. Of course not. But you seemed distracted. I thought I'd better wait to bring up the Christmas gala."

"Gala?"

"*Party.*"

"I know what a gala is. I'm just wondering why we need to discuss it. The town council hosts one every year."

"I know, but this is the hundredth anniversary of the very first town Christmas party." Ida pulled on a pair of black gloves and hiked her purse up on her shoulder. "Daniel and Miriam Riley hosted that party, and the way I've heard it told, a better party has never been had in this town. This year, we should top it. Have everyone dress in period costumes, have old Christmas—"

"Gran, you know this isn't my kind of thing, right? Shouldn't you be discussing it with the council?"

"I already have. We agreed that it's a wonderful idea, but we need a few young men to help set up the town hall. I thought it might be a good job for your boys' club."

"I'll see what I can do."

"Thank you, dear. Tell the boys we'll need them the Friday before Christmas. Maybe you can get a few of your friends to come along, too." She smiled and walked into the hall, obviously satisfied that she'd accomplished her goal.

And, of course, she had.

Trying to stop Ida was like trying to stop the tide. Didn't matter how much a person wanted to, he just couldn't hold her back once she got started on something.

He sent a quick e-mail to the boys' club members, dropped the mystery meat into the trash, and lifted one of the sticky notes that Emma had left on his desk while he'd been out on morning patrol. There were four others. He grabbed them all and tossed them on top of the meatloaf.

"I saw that," Emma said from the open doorway.

He waved her into the office. "We have more important things to worry about than the mess at the Riley property."

"Like what? Angus Grim's lost donkey?"

"Is it missing again?"

"I'm afraid so. What that man needs to do is get a stronger gate," Emma said wearily. There were circles under her eyes, and her hair hung limp around her pale face.

"You okay?" he asked.

"Just tired. And I've about lost patience with Zimmerman Beck. He called again." Emma slapped another sticky note down on Cade's desk.

He tossed it into the garbage with the rest of

them. "Give him a call. Tell him that I'll be there at four, and we can discuss the situation then."

"Will do, boss. Do you need anything else?" she asked.

"A cup of coffee?" he suggested.

She scowled. "Get it yourself. I have better things to do."

Cade laughed as she turned away.

Despite her mousy appearance, she had a backbone. No way could she have survived being raised by her father if she hadn't. Sherman wasn't the kind of guy people wanted to be around. Not in good times, and not in bad times. He was damn lucky that his youngest daughter was willing to put up with him.

Cade grabbed his keys and coat, feeling only a little guilty for going out for lunch when Ida had provided a plate of food.

He walked into the station's reception area, waving to Emma as he crossed to the door. Watery sunlight shone through the front windows, and he could see a half a dozen people walking toward Riley Park. Even in late November, with ice glazing the surface of the pond, the area attracted locals and any tourists who happened to find their way to the tiny picturesque town.

As always, Ida and the rest of the town council had planned the park's Christmas decorations. Wreathes and bows were tied to every streetlight, and every pine and spruce tree was covered with Christmas lights. Above the park, on a small knoll that over-looked the town, Apple Valley Community Church gleamed in the sunlight, its whitewashed walls and tall steeple as much a piece of town history as Daniel and Miriam Riley were.

Cade stepped outside, his gaze drawn to the church for just a moment before he headed up Main Street.

"Sheriff!" someone called as he turned onto First. Zim.

Shit!

"Hey, Zim." He turned and faced the older man, his best fake smile plastered to his face. "Did Emma tell you that I'd be stopping by at four?"

"She told me squat. That's why I came out here." Zim propped knobby fists on his scrawny waist. "I have rights, you know. Just like them Rileys."

"The Rileys are dead," Cade pointed out.

"That doesn't mean they're not responsible for the mess they left. Someone needs to get it cleaned up!"

"It's not a bad thing to have some compassion, Zim." Cade started walking again, hoping the old man would get the hint and give up the argument.

He didn't.

"What about compassion for me having to live next to that mess all these years? What about that?" he cried, his hair vibrating with the force of his irritation.

"You know, Zim, some people think you're not all that concerned about the mess. Some people think that you're just hoping to force the family out so you can buy up the property." Some people being Cade. He kept that little piece of information to himself.

"I don't know what you're talking about," Zim protested, but his ruddy cheeks were even ruddier than usual.

"You used to be a Realtor, Zim. You can't tell me

that you're not interested in fixing that place up and selling it for a profit."

"I'm not going to deny it, but you can't deny that I've been patient. I didn't push as hard as I could have before Dave and Emily . . ." Zim's scowl deepened.

"Were killed by a drunk driver?" Cade offered. "You're a saint, Zim. Come on. I'm hungry, and if we're going to be talking about this for the next few hours, I'd like to have something in my stomach while I do it."

"Where are you planning to eat, Sheriff? Because I'm not made of money," Zim griped as he panted along behind Cade.

If Cade wanted to give the old guy a heart attack, all he had to do was walk a little faster. He slowed down, because no matter how annoying Zim was, Cade didn't want to be responsible for killing him. "I'm heading to the diner."

"You know you can make twenty sandwiches for what it costs to buy one there?"

"Zim, I'm just about out of patience, so how about you keep your opinion about my lunch choice to yourself?" Cade shot Zim a hard look.

"I'm just saying that a smart man keeps a close eye on his budget." Zim didn't seem at all fazed by Cade's warning. "Take me, for example . . ."

Cade decided not to.

As a matter of fact, he opted out of the lecture, Zim's words just a backdrop to other town center noises. Cars passing, people calling out to one another, Christmas music drifting from a toy store at the corner. Cade would have to stop in there on his day off, grab a few gifts for his nieces and nephews.

A small figure rounded the corner, bypassing the toy store and moving across the street toward the park. Shoulders hunched, hood up, dark blue coat flapping open, it could have been anyone, but Cade knew the shuffling steps, the strange, almost disjointed movements of the arms. Alex Riley. The kid should be in school, not wandering around town.

"Hold that thought, Zim," he said, interrupting the other man's diatribe. "I need to take care of something."

"You need to take care of my complaint. I'm not going to wait another ten years," Zim sputtered as Cade sprinted across the street.

"Alex!" he called out.

The boy hesitated, then just kept walking, definitely heading for the park or somewhere beyond it.

Cade put a hand on Alex's shoulder as he caught up to him. "Hey, buddy. Where are you heading?"

Alex shrugged.

"Do your aunts know that you're not in school?" He tried again and was rewarded with a quick head shake. "What about your teacher? Did you tell her you were leaving?"

"It's recess," Alex said simply, his voice still rusty and rough, his gaze on the ground as he walked along the sidewalk.

"That doesn't mean you get to leave the school. You're a smart kid. I'm sure you know that."

"Yes."

"Your teacher is going to be worried when she realizes you're missing."

"I'm not missing," Alex pointed out, his hands patting his sides in a quick, frantic motion. "I'm here."

Cade couldn't argue with that, but he couldn't let

a ten-year-old wander around town unsupervised, either. "But you're not where you're supposed to be. That's a problem."

"I think that I need to be here."

"Why?"

Alex didn't answer. Cade had gotten more out of him than he'd expected to, but they were approaching the entrance to the park, and Cade couldn't let him go in. At just over seventy acres, the park stretched out from the town center to the cemetery at the old church. Aside from the pond and flower garden, there were thick copses of trees and deep ravines. Not a place he'd have wanted his ten-year-old son to be wandering alone.

"Alex." He snagged the back of the kid's coat and pulled him to a stop. "I'm going to have to take you home or back to school. You choose."

Alex stared up at him, his eyes wide, his hair a lighter shade of red than his aunt's, his eyes the same sky blue as his mother's had been.

"Home," he said and turned back the way they'd come.

Cade made a quick call to the elementary school and then called This-N-That. No one answered. Not a surprise. Tessa and Gertrude were probably too busy arguing to answer the phone.

"Hold on, Alex." Cade snagged the back of Alex's jacket again, and the little boy stopped, glancing over his shoulder. This time he looked irritated. Obviously, he had some of Tessa's impatience. "Have you ever ridden in a police car before?"

"I am not a criminal," Alex replied.

Cade couldn't quite help laughing, but Alex didn't seem amused.

"*I'm not.*"

"I'm not either, but I ride in a police car all the time."

"Because you're the sheriff, and it's your job."

"It's also my job to make sure kids are where they're supposed to be. So, how about I give you a ride back to your place?" He steered Alex toward the police station and down the alley that led to the parking area.

Sure, he needed to get the boy home, but he couldn't deny a little zing of excitement, a little heat racing through his blood at the thought of seeing Tessa again. He buckled Alex into the backseat of the cruiser, offering a quick smile as he closed the door.

He could have put on the sirens and lights, given Alex something to talk about at school the next day, but he didn't think Alex was the kind to talk about anything to anyone, so he just pulled out of the parking lot and drove toward This-N-That, the sirens off, the car silent, the boy who might have been Cade's sitting stiff and tense in the backseat.

Chapter Six

Cream-colored siding with dark blue shutters and trim. That was the goal. First, though, Tess had to get rid of several layers of peeling grayish-brown paint. She stepped back, eyeing the progress that she'd made on the lower level of the house. Not bad for four hours of work, but she had more to do and, if the dozen messages Zimmerman Beck had left on the store's answering machine were any indication, a limited amount of time to do it.

One thing at a time.

That was about all Tess could do.

"Looking good," Gertrude said as she lugged a trash bag from the house to one of the seven trash cans Tess had bought at the local Walmart. "You going to stop for lunch anytime soon?"

"Not until I get the second story finished." Tess dragged an old ladder from the side yard and propped it up against the house. For now, she and Gertrude seemed to have a truce. That suited her just fine.

"It'll be midnight by that time."

"I just have to scrape off the stuff that is peeling. It shouldn't take long." Not more than another four or five hours. She tried not to think about it as she climbed up the ladder. The sun was out. For now. It was at least forty degrees. She couldn't complain, and she couldn't waste energy thinking about how much she still had to do.

The key was to make as much progress as possible so that Zimmerman Beck would get off her back *and* her answering machine.

The acrid scent of cigarette smoke drifted from below.

Obviously, Gertrude wasn't as concerned about hurrying to clean up the house as Tessa was.

"You promised to finish the kitchen today," she reminded her, doing her best to keep accusation from her voice. Truces were nice. Especially after days of fighting.

"I may be a prisoner, but I'm entitled to a smoke break and lunch."

"No one said—"

"Dear God in Heaven! The boy's come home in a police car!" Gertrude shrieked so loudly, Tessa nearly lost her balance.

The ladder wobbled but held steady.

Thank God.

"What are you talking about?" She turned her head, saw the cruiser pulling into the driveway. Not just any cruiser, either. The sheriff's car.

She squinted against the afternoon sun, hoping Gertrude was wrong and that Alex wasn't actually in Cade's car.

He was. She could see him clearly, his coppery

head bent close to the window, his fingers tapping frantically on the glass.

"Shit!" she muttered, glad her nephew was still in the car and couldn't hear. He was supposed to be in school, for crying out loud. How in the world had he ended up being picked up by the police?

She climbed down the ladder as quickly as she could without breaking her neck, her heart tripping all over itself with fear and something else. A tiny little bit of anticipation. She was woman enough to admit it, but not quite woman enough to meet Cade's eyes when he got out of the car.

"What's going on, Cade?" Gertrude said before anyone else had a chance to. "You taking my nephew into custody until we get this mess cleaned up? Because I can tell you right now—"

"No need for dramatics, Gertrude," Cade said, cutting her off. He opened the back door of the cruiser, smiling gently at Alex, and Tessa's heart burned hot in her chest.

Why did he have to be good with kids?

Why couldn't he be just another pretty face? Shallow and vain and completely superfluous?

"You're home, buddy," he said.

Alex nodded, and Tessa's heart sank as she looked into her nephew's face. He was sliding away, back into the comfort of his own mind, and there didn't seem to be anything she could do to stop it.

"You're supposed to be at school." She touched Alex's soft hair, but he just shuffled past.

"He said it was recess," Cade explained.

"You can't just leave school because it's recess. You know that." Gertrude pulled Alex to a stop, holding on to him when he tried to shrug away.

"Alex." Tess crouched so that they were eye to eye, touching his chin to force him to meet her gaze. "You know what you did was wrong. What were you thinking?"

"I was thinking about finding her," he responded in his matter-of-fact way. No emotion. No hint of sorrow or grief.

Tess hugged him, not letting go even though his body was rigid and tense. "She's gone. She died. You know what that means, right?"

"She can't die."

"Everyone dies, Alex. When they do—"

"*She* can't," Alex cut in, slipping from her embrace and shuffling away. He moved like an old man, his steps brittle and unsure as he walked up the porch stairs.

"Son—" Gertrude started, but Alex disappeared inside without a backward glance.

Silence fell, thick as morning fog.

None of them seemed to know what to say, but Tessa felt the absurd urge to speak anyway. He was her responsibility, right? That meant she had to solve the problem, fix things. Make sure he stayed safe.

"I'd better go talk to him," she finally managed.

"What are you going to say, huh? You don't even know him, and you barely knew Emily," Gertrude said bitterly. "Stay out here and scrape the damn house. I'll take care of Alex."

"Ouch," Cade murmured as Gertrude slammed the front door.

Ouch was right.

But that was Gertrude and always had been. Mercurial and temperamental. Just a little resentful of the fact that she'd been left to raise her much younger sister's girls. "She's upset about Alex. It's just a lot easier to be angry with me."

"That's not an excuse." Cade frowned.

"It's a reason, and I guess after everything we've all been through, I need to give her a little leeway."

"She doesn't give you any. But"—he smiled, and Tessa's heart did a stupid little happy dance—"I admire your charitable spirit."

"You wouldn't be saying that if you could spend about three minutes in my head." She laughed, lighter than she'd been a minute ago. Happier, because being with Cade had always made her feel that way.

"Then I guess it's good that I can't." He propped his hip against the car, his arms folded across his chest. "What are you going to do about Alex, Tess? He was heading to the park when I found him. That's not a good place for a kid to be wandering around alone."

"I wish I knew." She rubbed the back of her neck and glanced at the house. "He's not a typical kid, and I just can't figure out how to reach him. Not that I'd know how to reach a kid who *was* typical."

"You've always handled whatever life sent your way. You'll handle this."

"You have a lot of confidence in me, Cade. I wish *I* did." The lump was back in her throat, and she looked away because she didn't want Cade to see how close she was to crying.

"Come here," he said, sighing, and the next thing she knew, she was in his arms, her nose buried in cold leather. Years ago, she and Cade had shared secrets and dreams. She'd told him everything, and he'd done the same. Standing there with him felt like going back in time, and she was ready to spill her guts, tell him just how unsure she was, how afraid she was of failing her nephew.

"You're going to be great, Red," he murmured against her hair. "I promise."

If only his promise could make it so, but promises were about as useful as sand in a desert.

And standing in his arms could only make her want things that weren't meant to be.

She stepped away, her hands shaking a little as she brushed paint chips from her jeans.

"Thanks." She looked at the house, all the work that still needed to be done, and felt so tired, she thought she could sleep for a month. "I'd better get back to work. The house won't scrape itself."

"What's the hurry?" He grabbed her hand, pulling her to the swing. "You look like you could use a break."

"I don't nee—"

He sat, yanking her down beside him. "Shut up, Tess, and just sit for a minute. You're going to wear yourself ragged trying to get this house done, and then where will Alex be?"

"Apparently inside with Gertrude," she muttered, trying hard not to notice how firmly their thighs were pressed together, the heat of his hip against her, or—and this was the most difficult of all to ignore—how good he smelled. Leather and outdoors and something indefinable and completely masculine.

"I talked to Zim today," he said, his words like a splash of ice water in her face.

Here she was, mooning over Cade when her whole life was going to hell in a handbasket.

She would have jumped off the swing if she hadn't been firmly wedged in place by Cade's hard body. "That doesn't surprise me. Unfortunately, I'm cleaning up as quickly as I can, but it's still going to take time."

"You're not going to scrape all the paint yourself, are you?"

"I don't really have a choice. Gertrude is too old and ornery to help, and Alex is too young. That leaves me."

"You could hire a crew and have it done in a day or two."

"That would be a great idea if there was money to do it." She had a nice little nest egg saved, but she needed to keep that for emergencies. Besides, getting her hands dirty and keeping herself busy was the best way to keep from focusing on what she'd lost.

And what she'd gained.

"Emily and Dave didn't have life insurance?" Cade's dark brows pulled together. He wasn't the kind of guy who'd have a family and not have life insurance. He'd have had everything in place to provide for his son.

Obviously, he couldn't understand how a person could die and leave the care of his child to chance.

Tess couldn't either.

"Look around." She waved toward the house. "Does this place look like it was being cared for by people who planned for the future?"

"I don't think either of them ever thought about much more than the moment."

"They were good people, though." She jumped to

their defense. It was fine for her to think they'd sucked, but not for anyone to say it.

Double standards, and she couldn't have cared less.

"I didn't say they weren't. But being nice doesn't always cut it when it comes to life." Cade's hand dropped to her thigh, the heat of his palm searing through her jeans and wiping out just about every thought she had in her head.

She wanted to tell him to move his hand so she could think again, but since coming back to Apple Valley, thinking had become highly overrated. She'd spent way too many hours thinking about all the things she should have said to Emily. Thinking about all the times she could have come for a visit and hadn't. Thinking about the job she was going to have to quit.

Soon.

Very soon.

Because Alex needed to be in Apple Valley.

Her eyes burned, and she blinked rapidly.

"Don't cry." Cade's hand slid from her thigh to her waist, his fingers wrapping in the belt loop of her jeans.

"I'm not," she mumbled, her throat so tight she almost choked on the words.

"You were thinking about it, though."

He was right. She'd been thinking about crying, but it was a colossal waste of time and energy. So was sitting with Cade. Seriously! Hadn't she learned anything during the past ten years? Men were trouble for women like Tessa, because she was just like her good-for-nothing mother . . . attracting guys who were good at acting the part of caring, concerned boyfriends, but who weren't so good at being them.

Take Kent for instance. He'd had it all. A great job as an electrical engineer, money, looks, charm. What he'd lacked was heart. And, apparently, a conscience. He'd barely blinked an eye when she'd thrown the sexy little silk teddy that she'd found under their bed in his face.

She didn't wear sexy lingerie. She wore boxers and tanks. Which, according to Kent, had been part of their problem.

Bastard!

She brushed Cade's hand away and extracted herself from his very warm, very tempting embrace. "I'd better get back to work. Thanks again for bringing Alex home. We'll talk to him and make sure he doesn't leave school again."

He nodded, his eyes dark with something she didn't plan to acknowledge, his gaze raking over her in the kind of slow once-over a man usually reserved for a woman who'd captured his attention.

A dozen years ago, she probably would have swooned at the thought of Cade Cunningham looking at her like that. Now, she just felt tired.

She stalked to the ladder and clambered up, setting the scraper against a chunk of old paint.

A car door slammed, but she didn't glance down at Cade's police cruiser. She wasn't going to wave good-bye. She'd thanked him and that was good enough. A few seconds ticked by. Nothing. Not a cough or purr. No sign that Cade was heading back to work.

"Hey, Red!" he called from right below her, and

she nearly tumbled off the ladder. "Hold tight. I'm coming up."

"You can't—"

Too late. The ladder shimmied under his weight, and she grabbed a windowsill to hold herself steady. "What in the heck are you doing, Cade?"

"You need a hat." His body brushed hers, every inch of his chest and thighs pressed to every inch of her back and hips.

She froze. Afraid to breathe. Not because she was afraid she'd tip the ladder if she did, but because inhaling brought her that much closer to Cade. "I do *not* need a hat," she muttered.

"It may be forty degrees, but the sun is still brutal." He plopped a baseball hat on her head, his fingers brushing through her ponytail. "There you go," he murmured, his lips so close to her ear, she could feel the warmth of his breath.

If she turned her head just even the tiniest bit . . .

But of course she wouldn't.

Ever.

Because she was done with men. Completely and forever done.

"Thanks." She made a big show of working off a chunk of paint, her body so stiff from trying not to touch any part of Cade that she thought a gentle breeze would snap her in two.

"No problem," he responded easily, his voice completely unchanged. No hint that he felt anything other than what they both should . . . the cold ashes of old friendship. The ladder shimmied again as he made his way down.

This time he didn't return.

The car door slammed. The engine roared. The cruiser rumbled away.

Good. Great. Wonderful even, because standing on a ladder, scraping paint off her sister's house, was exactly what Tessa wanted to do.

And she wanted to do it alone.

Even if forty degrees did suddenly feel like seven below, and even if the weight of Cade's baseball hat felt like every dream Tess had ever let die.

She sniffed hard, because it was cold and her nose was running. Not because she still felt like crying.

Behind her, the old swing creaked, its rusty chains groaning quietly. She didn't look down. She was almost afraid of what she'd see. Maybe Emily's ghostly form, looking up at her and laughing, telling her to go with the flow and let things happen.

Only letting things happen had never gotten Emily anything but trouble, and Tessa had always been the one walking along behind her, cleaning up the messes she left behind.

Piano music drifted from the house, the same sad and haunting melody Alex had played before, each note a wordless cry for something he needed that Tess couldn't provide.

Maybe she'd figure it all out eventually. Maybe she wouldn't be as colossal a failure at parenting as her mother had been.

Either way, she could fix the house up. Find a way to make some money and keep Alex in the place he loved. If that was all she could give him, at least he'd have that.

The rest . . . ?

A wing and a prayer. That's what Gertrude used to say when they'd been so poor that she'd stalked the garbage bin behind Goodwill to find school clothes for Tess and Emily.

We may make it on a wing and a prayer, but we'll make it.

Hopefully, that would prove true this time, because Tessa didn't have a plan B. She wasn't even sure she had a plan A.

Chapter Seven

Tessa scraped paint until her palm was raw and her fingers ached. If the sun hadn't started to go down and a cold wind hadn't started blowing, she probably would have kept going until she didn't have a bit of skin left on her hand. It just seemed so much easier than going inside.

She lugged the ladder into the backyard and shoved it into the old storage shed, pushing it in between an old table and an older rocking chair. She didn't know what else was in there. She hadn't had the courage to look through the stuff crammed into the building. Dave and Emily hadn't believed in throwing things away.

She dragged the rocking chair out and brushed off a thick layer of dust. An eon ago, someone had painted it baby blue and covered the seat in 1970s plaid, but the chair dated from the 1860s, the high back stylized with gorgeous lines. Restored, it would be worth a pretty penny.

"You planning to come in anytime tonight?"

Gertrude called from the corner of the house. "I made fried chicken."

Tessa wasn't hungry, but she couldn't say no to Gertrude's fried chicken. It was a peace offering. A truce. The same thing she'd offered when Tessa was a kid and they'd been at odds. Neither willing to back down. Both sorry. A stalemate with no way out. Every time it happened, Gertrude pulled out her great-grandmother's fried chicken recipe, and every time, Tessa ate it.

She'd eat it this time, too. Even if it choked her.

"I'll be right in," she said.

"What have you got there?" Gertrude walked across the yard.

"An old rocking chair." She refrained from mentioning that it had been left to rot in a cluttered shed. This was a truce, after all.

"It was probably in the house when Emily moved in. She wasn't keen on the old-fashioned furniture that was here, but Dave wouldn't let her throw it out."

"Smart guy."

Gertrude frowned, and Tessa hurried to continue. No way did she want to start the feud again. "I mean that, Gertrude. This is a good piece. Once all this paint is stripped off—"

"How about you tell me about it over dinner? Alex hasn't eaten yet, and he's probably hungry." There was no denying the worry in her voice, and Tessa couldn't find it in herself to be even moderately annoyed at being cut off.

"Sure." She lifted the rocking chair, grunting a little under its weight. She really needed to get back into some kind of workout routine. A week and a half away from the gym, and she was already starting to feel soft.

"You're bringing that inside?" Gertrude asked as they walked around the side of the house together.

"For now," Tess panted. The thing was heavy. Much heavier than she'd anticipated.

"Weren't you the one who was talking about clearing things out of the store?"

"Yes, but this is something we can sell once it's restored." She stumbled up the porch stairs and dropped the chair near the door.

"How much do you think something like that will bring?" Gertrude lit a cigarette and blew a puff of smoke into the frigid air. "Once it's fixed up."

"If I were selling it in Annapolis, five hundred. Here? Maybe two."

"Two, huh?" Gertrude touched the faded plaid cushion. "That's not bad."

"No, and there are dozens of pieces stacked around the house. Nice vintage pieces, some really nice antiques. If we sell some of those—"

"It's a good thought, Tess. It really is, but there are certain things we've got to keep. They've been in the house for a hundred years. They need to stay here."

"Like the angel you gave to Cade?" The question just slipped out, landing right square in the middle of their very nice truce. Damn it!

Gertrude tensed, her lips pressed together, the cigarette dangling from between her fingers. "You're probably right. I probably shouldn't have done that."

The acquiescence shocked Tess speechless.

She stared at her aunt, not sure if she should feel

her forehead for a fever or call the men in white coats to come and take her away.

"What?" Gertrude took a puff of the cigarette and then flicked it out into the yard.

"Are you sick, Gertie?"

"What kind of fool question is that?"

"I've known you for twenty-three years, and I've never, ever heard you say you were wrong before."

"There's a first time for everything. Come on. Let's go eat." She led the way into the house, and Tess followed, leaving the heavy chair exactly where it was. No one would take it off the porch. Not in Apple Valley.

The house was quiet, the stairs creaking as Tessa hurried upstairs. No piano music. Thank goodness! Alex had given up on his melancholy song soon after he got home from school. The music had been ringing through Tessa's head since then, though. No matter how hard she'd tried, she hadn't been able to shake it.

The scent of fried chicken and chocolate cake filled the apartment. Gertrude had gone on a cleaning frenzy, too. Every piece of furniture gleamed and the old wood floor nearly sparkled. There wasn't a dirty pan in the sink or on the counter. Not a speck of dust anywhere.

"You've been busy," she said.

"We both have been. Now it's time to take a break." Gertrude grabbed plates from a cupboard and dropped them onto the table. "Alex, come on, son! It's time to eat."

The door at the end of the hall opened, and Alex shuffled out, his skin pale, his hair ruffled. He had a block car in his hands. Some snapped-together creation. He was almost as good at making things as he was at composing music.

"What did you make?" Tessa asked as he sat at the table. He didn't respond, his head bent as he stared at something on the table. A spot? A speck? Whatever it was, it was obviously more interesting than Tessa.

"Don't be rude, Alex," Gertrude chided. She sounded tired, the weary edge to her voice reflecting the weariness of the house. The faded paint and worn throw rugs, the tired furniture that made a sad attempt to be cheerful. Emily had done well with what she'd had, but there was a vibe of unhappiness to the place, a hint of discontent.

"It's okay. I think we're all a little tired," Tessa offered, smiling at Alex even though he was still staring down at the table.

"That has nothing to do with being rude. Alex knows he's supposed to respond when he's spoken to." Gertrude put a plate of steaming fried chicken on the table and shot Tess a hard look.

It seemed like their truce was going to end before it even began. Tess put chicken on Alex's plate and a piece on her own. Dug into the baked macaroni and the fresh coleslaw that Gertrude slammed onto the table.

Yeah. The truce was over.

But at least they'd tried. For all of three seconds.

The doorbell rang, the sound cutting through the tension and the silence. It was as good an excuse as any for Tessa to leave her plateful of food and the table. "I'll get it."

She ran down the stairs, tripping all over herself in her hurry to get out. She braced herself as she opened the door, sure it was Zim coming to tell her that she hadn't done enough to clean up the mess. "Don't worry . . ."

The words trailed off as she looked into Ida Cunningham's stunning face. The woman had to be eighty, but she looked a couple of decades younger, her face lined with years of smiling, her eyes the same deep denim blue as Cade's.

"I wasn't worried. Not particularly," she said with a smile and stepped into the house, her high heels clicking, her black wool pencil skirt perfectly tailored to her shapely figure.

"I'm sorry, Ms. Ida. I thought you were someone else."

"More than likely, you thought I was Zimmerman." She unbuttoned her coat and looked around. "I'm happy to say that I'm not. The man has spent one too many years alone, if you ask me. But since no one has, I'll keep quiet on the subject."

She would.

That was the thing about Ida. She was one of the few people in Apple Valley that didn't love a juicy piece of gossip.

"It's really nice of you to stop by, Ida. We're just eating dinner. There's plenty if you want to join us."

"I'd love to, dear, but I have a dozen things on my plate right now. A whole list that I need to get through before the end of the week." She pulled a small notebook from her coat pocket and thumbed through it. "And here you are on it. Item number five."

Coming from anyone else, the announcement would have seemed rude, but Ida was one of the kindest, most sensible women Tess had ever met.

She lived by lists, and if you were on one of them, it meant she cared about you deeply.

"I made it onto your list? I'm touched," Tessa teased, and was rewarded with another of Ida's smiles.

"You are, and you should be. This, though"—Ida tapped the notebook page—"is about that angel your aunt donated to the historical society. We're going to have a little ceremony on Friday to honor the Riley family and to allow the public to see it. We'll have tea and sandwiches, cookies. All kinds of wonderful treats. Have you met Charlotte?"

"Yes." Not under the best of circumstances, but Tess kept that little tidbit of information to herself.

"She's doing all the cooking and baking. That girl is a rock star in a kitchen."

"It sounds great."

"Of course, once we're finished with our little tea, I'm going to have Cade bring the angel back here. Now that you're staying, I'm sure Gertrude wishes she hadn't donated it."

"How did you know—"

"Dear"—Ida patted her arm—"I know just about everything there is to know about this town."

"Who's down there?" Gertrude appeared at the top of the stairs, her hair still a strange shade of pink rather than red and sticking up around her head like she'd just stuck her finger into a light socket. Old sweats hung from her bony hips, and her T-shirt had food stains on the front. The unlit cigarette dangling from her fingers just added to the overall picture.

Compared to Ida . . .

Well, there *was* no comparison.

Which had been of huge concern to Tessa when she was a hormonal teenager and everything Gertrude did was an embarrassment.

"Hello, Gertrude!" Ida offered her trademark smile. "How are you doing, my dear?"

"Holding up." Gertrude picked her way down the stairs as if her bones ached and her body hurt. She looked older than Tessa wanted her to be, more fragile than seemed possible for someone with so much personality. "It's been tough, though."

"I can't even imagine, Gert." Ida touched Gertrude's arm. They were as different as night and day, but they were friends and had been for as long as Tessa could remember. "She was your daughter."

"Yes." Gertrude swallowed hard and nodded. "She was. Never could have kids of my own, and she was a piece of my heart. Now I've got her son, but it's not the same."

"And you have Tessa." Ida's gaze jumped from Gertrude to Tessa. She wasn't smiling now, but then she knew how difficult things had always been between them.

"For now." Gertrude offered a quick nod as if conceding a point she didn't quite agree with.

"I, for one, am glad to hear it. I've missed having you around, Tess. But what about your work? You're an interior designer, aren't you? What's going to happen to your job?"

"I'm going to submit my resignation. Hopefully, I can find something here." *Nice of you to ask*, she wanted to add. *Since my aunt chooses not to.*

"You worked there for quite a while, didn't you?"

"Seven years."

"Your boss will probably be very sorry to lose you."
Once again, Ida said all the right things while Gertrude scowled.

"I'm sure he'll be sorry to see me go, but the firm is large, and he won't be hurting without me." Large was actually an understatement. James Winthrop's firm was one of the largest in the Annapolis–D.C. area, and he had clients up and down the East Coast. Dozens of employees, hundreds of clients, James had built a reputation that had made him one of the most sought-after interior designers in the nation.

He'd do just fine without Tessa.

She wasn't sure she'd do all that well without him.

Or, at least, without the income working for him had provided.

"Are you sure staying here is the right thing for you, though? You worked so hard to establish yourself there, and—"

"She said she's staying here, Ida."

"And I said I was happy to hear it, but a family needs money to support itself. If Dave and Emily didn't leave enough money to pay the taxes on the house and to cover Alex's therapy, Tess is going to have to have a job. Finding one here may be—"

"Emily and Dave didn't leave squat, but it doesn't matter. Tess said we're staying. Stop trying to change the girl's mind," Gertrude barked, then sighed, rubbing her forehead. "Sorry. I didn't mean to snap. This has been . . . tough, and I'm just plumb wore out."

"I know, and you don't need to apologize. We've been friends far too long for that." Ida patted Gertrude's arm.

"Which is why I shouldn't have taken my mood out on you." Gertrude glared at Tess, apparently more than happy to take it out on her.

"Water under the bridge, dear. Now, how about we get back to why I came knocking on your door at dinnertime? I already told Tessa. We're going to have a lovely community tea this Friday. Give everyone a good look at Miriam's angel. Once it's over, I'm going to bring her back here. Since you're staying, the angel really should stay, too."

"You don't know how relieved I am to hear that. I should never have donated it. The angel was meant to stay with the house, or at least with the last Riley," Gertrude said.

To Tessa's shock and horror, Gertrude's voice broke.

Was she going to cry?

"You're in the midst of a very emotional time." Ida pulled Gertrude in for a hug. "I knew when Cade brought me the angel that you'd regret giving it up. Alex deserves to have every part of his legacy. His family was such an important part of Apple Valley's history, and I'm sure it will continue to be part of our story for years to come."

"Thank you, Ida," Gertrude mumbled, her voice a little stronger. "You're a class act."

"As are you. Now"—Ida stepped back and brushed a wrinkle from her skirt—"you two come to the tea on Friday afternoon. We're starting at three and ending at six. You don't have to stay the whole time, but it would be really nice to have you there."

"We will be. Won't we, Tess?"

Tess supposed that they would be, but she wasn't sure how excited she was by the idea. It wasn't that she didn't want to reconnect with old friends. It was just that she didn't want to see what she knew would be in the eyes of every one of the people she'd gone to high school with.

That I-told-you-so look that made it clear that Tessa had thought way too much of herself and her talents when she'd driven away from town.

It wouldn't matter that she'd gone to college, gotten a degree, had had a good-paying job with a prestigious company. No, all that would matter was that she was back, living in a run-down house on an overgrown piece of property.

Ida walked outside and Tess followed, standing on the porch and watching as the mayor picked her way across the yard and got into her black sedan.

A quick honk of the horn and Ida was gone, the taillights of the car disappearing from view.

Across the street, Charlotte's house was dark. Not one light shining from the windows. Apple Valley didn't have much of a nightlife, but there were things to do if a person looked hard enough. Reading groups at the library, bowling at Mike's Bowl City. As far as Tessa knew, in the summer the drive-in theater still ran G-rated movies.

Eventually, Tess would get back into the swing of small-town life. Whether or not it would drive her stark-raving mad remained to be seen.

She glanced at Zim's house. *It* wasn't dark. There were Christmas lights shining from the porch railing, lights spilling out from the front windows, and more lights glowing on either side of the door. The curtains in the front window were open, and beyond it a decorated Christmas tree sparkled in a well-lit room.

Zim might be worried about his neighbor's messes, but he wasn't worried about his electric bill.

A figure walked past the window. Not the old stoop-shouldered man Tessa expected. Someone taller, broader. Someone who looked a lot like . . .

Zim's front door opened, and Cade stepped outside with Zimmerman.

Dark hair glinting with reflected Christmas lights, his leather jacket unzipped and revealing his uniform shirt. Man! He filled it out well, his abdomen flat and taut beneath the light blue cotton.

She shouldn't be noticing that. Just like she shouldn't have noticed how good he smelled earlier, or how nice it felt to be back in his arms. Funny how easy it was to fall back into old patterns.

She hadn't seen the guy for ten years, and then suddenly, all she was doing was seeing him. Every place she went, there he was. Just like when they were kids.

Only she wasn't a kid, and she knew exactly where all that seeing him and thinking about him would lead.

He glanced her way, and she took an unconscious step back, nearly tripping in her haste.

"Idiot!" she hissed, hurrying into the house and closing the door. Locking it tight as if Cade were going to come bursting in demanding her attention again.

No. He wouldn't do that. He'd wait for her to come looking for him. That's what the pattern had always been. Not this time, though. She'd grown up a lot since the days when she'd chased him around town, hanging on his every word and laughing at his jokes.

She'd been so desperate it was almost embarrassing to think about.

It *was* embarrassing to think about.

A soft noise drifted from the depth of the house. Not a sigh exactly, but something close to it.

Tess stiffened, all thoughts of Cade gone as she cocked her head and listened.

Upstairs, pots and pans were clanging and Gertrude was humming. Ida's visit must have cheered her up. Downstairs, the air felt thick and heavy, the musty scent of dust still hanging in the air after days of cleaning.

There!

She heard it again!

The same soft sound. Not quite a sigh. Not quite a whisper.

The hair on the back of her neck stood on end, and she was tempted to go upstairs and pretend she hadn't heard anything, but that wasn't her style.

She'd always been a realist. Always been pragmatic and grounded. Aside from her little foray into puppy love as a teen, she'd never lost her head over anyone or anything. Even Kent, the man she'd planned to marry, hadn't been able to sweep her off her feet.

That's probably why she'd been more irritated than brokenhearted when she'd realized what a lying, cheating ass he was.

She flipped on lights as she walked through the front room and into the dining room. She didn't know what she expected to see. A ghostly apparition? A creepy doll swinging in one of the old baby swings?

There was nothing. Everything was still and quiet,

the clutter weeded down to a manageable pile of crappy stuff that someone might want. Gertrude had been working hard while Tess was scraping the house. She'd give her that.

She walked into the old kitchen, completely sure that there was going to be nothing there, either.

A dark shadow moved in front of her, darting to the left as she entered.

She screamed, her heart nearly bursting from her chest before she realized what she was seeing.

Who she was seeing.

"Alex! What in the he—world are you doing down here!" she hollered, flipping on the light and looking into her nephew's startled face.

He blinked, his blue eyes wide and empty.

"Alex?" She gentled her voice. "You weren't trying to go outside, were you?" She glanced at the mudroom. No way could he squeeze his way through the mess in there to get out the back door. She wasn't sure he knew that, though.

"No," he answered.

"What—"

He turned his back to her, walking across the nearly clean kitchen and touching the old china cabinet that stood against the wall. He pressed his forehead against the glass.

"We need to bring her back," he said so quietly Tessa almost didn't hear.

"What?" She put a hand on his shoulder, wincing when he tensed.

"My angel."

"You mean the one Gertrude gave away?"

"Yes. She goes here." He shrugged away from Tessa and opened the cabinet. It was stuffed full of trinkets. Old chipped china cups and porcelain knickknacks. Yellowed lace doilies. Things piled on top of things, none of it seeming to have any particular order or value.

Alex seemed to know what he was looking for, though.

He lifted a pile of doilies and revealed a wooden box. Maybe five by seven inches, it had an intricate mother-of-pearl inlay on the top and a tiny lock on the side.

Alex handed the box to Tessa, replaced the doilies, and closed the cabinet.

"What is it?"

"Miriam's," he said as if she should know exactly what that meant.

"Okay, it was Miriam's. But . . . *what* is it?"

"'Night, Tessa," he responded, walking out of the room.

She would have followed, but she was too busy basking in his words. *Tessa.* It was the first time he'd called her that. Ever.

She hugged the box to her chest and turned off the kitchen light, her heart thumping the painful, slow rhythm of love for her nephew. She'd been at the hospital when he was born, had looked into his eyes and been lost.

When he was diagnosed with autism, she'd flown in to be with her sister, hoping to offer support. She'd watched Alex sit at the piano. Three years old and tapping out a melody that was both boisterous and lively. He hadn't spoken a word in his life at that point. Not one, but Tess had believed he would. She'd told Emily that one day he'd say Mommy,

Daddy, Aunt Gertrude. And, one day, he would say Aunt Tessa.

Eventually, he'd started calling his family members by name, but he hadn't seen Tessa frequently enough to include her in the small group of people that he communicated with.

The day had finally come.

Too bad Emily wasn't around to see it.

Chapter Eight

Seeing Tessa three times in one day was probably overkill, but Cade couldn't seem to make himself care. He walked up the creaky porch stairs and knocked on the door.

An hour with Zim had calmed the older man down and elicited a promise to leave the McKenzies alone for a while. Zim hadn't been all that excited about it, but he'd agreed to give Tessa and Gertrude time to clean things up. Tess would be happy to hear that, but that wasn't the real reason Cade was standing outside her door.

He wanted to see her again.

It was as simple as that.

The door opened a crack and Tess peered out, a chain pulled tight across the crack in the door. "What are you doing here?"

"Standing on the porch waiting for you to open the door."

Most of Tessa's face was hidden, but he was pretty sure she smiled. "Smart-ass."

"True. Are you going to let me in, or am I going to have to stand out here freezing my—"

"Hold on." She closed the door, and the chain rattled as she unhooked it. Seconds later, the door opened wide.

"Come on in. Even though I'm not sure I want to hear what you have to say." Tessa stepped back, a small wooden box in her hands. It was a pretty little thing. Much prettier than most of the stuff Cade had seen in This-N-That.

"What's this?" he asked, plucking the box from her hand and studying it.

"I don't know. Alex pulled it out of an old china cabinet."

"Anything in it?" He tried to open the box, but it was locked.

"I have no idea."

"Want me to break it open?"

"No!" She snatched it back, her eyes blazing. "This is over a century old, Cade."

"Sorry."

"You should be." She set the little box on a table and put her hands on her hips, her jaw tilted up. *This* Tess was a Tess he knew. Strong, determined, and just a little belligerent.

"What are you smiling about?" she asked impatiently.

"You."

"Well, stop. I'm trying to maintain my sour mood." But a tiny smile curved the corners of her mouth.

"Now, why would you want to do a thing like that?"

"Because, you're about to tell me what old Zim said."

He laughed and was rewarded with a full-out smile. She had beautiful lips, silky and deep pink, and he couldn't quite stop looking at them.

"So, go ahead. Tell me what he said," she demanded, raking her hand over her hair, smoothing some of the wild curls.

"Not much. Mostly he listened to what I had to say."

"You're kidding, right? Because Zimmerman Beck does not seem like the kind of guy who likes to spend a lot of time listening."

"Zim may be a grumpy old man, but he can be reasonable. He's agreed to back off for a while. I think the progress you've made on your house might have had something to do with that." The fact that Cade had told Zim that he wasn't going to win any points in the community by harassing a grieving family had helped, too.

"Well, that's a relief. I'm working as fast as I can, but the man has called at least a dozen times today. I was beginning to think that if Gertrude didn't kill the guy, I would have to."

"Murder is against the law, Tess. I can't recommend it." He tucked a curl behind her ear, just because he wanted to touch her silky hair and velvety skin.

She stilled, her eyes going wide, the pulse in the hollow of her neck beating rapidly. He almost slid his finger to the spot, just to see how far he could push things before Tess pushed back. To see if maybe she *wouldn't* push back. But she was pale, her eyes deeply shadowed, and he figured that what she needed more than some jackass making a pass at her was a friend.

"I was kidding," he said, to break the silence and the tension.

"I was, too." The huskiness in her voice made his gut tighten. "But I'd be lying if I said Zim hasn't driven me to the edge of sanity today. I don't blame him for being upset about the house, but I have other things to worry about."

"Like?"

"The fact that Alex left school without permission today. The fact that I don't really know how to reach him, Gertrude thinks I'm a loser, and I'm wondering if she's right. And then there's my job . . . I'm going to have to quit, but if I do, I won't have an income or any way to pay the bills Emily and Dave left behind. If I can't . . ." She shook her head. "Sorry. That's probably way more than you wanted to know."

"I want to know it all," he responded, holding both her hands, palm to palm, fingers woven together. Just like they had when they were little kids sharing each other's deepest dreams. He couldn't believe he'd forgotten that for so long. Forgotten how much he'd enjoyed just being with her.

"Look, Cade. I'm fine, okay? You don't have to worry about me." She tugged her hands from his, and his palms felt cold, his hands empty.

"I'm not worried. I'm just trying to understand."

"What? How my sister and brother-in-law could have left such a mess? Or how I ended up being the one who had to clean it up?"

"How you ended up so damn responsible when your sister was—" *A loser* didn't seem like the right way to describe a dead woman, but Cade was tempted. He knew how many times Tess had gotten

Emily out of trouble. She'd written term papers for her sister, paid for items that Emily had stolen from local shops. She'd cleaned up puke when Emily drank too much, and she'd snuck out in the middle of the night to follow Emily to parties, staking out whatever house or apartment her sister went into and escorting her home.

"Someone had to be responsible," Tess said wearily.

"You were a good sister to her, Tess. I know she thought so."

"Maybe when we were kids, but it's been years since I spent any amount of time with her."

"She still loved you," he said, mostly because it seemed like what he *should* say. The fact was, love had been something Emily wanted, but not something she knew how to give. Not for any length of time, anyway.

"As much as she could love anyone, I suppose." Tess walked into what had once been a parlor and stared out into the dark yard.

She and her sister had been about as opposite as two people could be. One driven. The other lackadaisical. One focused. The other flighty. One loyal. The other . . .

He couldn't call Emily traitorous, but she *was* a cheat. He'd found that out the hard way right around the time Emily had announced her pregnancy. He'd assumed the baby was his, even though their relationship had been rocky since he'd gone off to college, and he'd been prepared to do the right thing. He had a ring, had perfected his proposal speech, and he'd even been excited about the idea of being a father.

He'd told Tess all about his plans, the two of them

sitting on his parents' porch swing. She'd smelled like vanilla and cinnamon. He remembered that. What he couldn't remember was what she'd said after he'd told her. *Good luck*, maybe. Or, *I hope you'll be happy.*

"You weren't happy when you found out Emily was pregnant, were you?" He'd never thought to ask before, didn't know why he felt the need to ask ten years after the fact.

She shrugged, her shoulders taut beneath a faded sweatshirt. She'd pushed the sleeves up, and her forearms were smooth and flecked with gray paint from the hours she'd spent scraping the house. Even after her death, Emily had the power to make her sister work for her. No wonder Tess had left town and never looked back.

"Did you leave town because you were afraid you'd end up taking care of her baby?" That was another thing he'd never asked. She hadn't given him the chance. Just packed up and gone. *A day past eighteen and determined to make her way in the world*, Gertrude had said bitterly Christmas morning. Cade had been surprised. Shocked even, but he'd been too nervous about the proposal to think much about Tess.

"I'm not really in the mood for a jaunt down memory lane, Cade." She swung around, and he was struck by her beauty, the delicate line of her jaw, and the almost harsh angle of her cheekbones. And those eyes. Large and purplish, and right at that moment, filled with a truckload of irritation.

"No jaunt, Red. Just curiosity. You never even said good-bye."

"You were preoccupied." She frowned and brushed paint from her arms.

"So, you had it all planned out? It wasn't just a spur-of-the-moment thing?"

It had been, but Tess wasn't going to tell Cade that. She wasn't going to admit that his announcement had been the catalyst. That she'd actually been looking forward to spending Christmas with her family, or that she'd planned to finish out her senior year of high school even though she already had enough credits to graduate. "You know that I never planned to live in Apple Valley. From the minute I got here, all I wanted to do was go somewhere else."

Now that she was back, though, the small-town ways that she'd despised as a kid seemed comforting. Ida stopping by to announce a community tea, Charlotte waving from her house as Tess worked, bringing slices of gingerbread and cups of hot chocolate.

Cade . . . standing in her house, close enough to touch.

She fisted her hands, stared out the window again.

"Tess." Cade urged her back around. "You didn't answer my question." He touched her arm, and she shook her head because she was afraid of what she might say, of the things she might reveal. She wasn't like her sister; she didn't need to be taken care of. She didn't *want* to be taken care of.

But she *did* want Cade. Even after all the years she'd spent telling herself she didn't, hadn't, wouldn't ever again.

"You should probably go," she said.

He nodded, his palm sliding up her arm and cupping her nape, his fingers warm and rough, calloused from his work, but gentle, because he was

Cade. He pressed a kiss to her forehead, just a brush of his lips, but it burned through her, made her breath catch and her heart jump.

She didn't walk him to the door, just watched as Cade crossed the yard to Zim's place and got into his truck. Headlights splashed across the yard as he backed out of the driveway and pulled away.

It took a few more minutes for her to get up the gumption to move. Her legs felt heavy, her chest tight as she grabbed the box and headed upstairs.

Gertrude was still in the kitchen, humming some old tune, her bony hips gyrating as she shoved a plate into the cupboard.

Tessa decided not to disturb her. Knowing Gertrude, it would ruin the mood, and they'd be fighting again. She carried the box into Emily's bedroom and left it on the bed, then walked to Alex's room. He'd closed the door, and the room beyond was silent.

"Alex?" She knocked softly, almost hoping that he wouldn't respond.

The door opened, and he stood on the threshold, his golden-red hair standing up around his head. He had a few freckles, and his thin face was shaped more like Tessa's than like Emily's. As a matter of fact, more than one person had commented on the photo of him that Tess kept on her desk at work, asking if Alex were her son.

She'd always laughed and said she didn't have time for kids. She wasn't laughing now.

"Can I come in?" she asked, and took his silence as consent.

His room was neat as a pin. The shelves free of clutter, the piano free of dust. His books were lined up from smallest to largest, thickest to thinnest, the blue duvet on his bed wrinkle-free. The only hint at what he'd been doing was the rocking chair slowing to a stop in the corner.

"Were you rocking in your chair?" she asked, feeling inane and inept and just a little foolish.

He stared up at her, his eyes big and Emily-blue.

"It's okay if you were. What I mean is, it's your rocking chair, and of course you can rock in it anytime you want."

Good one, Tess. Great piece of motherly advice.

She cleared her throat. Wondered if Alex was getting as sick of her as she was getting of herself. He was a little boy, after all. Not some exotic creature.

"Listen," she tried again. "I wanted to talk to you about what you said downstairs. About looking for your angel. Are you upset that Gertrude donated it?"

"It's mine now," he responded, and he sounded like a young man, not a little boy. Sounded like someone who understood all about death and life, and what happened when the person you loved was gone.

They hadn't been giving him enough credit, and that made Tessa feel like an even bigger failure. "I know, and I'm sorry that Ms. Ida has it right now. You know Ms. Ida, right?"

"She's the mayor."

"Exactly. And she also is the president of the town historical society. She loves everything that has anything to do with Apple Valley." Great! Now, she was babbling. She pressed her lips together, took a deep breath. "What I mean is, she's taking good care of it."

"The angel is mine."

"I know, and you're going to get her back. There's going to be a tea at the town hall on Friday. We're going to have some really wonderful food, and when it's over, the angel is coming home."

"She needs to be here now," he said as if it all made perfect sense.

"She can't be, Alex. Everything is already planned, and it wouldn't be right to insist that we have her back before the tea."

"Why not?"

Right. *Why not?*

"Because people are really excited that they're going to have a chance to see the angel, and we wouldn't want to disappoint them." That was it. All she had. She tensed, waiting for Alex's reply.

He rubbed his fingers and thumbs together and looked down at the floor, his head shaking to the left and then to the right.

"Alex?" She touched one of his hands, and he stilled. "Are you all right with that?"

"Is everything okay in here?" Gertrude peered into the room, her hair wild, water and soapsuds splattered all over her shirt. She narrowed her eyes and glared at Tessa. "What did you do?"

"Why are you assuming that I did something?"

"He looks upset. Are you upset, honey? You come on with Aunty, and I'll get you a couple of those cookies you like. The one with chocolate candies in them." She took Alex by the hand and led him out of the room, casting one last hot look in Tessa's direction.

There were a lot of things Tessa could have said, but she decided not to. Gertrude wouldn't listen, and she was too tired to try to make herself heard.

She turned off the light in Alex's room and locked herself into Emily and Dave's.

She was done for the night.

She'd scraped paint and played mother and kept her mouth shut when she hadn't wanted to. Now she was going to get some sleep.

Hopefully, she wouldn't dream.

If she did, she hoped she wouldn't dream about Emily or Dave.

Or worse, Cade!

She walked into the bathroom. Emily's pride and joy. The one room in the house that she'd actually asked Tessa's decorating advice on. She and Dave had spent way too much money. Tessa knew that for a fact, seeing as how there was still a stack of bills that needed to be paid.

The room was gorgeous, though. The paint soft yellow, the claw-foot tub set near corner windows. Not a big room, but a sanctuary with an antique cupboard converted to a sink and a nineteenth-century mirror hung above it. Tessa had refurbished both pieces and sent them from Annapolis for Emily's birthday in June. She'd never gotten a chance to see her sister enjoy the gifts.

She ran water into the tub, her palms stinging from all the work she'd done. Her shoulders ached. Her legs hurt. Working out at the gym five days a week hadn't prepared her for eight hours of hard labor.

The remodeler had built shelves into the wall, and Emily had stocked them with bath salts and bubble baths. Shampoos. Soaps. Little glass trinkets in a rainbow of colors. Those hadn't been Tess's idea, but the small perfume and medicine bottles fit.

She dropped a handful of bath salts into the water and stripped out of her clothes. In the kitchen, Gertrude was singing in a husky falsetto. Tessa thought she heard Alex singing, too, as she settled into the hot water and let the heat ease away some of the aches and pains.

Too bad it couldn't ease heartache and disappointment. If it could, she'd be as good as new when she got out.

Chapter Nine

Done.

Finally!

Tessa wiped the brush along the last rectangle of siding and stood back to look at her accomplishment. It looked good. Great even. The siding pristine, the gingerbread trim gleaming. Three full days of work, and she'd finally accomplished her goal. The house was no longer the ugliest one on Main Street.

Not on the outside, at least.

She still had plenty to do on the inside.

"Looks good, kid," Gertrude said. "Now, we have to get going or we're going to miss the tea, so you go in the house and get cleaned up. I'll have Alex wrestle into his suit. Hopefully, he hasn't outgrown it."

Right. The tea. The thing that Tessa had been trying to come up with an excuse to not attend.

"I'm a mess, Gertrude." She waved her paint-stained hands in front of Gertrude's face. "It's going to take me way too long to get cleaned up. You take Alex and go. I'll meet you there later."

Like after everyone else had left.

"We've got to arrive together. What would it look like if we didn't?" Gertrude smoothed her fuchsia suit jacket and fluffed her hair. She'd finally gone back to Adele, and the woman had made good on her promise to fix the mess she'd made, turning it from pink back to bright orange. Gertrude was pleased with it, so Tess had decided not to point out the fact that her hair and her suit clashed.

"It will look like one of us was ready to arrive and the other one wasn't," Tess replied. "Besides, since when have you ever cared about what anything looked like?"

"Since we became the keeper of Alex's legacy."

"What legacy?" Tessa asked, exasperated and unable to hide it. "An old house, a big piece of land, and back taxes?"

"You know it's more than that, Tess. It's the name. The history."

"You've spent a little too much time with Ida."

"I haven't said a word to the woman since she left here the other night," Gertrude protested.

"Then what's with all the talk about legacies? When I was a teenager and wanted to try to find my father—"

"Father? Is that what you call a guy who gets a woman pregnant and then walks out on her and the kid?"

"I didn't care about that. I just wanted to know who he was, and you told me that where I came from wasn't nearly as important as where I was going."

"And I was right. It wouldn't have done you one bit of good to look for that bastard, but things are different for Alex. He already knows who his family is, and he needs us to make sure that no one ever forgets it."

"I don't think anyone will forget. Not as long as we're in Apple Valley."

"What's that supposed to mean?"

"Rule number one for small-town living: Never forget anything."

"Ugly doesn't suit you, Tess."

"Neither does a bucket-load of paint." She held up her hands again. "I'd better get ready." She grabbed the nearly empty paint can and carried it to the shed. She'd managed to drag several good pieces of furniture from the old building before she'd spotted a nest of mice in the stuffing of a 1950s sofa. She hadn't been back in the shed since. She set the can right in the open doorway, because there was no way she was going any deeper into the gloomy mouse nursery.

"They're just mice, Tess!" Gertrude called from the corner of the house.

"I hate mice!" she replied.

"Well, now that Margrave is wandering around, they'll be gone soon enough."

"Margrave is evil," Tess responded, eyeing the huge tabby cat that was licking its paws a few feet away. Probably cleaning up after a three-course meal of mice. Borrowed from one of Gertrude's bingo buddies, the cat had narrow yellow eyes and a way of looking at Tess that made her wonder if she was next on the menu.

"Don't tell Lottie that. She loves that fat old cat."

Margrave stretched, walking over to Tessa and purring as he wove his way through her legs.

Okay. So maybe he wasn't as bad as all that.

"Nice kitty," she tried.

He swatted her leg, and she jumped back. "Geez, cat! You either like me or you don't. You can't have it both ways."

"Stop talking to the cat!" Gertrude yelled. "You have to get ready so we can go."

"Okay, okay," Tess muttered, following Gertrude back around the side of the house.

"Your boss called while you were on the ladder. Said he wanted to check in and see how you were doing."

Tess's heart jumped, and she stopped in her tracks. "What did you say, Gertrude?"

"I didn't say that you were resigning, if that's what you're worried about." Gertrude tapped a cigarette against her thigh but didn't light it. "You can't put it off forever, though."

"In case you haven't noticed, I've been a little busy, Gertrude." And yeah. Maybe she *was* a little reluctant to close the door on her old life. She'd been happy in Annapolis. She'd still be happy there if she had a choice.

"You'll be busy for the rest of your life, Tess. At some point, you're going to have to bite the bullet and make the call."

"Right now, I need to get ready to go to the historical society's tea. Give me twenty minutes to take a quick shower and throw on some clean clothes, okay?" she said, cutting off further discussion about her resignation. She'd deal with it. Eventually.

"You wear a dress or skirt, you hear? We're representing the Rileys today, and that's a big deal."

Gertrude brushed invisible lint from her skirt. She'd painted her nails. They were a garish red and clashed with her pinkish suit and orange hair. Maybe they'd distract people from the giant shoulder pads in the jacket.

Not that Tessa cared what people thought of her aunt.

She'd gotten over *that* a couple of decades ago.

"I'll wear a dress, but don't expect me to stick my nose in the air and act like royalty." She tossed the words over her shoulder as she hurried into the house and nearly ran Alex over.

"Whoa!" She grabbed his arm to keep him from tumbling backward, felt every muscle in his skinny body tensing.

"Sorry, buddy." She stepped back, surprised to see that Alex was wearing a dark blue suit and a blue striped tie, his white shirt pristine. "You look good. Did Gertrude tell you to wear that?"

"No," he said, swiping his hand over his hair. He'd slicked it down. Hopefully with water.

"Well then, you have good taste. I'll be ready in just a few minutes."

"Okay." He followed her up the stairs, loping along after her like a puppy following a new play-mate. Following her down the hall. Following her right into Emily and Dave's room.

He sat on the bed, his feet not even touching the floor. He was tiny for his age. Puny, even. Looking at him sitting there, his feet swinging to some silent tune, made Tessa's stomach churn. He was so vulnerable and, she imagined, so easily hurt.

How in the world could she ever protect him?

She knew he had some limitations, but Emily had always only talked about his strengths. His gifts. His sweet nature.

What about the rest?

She stared at him, but answers didn't magically appear over his head, and he didn't suddenly start explaining what made him happy, sad, or excited.

He was an enigma, and Tessa had to figure him out.

First, though, she had to get ready.

She grabbed a black dress from the closet.

"I have to take a shower. You go on downstairs and wait with Gertrude, okay? I'll be right out," she said and hurried into the bathroom. She closed the door firmly behind her, her heart doing a funny little jig as she listened to his footsteps on the wood floor, heard her bedroom door close quietly. Her eyes burned, her chest heavy with an emotion she couldn't quite name. It felt like grief and something more. Maybe a smidge of that thing she'd never had. The maternal instinct. The thing that turned ordinary women into mama bears.

She hoped so. For Alex's sake.

He deserved more than what she'd been giving him. That was for sure.

She showered quickly, dried her hair, and rubbed Emily's cocoa butter into her hands. It smelled like chocolate. Which made Tessa's stomach growl and reminded her that she hadn't eaten lunch. She might not have eaten breakfast, either.

"Hey!" Gertrude called from outside the door. "You ready? 'Cause we're going to be late if you don't hurry."

"Give me a minute!" Tess stepped into the dress, pulled it up, and wrestled with the dozen tiny little buttons that ran up the back. Silk and lace, with a boat neckline and three-quarter-length sleeves, the vintage dress had been languishing in the back of an antique store when Tessa had spotted it. It represented 1940s style at its finest, with its pencil skirt and tight bodice and covered buttons that were nearly impossible to reach.

Darn them!

She managed all but the last seven or eight.

Which was why she didn't wear the dress often. Too difficult for a single woman to manage. She'd have to get Gertrude's help after she finished applying makeup. No way was she leaving the bathroom before then. She wasn't in the mood for her aunt's nagging.

The doorbell rang, but Tess ignored it as she applied foundation and a light coat of mascara. No amount of makeup could hide the circles under her eyes, so she didn't bother with concealer, and decided against taming her curls. She ran her fingers through them, stepped away from the mirror and eyed what she could see of herself. Not bad. If she were attending an evening event in Annapolis, her outfit would be perfectly appropriate. Not too dressy. Not too casual. Just the right amount of vintage quirkiness to fit her business persona.

She wasn't in Annapolis, though.

Maybe a skirt and sweater set would be a better choice. She glanced at her watch. The tea had already begun.

Someone knocked on the door, and she yanked it open, ready to lay into Gertrude for being so impatient.

Only Gertrude wasn't standing on the other side of the door.

Cade was, and man, did he look yummy. His black suit fit perfectly, his hair just a little ruffled.

"What are you doing here?" she sputtered, holding the bodice of the dress to her chest like some young Victorian miss. Good God! Could she be any more idiotic? This was a guy she'd skinny-dipped with when she was twelve. He wasn't going to be shocked by a glimpse of skin.

"Ida asked me to make sure your family was coming to tea."

"That doesn't explain what you're doing outside my bathroom door." She let her hands drop away from the bodice. The tight-fitting top didn't so much as slide, but Cade's eyes did. From her face to her chest.

She should be disgusted. If he were any other guy, she would be, but because it was Cade, her toes curled and her insides turned to mush.

"Gertrude sent me to get you. She said you're taking too damn long." He scanned her from head to toe. "I say it was well worth the wait."

"Thanks. You can tell her I'm almost ready."

"Sorry. Not going to happen. She told me, and I quote, *bring that girl down here or I'll have your hide.*"

"Since when are you afraid of Gertrude?"

"I wouldn't say it was fear, exactly. Just a little healthy respect. Turn around."

"What?"

"Turn around. I'll get the zipper so we can get out of here."

"It's not a—"

"Just let me do this before my phone starts ringing with Ida's calls and Gertrude comes up to bust my balls."

"That rhymed," she said, and he chuckled, snagging her arm and dragging her around.

"We can make a song out of it *after* I get you to that tea. Now, hold still so I can do this." His cool fingers skimmed her back. Her very naked back. Her toes curled, her palms itched. She wanted to spin on her heels and throw herself into his gorgeous arms.

She held her ground, though.

Because she wasn't into making a fool of herself. Although, if he didn't hurry it up, she just might change her mind about that.

"Damn, these buttons are tiny," he murmured, his voice husky, his fingers trailing up her spine. Rough, calloused fingers that were probably snagging the vintage lace. She tried to make herself care, but there was something altogether too wonderful about those fingers against her skin. His knuckles skimmed her nape, his breath tickling her hair.

And, dear God, she felt like a teenager again. Felt that same little zing of excitement that she'd experienced then.

Only it wasn't such a little zing anymore. It was a big, huge, change-your-life kind of zap.

"Done. I'll meet you downstairs," he said, leaving her standing where she was.

She heard him walking down the hall, heard the stair at the top of the steps creak. She was ready. She could have followed him down, but she brushed a little blush on her already pink cheeks. Smoothed one of her brows, took a couple of deep breaths, waiting until her heart slowed and she felt . . . settled again.

She grabbed her purse and slid her feet into

two-inch stiletto boots, spritzed herself with a little of the perfume that had been her last birthday present from Kent. Extravagant and expensive, he'd had it created specifically for her. He hadn't cared that she didn't usually wear perfume or that she'd asked for an antique rolltop desk that she'd been eyeing for a year.

She'd cared, but she'd accepted the gift like she had most of the things Kent gave her. With a smile and a thank-you and a few minutes of wondering what in the hell he'd been thinking.

"Tess!" Gertrude shouted from the bottom of the steps. "Do *not* make me come up there and drag you down."

"I'm not ten, Gertie!" Tess hollered back, shoving her arms into the sleeves of her coat. She'd wasted as much time as she could. She was going to have to accept the inevitable and go to the tea. No matter how much she didn't want to. She sighed and reluctantly headed downstairs.

Chapter Ten

High heels on wood floors. If a sound could be sexy, that one was. Cade glanced up the stairs, his heart skipping a few beats as Tess walked into view. She wore the kind of boots that were meant for show—black leather that stopped just below her dress. A hint of knee peeked out every time she took a step. That glimpse of skin was a hell of a lot sexier than ten inches of thigh would have been.

"It's about time," Gertrude barked, her frizzy orange hair nearly tamed, her bright pink suit almost fitting her scrawny frame. She looked just like Cade had imagined she would when Ida had asked him to drive by and make sure the McKenzies and Alex were heading over to the tea.

Tessa didn't look anything like he'd imagined. He thought she'd be wearing an understated pants suit or a black skirt and sweater. Instead, she wore a dress that fit like a glove and buttoned all the way up her spine. Black lace over creamy skin. It had taken all he'd had to keep his hands from doing more than closing those damn small buttons.

"It took me"—Tess glanced at a slim silver watch—"twenty-two minutes. How long did it take you, Gertrude?"

"That has nothing to do with it. I was ready when it was time to leave." Gertrude patted her hair again, smoothed her pink skirt.

"I would have been, too, if I hadn't been finishing up the painting," Tess pointed out, the scent of some exotic perfume drifting on the air as she walked past Cade and touched her nephew's shoulder.

"Are you ready, Alex?" she asked.

"Yes." Alex walked outside, his coat bunched around his shoulders, the bottom of a suit jacket showing beneath it. He looked uncomfortable and a little awkward.

"What do you think about this tea thing, Alex?" Cade asked as he followed the family outside.

Alex shrugged.

"Alex, answer the sheriff properly," Gertrude chided, her tone gentler than any Cade had heard when she was raising Emily and Tess.

"It's okay," Cade started to say, but Alex glanced back, his hand on the door handle of Gertrude's old blue Pontiac.

"I like tea," he said. "And music."

"There will probably be some of both. Cookies, too. Charlotte made them, and they're really good. Don't tell anyone, but I snagged two before the tea started." Cade had also grabbed a slice of gingerbread from a platter Charlotte set out.

He'd been hungry, and she was a great baker.

"Never take things without asking," Alex responded solemnly. The kid liked rules. That was for sure.

"Don't worry. I asked." She'd said no, but could Cade help it if she'd left the treats sitting out unattended?

"Enough chitchat. Let's get this show on the road." Gertrude opened the car door and shooed Alex in. "Get in there now, and put your seat belt on."

He moved slowly, settling into the seat and pulling his coat over his knees. When he was done, he leaned over and touched the car floor, then his knees, then the floor again.

"Seat belt," Gertrude prodded and closed the door with her hip. "You going to the tea, Cade?"

"Ida gave me direct orders to escort you there, so I guess I don't have a choice."

"There's no need for an escort. I think we can find our way," Tessa said as she rounded the car and climbed into the driver's seat, showing off more than a glimpse of knee. Her thighs were as smooth and creamy as her back had been. Flawless. Touchable.

He clenched his fists and got in the truck, opening the window to cool his heated blood. He pulled in behind Gertrude's car, keeping a slow pace up Main Street, past the police station and out toward the edge of town.

Town hall sat on a bluff that overlooked Apple Valley, the Greek Revival–style building gleaming white in the setting sun. The parking lot was nearly full. At least sixty cars. That was a good turnout for a last-minute event, but it didn't surprise Cade. Ida had a way of making things happen.

Tess parked between a yellow VW Bug and a black Corvette. Cade pulled into an open spot a dozen yards away. It was farther from the building, but he caught up to the family before they reached the wide front porch. Christmas lights were wrapped around the railing and windows, the multicolored display one that Cade had seen every Christmas season for as long as he could remember.

"It looks the same," Tessa murmured, and he wasn't sure if she was talking to him or to herself.

"You know how it is around here. Things don't change unless they have to."

"If it's not broke, don't fix it?" she asked, offering a quick smile. She looked nervous, her eyes shadowed and wary. He guessed he'd be nervous, too, if he had to face a bunch of people he hadn't seen in years and who would probably wait anxiously for an opportunity to whisper about clothes, hairstyle, wrinkles, or weight.

He held the door open, letting Alex and Gertrude precede him. Tessa hesitated, biting her lip and craning her neck to see inside.

"Don't worry, Red," he whispered in her ear. "They don't bite."

"No, they just gossip and gawk." She sighed.

"You're a beautiful, successful woman who has come back to town to raise her nephew. Who cares if they gawk and gossip?" He pressed a hand to her back, urging her into the massive entryway. Built in the 1920s, town hall had retained all of its stately charm: marble floors and wide stairs that led to offices on the second story. Large meeting rooms opened out on either side of the entry.

There were people everywhere, and Cade didn't mind one bit that Tess kept close, her arm brushing his, her perfume tickling his nose. She smelled like

a garden at midnight, flowery and just slightly
mysterious.

Christmas music played from an intercom that
had been installed in the 1970s. People talked and
laughed. Gertrude and Alex had already disappeared
into the crowd. He hoped they were making their
way to Ida. She'd planned a speech and a presentation of the angel to the community. Sure, it was for
show, and the angel was going to be returned to the
family, but that hadn't dampened Ida's enthusiasm.

Charlotte was in the room to the right, doling out
her baked goods and talking to whoever stopped for
a snack.

"Want something to eat?" he asked Tessa.

She shook her head, the deer-in-the-headlights
look on her face. "I . . . think I'll get some water."

She sidled past a group of people who didn't
make any secret of the fact that they were staring at
her. Gawkers and gossips to the person, but she held
her head high and just kept going.

Cade followed because he couldn't think of any
reason not to. Life had been quiet since Darla had
walked out three years ago—no complications, no
troubles. A few dates with a few nice women who had
been undemanding and easy to please. Lately,
though, his house had been too quiet, his nights too
lonely, and he didn't see any reason to keep things
that way.

A few people called his name and waved as he
made his way down the hall. He nodded and smiled
but didn't stop.

Double doors led into a huge kitchen. Remodeled
in the 1970s, the room was one of the ugliest Cade

had ever seen. Mustard-yellow appliances, linoleum floors, and countertops that were so scuffed and worn they looked like weird abstract art.

Four round tables took up most of the floor space, each surrounded by metal folding chairs. A large window looked out onto the back of the property and the spruce trees that had been hung with white Christmas lights. Golden sunlight spread across the dusky sky, illuminating the small herb and vegetable garden that Ida had planted a decade ago. Like so many places in Apple Valley, town hall never seemed to change.

Cade didn't mind, but the monotony drove some people away. Darla, for one. His brother Tanner for another.

And Tess.

She opened a cupboard and grabbed a white coffee cup, apparently content to pretend that he wasn't there.

Too bad he didn't like to be ignored.

"There's coffee in the ballroom," he pointed out, and she shrugged just like her nephew had.

"It's quieter in here."

"There are a lot of people who are eager to talk to you. Hiding out in here isn't going to change that."

"No, but it's been a long week. I'm tired. A little coffee before I face the masses of curious people is a necessity." She lifted the carafe from a coffeemaker that had probably been plugged in in the eighties and stayed plugged in twelve hours a day, six days a week ever since.

"Not curious. Excited. Seeing the Riley place put to rights is making a lot of people really glad you came back to town." He'd been hearing murmurs all over town. People were talking about how hardworking Tessa was, how smart and thrifty to do the work herself rather than paying to have it done. She was the prodigal returned, and everyone in town seemed to be willing to open their arms to her.

The problem was, Tess didn't seem all that eager to step into any of them.

"That's . . . nice." She sipped coffee, her ankles crossed, her dress skimming her hips and thighs. She'd left her hair loose, and it fell in deep red curls to her shoulders, glossy, shiny, more than a little touchable. "There's still a lot to do on the inside. Another couple of weeks' worth of work. Once the ground thaws, I can start working on the landscaping."

"You have big plans. People around here will be happy to hear that."

"I'm not all that interested in what makes people around here happy." She looked into her coffee cup and frowned. "That didn't come out quite the way I wanted it to."

"How did you want it to come out?"

"Just . . . I spent most of my childhood running around after Emily, making sure she didn't cause problems and that if she did, I cleaned them up. I cared a lot about what the town thought of us. The old clothes we had to wear. The peeling siding on our house. The fact that we were always those *poor little McKenzie girls*. Everyone pitied us, and I hated it." She shook her head, and Cade was surprised at the sadness in her eyes.

"Hated it? You used to thumb your nose at everyone, Tess. Remember how we used to laugh at the rich kids?"

"Sure." She topped off her coffee, held the cup between her palms. "But it wasn't really all that funny to me, and you *were* one of the rich kids. I just didn't hold it against you."

"Rich? My father was the sheriff and my mom was a homemaker. We barely had two sticks to rub together."

"You had each other, Cade. That's way more than I ever had."

"Tess—"

"The caffeine has probably kicked in, and I should probably go out and face the hordes," she said, turning her back to him and rinsing her cup in the chipped porcelain sink.

"I hate to tell you this, but Ida stopped buying caffeinated coffee about five years ago."

"Oh." She turned, laughing, all the sadness gone.

But he'd seen a glimpse of the girl she'd been, and it surprised him. All the things they'd shared, all the dreams and secrets they'd told each other, and he'd never known just how much Tess had wanted the things he'd taken for granted. Family and love. Security.

Now that he'd seen it, he wouldn't forget.

She must have known that, because she didn't meet his eyes as they walked out of the kitchen together.

She stopped to chat with a few people on the way through the hall. Cade stood beside her, not really listening. He was still thinking about the past. How young they'd both been, how oblivious *he'd* been.

"Good evening, Sheriff!" Reverend Jethro Fisher bellowed as he and his wife, Natalie, wove their way through the crowded entryway.

Thin-faced and gangly, Jethro looked like a younger, happier version of Abraham Lincoln.

"Hi, Jethro. Natalie. How are things at Apple Valley Community Church?" Cade asked, smiling at the couple. They'd moved from Mississippi a few years ago, taking over when old Reverend Scotts had retired. It had taken a good year for them to be accepted by the townspeople. They'd proven to be kind and charitable, with just enough humor to help them survive the tight-knit community.

"Why don't you come this Sunday morning and find out? If I recall correctly, you haven't graced the door of our beautiful church for a month," Jethro responded with a grin.

"Hon, leave the poor guy alone. You know he works most Sundays." Natalie elbowed her husband, her dark eyes flashing with humor. Small and fragile-looking, Natalie had enough energy to keep up with her husband, their congregation, and the tenants who rented rooms in their parsonage.

"You can't fault a pastor for trying, my dear." Jethro wrapped his arm around Natalie's waist and kissed her head. "Besides, I'm just looking out for my congregation. It will be much safer on Sundays with a sheriff in the pews."

Cade laughed at that. He had to give the reverend credit. He knew how to stick with a topic. "You know I come when I can, Jethro. If I'm not there, half my deputies are. Plus, the way I hear it, you're packing heat."

"Not on Sunday, but I *was* a sniper in the army,

so I know my way around a firearm." Jethro's gaze jumped from Cade to a point just beyond his shoulder. "How is Tessa holding up?"

"She seems to be doing okay." Cade turned in the direction Jethro was looking and just managed to catch a glimpse of Tessa disappearing into one of the banquet rooms.

"Such a shame about Emily and Dave," Natalie chimed in, her eyes filled with sorrow. "They were lovely people."

"That's what everyone is saying. Now that they're gone." Not many people in town would have said it *before* they'd died. Cade sure wouldn't have.

"Death often makes friends of even bitter enemies. Besides, people in town know that Emily and Dave tried," Jethro said, his tone suddenly serious. "You and Tess are pretty close, aren't you?"

"We used to be," Cade responded, hoping that would be enough to satisfy the reverend. He liked Jethro and Natalie, but they had a way of getting involved in the lives of everyone.

"Do she and Gertrude need anything? Maybe some help around the house? Natalie and I could ask the congregation to hold a workday. We could get that placed fixed up quick," Jethro offered.

"Why don't you ask Tessa or Gertrude? I don't want to speak for them." But he would like to be speaking *to* them. One of them, anyway. He glanced in the direction Tess had disappeared. Dozens of people were crowded around something. Cade caught a flash of deep red hair and a pale face. Okay. Not something. Some*one*.

"You know how Gertrude is. It's hard for her to accept help."

"True," Cade murmured, wondering if Tess was in need of rescue and caring a whole hell of a lot more about that than about Gertrude's difficulty accepting help.

"Talk to them, will you? Just feel them out and see if there's anything we can do to make this transition easier for everyone." Natalie smiled, her eyes soft chocolate brown. She looked like a mother, sister, best friend, and Cade couldn't resist her plea any more than he could have a plea from his family.

"All right. I'll talk to them."

"You're a dear." She patted his cheek and nearly skipped over to a small group of elderly ladies.

"She's hard to resist, that one." Jethro sighed dramatically, his green eyes flashing with humor.

"Is that why you let her do the talking when the church needs something?"

"That is exactly why. Now, if you'll excuse me, I need to go do a little mingling. We're getting near the end of the fiscal year, and our coffers are about five thousand dollars short. Feel free to make a donation the next time you visit."

Cade laughed as the reverend walked away.

He liked the guy. He really did.

Right now, though, he wasn't all that concerned about Jethro's coffers or Gertrude's inability to accept help. More folks were crowding around Tess, and Cade thought she might be in danger of being crushed. He pushed his way through the wall of people, "White Christmas" playing over the intercom.

It took a minute, but he finally managed to fight

his way to the center of the crowd. No Tessa, though. She must have slipped through a crack and gone into hiding.

He glanced around the room. Pine boughs hung from the windows, white lights sparkling from between deep green needles. Two large fireplaces were decorated with Christmas lights and deep red and green stockings that would be filled and handed out at the annual Christmas party. This year, the stockings reflected Ida's theme. They were long and hand knit, and looked like something that would have hung there at the turn of the last century.

At one end of the room, several large tables were laden with snacks. At the other end a display case stood between floor-to-ceiling windows, the glass front revealing the small white angel Gertrude had donated.

"You heading for the food, Cunningham?" someone drawled, and Cade glanced over his shoulder, not surprised to see Max Stanford walking up behind him.

"If I can get there before the seniors and juniors demolish whatever is left. Good job on the display case." He eyed the other man's starched uniform and polished shoes. "You heading to the office?"

"I'm out on patrol. The mayor asked me to stop in to make sure that things were going smoothly. Crowd control and all that." He glanced around. "Looks like everything is under control. That being the case, I may as well partake of Charlotte's cooking."

"That worked out nicely for you."

"What can I say? I'm just one of those people who touches something and watches it turn to gold."

"You're full of shit, Maxwell. You know that."

"I do, but right at this moment, I'd rather be full of whatever Charlotte made. That lady can co—" He stopped, his eyes tracking something behind Cade. "Now, would you look at that? She *is* a fine specimen of a woman."

Cade knew who he was going to see before he turned, but he turned anyway and saw Tessa a few feet away, talking to one of the blue-haired ladies from the diner. She'd taken off her coat, and her dress fell from her neck to her knees, covering every inch of skin in between. She shifted, and he caught a glimpse of all those buttons, the ones that went from her nape down to the small of her back. Fire roared through his blood, and he took an unconscious step toward her.

"I think I'd better get what I came for and get back to work," Max mumbled, but he wasn't looking at the buffet tables; he was eyeing Tessa. So was just about every adult male in the vicinity.

For some reason, that really pissed Cade off.

Max stopped at the elbow of one of the ladies, touched her shoulder, and said something Cade couldn't hear. The woman laughed, and Tessa smiled a warm, you've-caught-my-interest smile.

It took about two seconds, and then Max had his hand on Tessa's arm and was leading her to the buffet table. Not one blue-haired lady followed. They were probably already planning the wedding.

Which maybe should have been just fine with Cade.

It wasn't, and he'd be damned if he'd stand by and let the biggest player in town turn Tessa's head.

Chapter Eleven

Being hounded by half the population of Apple Valley was *not* the way she wanted to spend the evening, but Tessa kept a smile on her face as she grabbed a dessert plate and filled it.

"So, you're from Annapolis?" the good-looking police officer with the overconfident smile asked.

She wanted to tell him to buzz off. He reminded her a little too much of Kent, every pore oozing refinement and polish. She was surprised the guy hadn't donned a tuxedo instead of his uniform.

"Yes."

"I attended the naval academy there," he offered, despite the fact that she was trying really hard to give off a not-interested vibe.

"That's nice."

"You've visited the campus?"

"No." So, go on your merry little way and find a woman who wants to hear all about it.

"Too bad. There's a lot of history there. Of course, there's a lot of history in Annapolis, period. The architecture itself is astounding." It was the first interesting thing he'd said since he'd asked if she was hungry.

Maybe he wasn't just a pretty face.

A *very* pretty face, btw. The guy looked like he'd just walked off the cover of a magazine. Sandy hair perfectly in place, his teeth too white and too perfect.

Yep. A Kent clone.

"I couldn't agree more," she offered anyway and was rewarded with a warm smile.

"I've heard you're an interior designer."

"Yes." She bit into a cookie, hoping that would forestall more conversation.

"My grandmother was one. She taught me to appreciate fine furniture and decor."

"Um . . . wow?"

He smiled again, this time with just enough mischief in his eyes for her to know that he'd heard her sarcasm. "Just thought I'd give it a try. After all, you are the most stunning woman I've seen in years."

She couldn't help it. She laughed. He might be a Kent clone, but he was funny and very overt in his efforts to gain her interest.

She liked that. Even if she wasn't at all tempted by him. "Thank you, but I—"

"Weren't you heading back to the office, Stanford?" Cade interrupted, his hand sliding around Tessa's elbow.

And suddenly she knew exactly what temptation felt like. She wanted to lean into him so badly her body swayed with the force of it.

She stepped away, shoving an entire cookie in her

mouth so she wouldn't say something stupid like *I've been wondering where you were.*

"Right after I eat this." The officer popped a quarter of a sandwich in his mouth and grabbed a cookie from another tray. "And this. It was nice meeting you, Tess. I'm sure we'll see each other around town."

He sauntered away.

Every under-eighty woman in the room watched him go. Even Tess. It was difficult not to watch a guy like him.

"He's trouble, Tess," Cade said as he grabbed a plate and piled it with sandwich quarters and cookies. "Just so you know."

"What guy isn't?" She focused her attention on Cade and then wished she hadn't. He didn't have the cocky confidence of Stanford, the stuff that oozed out of pores and looked a heck of a lot like arrogance. Cade's confidence was more the hard-earned kind that came from years of working hard and doing well at it. The kind that didn't need to ooze because it just . . . *was.*

No wonder he'd made sheriff at such a young age.

Who wouldn't put their trust in him?

"That's pretty cynical. Even for you." He snagged a couple of slices of gingerbread, and she took one of two that were left. She might be in a mood, but she wasn't stupid.

"I'm not cynical. I'm a realist." She bit into the spicy sweet bread and nearly swooned with joy. She'd been working hard from sunup until sundown, a smidge of an idea in her head. Something she might just be able to make work. But she had to give the house an upscale look first. Had to take it all the way back to the time when the Rileys had been Apple

Valley royalty. Then she might be able to convince people to start shopping there. Better yet, she might be able to pull people in from Spokane and Coeur d'Alene.

With a good enough reputation and impressive enough product, people might even come from Seattle and Portland. Quite a drive, but if she made it worth their while—

"I've lost you, Red," Cade said quietly, his finger brushing her cheek. "Where have you gone?"

"Back to the house. I have a lot to do if I'm going to make a phoenix rise from the ashes of what Emily and Dave left behind."

"If anyone can do it, you can." It wasn't just flattery; he meant it, and that meant more to Tess than it should have. More than she wanted it to.

"Thanks," she mumbled, frantically looking for Gertrude and Alex. She'd been sidetracked by Ethel Morris and Lucy Candlewick. Twin sisters who'd married, raised a couple of kids, and then opened a quilting shop on Main Street when Tess was a kid, they'd been at the funeral and had brought at least three chicken casseroles to the house since Tess had begun renovations.

She suspected they were more interested in seeing her progress than in charity, but they were sweet, and she couldn't hold it against them.

"There's no need to search for the nearest escape route, Tess," Cade said quietly, and she found herself looking in his eyes again. Blue, blue eyes with laugh lines that fanned out at the corners.

"I wasn't."

"Sure you were, and I'm wondering why."

"I told you—" She caught a glimpse of Gertrude's

fuchsia suit moving through the entryway. Saved by
her aunt! "I see Gertrude and Alex. I'd better go
make sure they're okay."

She didn't run, but she might have if there hadn't
been so many people to navigate around. She finally
made it through the crowded banquet room and
into the entryway.

Gertrude and Alex weren't in the hall, so she
walked into the spacious room to the left of the
foyer. Chairs had been set up facing a raised platform and podium, and a couple of dozen people
were seated in them. A few more were gathered near
the large fireplace, sipping coffee and talking.

A baby grand piano sat on the platform, pushed
far back toward the wall and covered with a thick
blanket. Only its legs were visible, hand carved and
swirling in an Art Nouveau style.

Tess wanted to lift the blanket and get a look at
what was underneath. Apparently she wasn't the
only one. Alex hovered over the piano, tugging at
the blanket with just enough force to make it lift and
fall again. Gertrude had her hand on his arm and
was trying to manhandle him off the platform, but
he wanted none of it.

Tess couldn't blame him. If there was one thing
she knew her nephew loved, it was playing piano.
Still, this wasn't the place or time.

The easiest thing would be to walk away and let
Gertrude deal with it. Throw up her hands and pretend the problem wasn't hers or that she didn't
know it existed.

It's what Tessa's mother had done: turned her
back and acted like she'd never given birth to her
daughters. The night Tessa had watched her mother

back out of Gertrude's driveway, she'd sworn she'd never be like the woman who'd birthed her.

Until now, she hadn't had an opportunity to challenge that childish promise.

"Alex Daniel Riley, you come away from there!" Gertrude hissed, tugging harder on Alex's arm as a small crowd gathered around, murmuring not so helpful advice.

Tess was pretty sure Alex was about to drop down in front of the piano and hang on to its legs for dear life.

Move your ass and take care of this, her childhood self shouted, and Tess hurried forward, her heart racing with the need to do things right. "What's going on?"

"What does it look like?" Gertrude huffed. "The boy has decided he needs to play piano, but this thing is nearly a hundred years old. It's not an instrument for a little boy, Alex. Even if it was, this isn't the time to be playing it."

"Why not?" Alex said reasonably, his fingers curled in the blanket.

"Because we're here about that angel you've been worrying about. The whole town is. They're not here to listen to piano music."

"Maybe they want to," Alex responded, and Gertrude looked like she was about to lose whatever patience she had left.

"Alex—"

"I'll take care of this, Gertrude." It seemed like the right thing to say, but when Gertrude huffed again and walked away, Tess wasn't exactly sure how to follow through.

"You have a piano at home, Alex," she reminded

her nephew, as if he needed any kind of reminder about the thing he seemed to love most in life.

"Not like this." The awe in his voice was unmistakable. He lifted the blanket and peered underneath.

Tess couldn't help it. She looked, too. Seriously. An antique piano that looked to be in pristine condition? She would have been all over it if she'd seen it in a store or at an estate sale.

Sure enough, the keys were yellowed ivory, the wood tiger maple, stained to a rich burnt red. She whistled under her breath, and Alex glanced her way, their eyes meeting for a surprisingly long moment. He never looked straight into her face for any length of time—certainly not into her eyes—but he had, and she recognized something in his gaze. Zeal. Passion. Fervor. Whatever it was that drove Tess to hunt antique stores and haunt estate sales. The thing that pounded in her chest when she spotted a beautiful old item.

Suddenly, her intention to lead Alex off the platform and to the snack table or the angel or outside disappeared.

They both wanted to lift the blanket and reveal the piano. So, why not do it?

"All right," she said, making up her mind. "Let's take a look." She backed out from under the blanket and waited for Alex to do the same.

His hair stood on end from static, and she smoothed it down, wishing that he'd look into her eyes again.

"We're not going to touch it, though, okay? No playing it. We wouldn't want to get into any trouble with the mayor." She lifted the blanket and folded it,

her breath catching at the beauty of the wood and
those ivory keys.

"Wow!" Alex breathed, and sat on the piano bench,
his fingers running along the keys before Tess could
react.

"Alex . . ."

He played the Christmas carol that was drifting
from the intercom, the mellow sound of the piano
more beautiful than the canned chords and notes
Alex was matching.

God, he was good, his small hands flying up and
down the keyboard. First he played "I Saw Mommy
Kissing Santa Claus" and then "Frosty the Snowman."

Conversation died down, the murmur of laughter
and chatter drifting away as people found chairs and
settled down to listen. Soon the room was filled,
every seat occupied, every bit of space taken up.

Ida walked up to the platform and took Tessa's
elbow. "Let's sit down and enjoy the concert."

"Are you sure you don't mind him playing—"

"That is not playing, Tess," Ida chided. "That is
creating. He's telling a story. Can't you hear it?"

Tess could. Every note, every chord, every touch
on the piano. If she closed her eyes, she could probably see it in colors and shapes and patterns. Not
words, but that was Alex. Caught in a world that he
didn't understand, forced to use a language that
didn't make much sense to him. No wonder he
spoke so infrequently.

Someone turned off the intercom, but Alex didn't
stop playing. His next song was one that Tessa was
familiar with, but that she doubted anyone else had

ever heard. That sad melody that he'd played the night she'd decided not to move him to Annapolis.

It burned in her chest and in her heart. She loved it and hated it, because it seemed to say all the things Alex couldn't and probably a hundred things that *she* couldn't say and wanted to.

When he finished, the room was silent except for a few quiet sniffles. His hands fell away from the keys, and he sat quietly, apparently done with his impromptu concert.

"Well," Ida finally said, her voice huskier than normal. "That was beautiful, Alex. Just beautiful." She cleared her throat. "I don't think I've ever heard that last song before. Does it have a name?"

Alex scraped his foot along the floor, his head still bent over the piano.

"'My Angel's Song,'" he said clearly, and a quiet murmur went up in the room. Most of the people there had probably never heard him speak, but that didn't mean he was a circus sideshow.

Tess tightened her hand into fists, ready to come out swinging.

"That's a beautiful name," Ida said before Tessa could tell the crowd to keep their oohs and aahs to themselves. "Is it about Miriam's angel? The one we have here?"

Alex nodded, and Ida smiled. "Let's go see her, shall we?" She looked at the audience. "This would be a wonderful time for Gertrude to read the letter Miriam's great-great-niece sent. Are you in here somewhere, Gertrude?"

"Right here!" Gertrude called from the back of the crowd, waving her arm frantically.

"Wonderful!" Ida took Alex's hand and smiled into his face. Alex smiled back, and the entire room seemed to sigh in unison.

Even Tess sighed, because it was so good to see that smile.

"Let's go, then. Make sure there's room for the Rileys and McKenzies around the angel," Ida said as she stepped off the platform and led Alex through the room.

As was the Apple Valley way, people followed in an orderly and quiet fashion, walking through the foyer and into the banquet room.

Gertrude was already standing near the display case, a piece of paper in her hand, a look of horror on her face. Every bit of color was gone from her cheeks, and Tess rushed forward, terrified that her aunt was having a heart attack.

"Gertrude! What's wrong?"

"She's gone," Gertrude responded, her lips colorless.

"Who's go—" Tessa's voice trailed off as she caught sight of the display case. The glass door hung open, and the shelf was empty.

"What's going on?" Ida asked, her wrinkled hand still wrapped around Alex's smooth one.

"My angel is gone," Alex said, and the entire crowd gasped.

It would have been funny if it hadn't been so awful.

Tess reached for Alex as Cade shoved his way through the throng of people, still looking sexy as sin and gorgeous. But tears were streaming down

Alex's face, and all Tess cared about was getting her nephew to a private place where he could cry.

She lifted him, not caring that he was ten and probably way too old to want to be carried, and shoved her way through the crowd.

Chapter Twelve

Alex cried himself to sleep.

Tess wanted to.

She also wanted to murder whatever bastard had taken the angel.

No. Not *the* angel. *Alex's* angel.

She paced the hallway outside Alex's room, peeking in every few minutes to make sure he was still sleeping. She had this fear that he'd wake up and go searching, even though she, Gertrude, and Ida had spent an hour assuring him that the police would do everything they could to find the angel.

They'd better find it quick, too. Tess didn't think she could spend another night listening to her nephew cry.

Gertrude's bedroom door opened, and she peeked into the hall. Not a bit of makeup on her face, her hair scraped back, she looked older and frailer than she had that afternoon. "You can't stand guard all night, Tess," she said quietly.

"Sure I can." She settled on the floor next to Alex's door and leaned back against the wall.

"He won't go anywhere."

"He has before."

"It's been years since he wandered away from home."

"He wandered away from school last week, Gertie. We can't pretend that didn't happen."

"I'm not pretending. I know there's a possibility he'll go looking for the angel. I dead-bolted the door to make sure he doesn't."

"He composes music, Gertrude, and he plays complicated pieces by ear. Do you really think he won't figure out how to open a dead bolt?"

"It's not that he can't figure it out. It's that it's too high. Way up at the top of the door. Dave put it there when Alex was four. He was fascinated with the stars then. Used to play little songs about the sky." Her voice broke, and she sank to the floor beside Tessa in a heap of faded cotton fabric. "I had no idea he even knew that angel existed, Tess. If I had . . ."

"It's okay, Gertie." Tess patted her aunt's hand. For once they were on the same page, worried about the same thing, determined to accomplish a common goal.

"It is not okay, damn it!" Gertrude pulled a cigarette from somewhere within the folds of her nightgown and stuck it between her lips. "The boy cried himself to sleep, and it's all my fault."

"You said yourself that you didn't know."

"I should have."

"And I should have known I had limited time with Emily, but I didn't. Now it's too late to spend the time with her that I wish I had," Tess responded tiredly. "Sometimes, all we can do is keep moving forward."

"You've got a point there, kid, but I still feel bad. I let my emotions rule my head, and it got me into trouble."

"Has there ever been a time when it hasn't?"

"Nah." Gertrude smiled. "You'd think I would have learned something from that by this point in my life."

"You'd think I would have learned something, period," Tess said with a sigh.

Gertrude touched her hand. "You've done good, kid." She took the cigarette from her mouth and frowned at it. "I know I haven't told you that much. Fact is, you always had your head screwed on straighter than your sister."

"You'd better stop, Gertrude. Or I'll start thinking you're sick or dying or something."

"I'm too old and ornery for that." Gertrude got back on her feet with a couple of loud grunts and a groan or two. "There's nothing we can do about any of this tonight. It's best if we both go to bed."

"I'd rather call Cade and find out what he's doing to get the angel back," Tess grumbled.

"At midnight? I don't think he'd appreciate it, but his home number is in the phone book down in the kitchen if you're hell-bent on giving him a call. Me? I'm going to get these old bones in bed. I need my beauty sleep. It's date night tomorrow at the seniors' center. Bowling first. Then a movie. Then, if my man is good, a little trip to Pike's Hill."

"Pike's Hill?" The Lover's Lane of Apple Valley.

Tess didn't want to even imagine Gertrude and her "man" there.

"Don't act like you haven't heard of it, Tess. I know you and that scuzz-bucket Orlando used to park there every Friday night after work."

True. They had.

Also true that Orlando had been scum, but he'd been cute, and Tess had been trying to pretend she didn't have a crush on Cade.

Crush?

It had been more than that.

She'd been planning their wedding, for crying out loud! Thank God, she'd never told anyone but Emily that.

"I didn't say I didn't know what it was. I'm just surprised that you might be going there."

"Why?" Gertrude scowled.

"Because I didn't even know you were dating." Tessa scrambled to her feet.

"Just because you didn't know, doesn't mean it wasn't happening." Gertrude patted her hair and smoothed the bodice of her old-fashioned nightgown. "Some of us just have it, Tess. It's a sad fact of life and a hard reality for those who don't, but it is what it is, and I'm not one to complain."

Tess snorted, and Gertrude lifted her sagging chin several notches. "I'm not. Now, I really do have to get some sleep. You'd be smart to do the same. Knowing the way things are in this town, everyone and her uncle will be on the doorstep when the shop opens in the morning." She retreated into her room and closed the door, leaving Tess to stare at the painted wood.

Gertrude dating? Tess hadn't been on a date since she'd kicked Kent to the curb. Was it pitiful that her aunt had a better love-life than she did? Probably, but she didn't plan to waste time worrying about it.

Tess got to her feet, her body aching to the bone. She felt ancient and defeated. She hated that feeling.

There was a phone book downstairs near the phone. Sure it was midnight, but Cade was a sheriff. He had to be used to being woken at odd hours. Besides, the last thing he'd said to Alex was that he could call anytime to find out how the search for the angel was going.

Alex was asleep. He couldn't call, but Tess could.

She eased down the stairs, careful to avoid the creakiest ones. It was colder on the lower level of the house, the shop somehow hollow and empty feeling despite how full it was. Even after all the work that had been done, there was too much stuff. Tess had put Gertrude to work weeding out the junk, and she had to admit, her aunt had a good eye. She'd managed to pull out items that would fit well into a fine antique store. They were lined up against the walls and set on shelves, still unorganized, but not nearly as cluttered as they'd been when Tess had arrived.

Tess walked down the hall and into the kitchen. The difference in there was almost miraculous, all the clutter gone, the deep porcelain sink scrubbed out, the cupboards dusted. She needed to pull up the old linoleum to check the tile floor beneath to see if it was salvageable. She thought it would be.

A few small tables, and the room would be

perfect for small social gatherings. Maybe book clubs or quilting meetings. She was sure she could get people in with the right motivation, and after attending the tea, she knew just what that motivation needed to be.

Charlotte.

That woman could bake like nobody's business. If she was providing refreshments, people would come to the shop. One thing at a time, though. There were hundreds of little projects and dozens of big ones that needed to be done before then.

An old-fashioned phone hung on the wall near the mudroom door. The phone book was on the counter nearby. Tess thumbed through it, reading through the Cs until she found Cade's home number. His address was listed, too. Tenth Street. That wasn't far. A hop, skip, and a jump away. As a matter of fact, Tess could jog there easily if she ever had the desire.

Fortunately, her days of running past a boy's house in the hope of getting his attention were long past. She'd grown up and matured. And yet, there she stood with her finger on Cade's number and her hand on the phone.

Was she really going to wake the man in the middle of the night to ask questions that could wait? It wasn't like she had anything new to say. She'd said everything at the town hall, and she'd said it loudly enough to shock several of the blue-haired ladies.

She wasn't proud of it. As a matter of fact, if any of them visited the shop, she was going to apologize.

What she was not going to do was call Cade.

She stepped away from the book and the phone and walked back through the dark hall. The front room was nearly cleared of clutter, an old couch that Tessa planned to restore and recover sitting in front of the windows. She knelt on the saggy cushions and pulled back the curtains. Snow had begun to fall. The first snow of the season, each flake fat and fluffy.

She felt a moment of deep yearning so intense that she wanted to walk outside and look up at the swirling snow, let the flakes melt on her face the way she and Emily had when they were kids. They'd been best friends before they'd moved to Apple Valley, because they were all each other had. Homeschooled because that had been easier for Gretchen than getting them up and ready in the morning. Not much schooling had ever gotten done, but Tess and Emily had spent lots of time telling each other stories and playing make-believe. Usually Emily was the princess, Tessa the maid, but she hadn't minded.

That had probably been the beginning of the pattern that had shaped their relationship. They'd been too young to realize it, of course. All they'd cared about was being best friends ever.

How many times had Emily said that?

She'd stopped after they'd moved in with Gertrude. Not right away, but slowly as they'd entered school and she'd made new friends.

Tess would give a lot to hear her say it now.

She sighed, dropping down onto the couch. It was cold, but she was too tired and lazy to look for a blanket, so she tugged her flannel pajama top down over her knees and curled up on the old cushions.

She closed her eyes, listening for the floor to creak or a door to open, waiting for Alex to try to make another pilgrimage to find his angel.

She fell asleep waiting.

Emily came to her in her dreams, but not the grown-up Emily of recent years. Young Emily, with her white-blond hair in pigtails, standing in the yard they'd grown up playing in. She walked toward Tessa, not smiling like she always was. Her eyes were wide, her mouth open. She looked up at the sky and then at Tess, her skin as white as the falling snow, her mouth blood red.

She needed something.

She didn't speak it, but Tess felt that need the same way she'd felt the yearning to walk outside and catch snowflakes on her face.

What do you need? She tried to say it, but no sound escaped.

Tears streamed down Emily's face, and she turned her back to Tessa, walking across the yard and disappearing into falling snow.

"Emily!" Tess woke yelling her sister's name, sweat beading her brow and her heart pounding so fast she thought it would burst from her chest.

She sat up, shaking with the remnant of the dream.

Wind howled, rattling the windows behind her, and icy air swept across her hot cheeks. She could swear a snowflake landed on her forehead. She turned, her gaze jumping to the foyer and the door.

It was closed.

Thank God.

She had a crick in her neck from sleeping on the couch, and a pain in her stomach that was probably from hunger, but at least the house was still locked up tight.

She glanced at an old grandfather clock as she walked into the hall. Just past two. She could get in bed, sleep until dawn, and then begin the interior work that needed to be done. The entire lower level was due for an overhaul. It wouldn't cost much for a few gallons of paint, but what she really wanted to do was buy vintage wallpaper prints for the parlor, wainscoting for the dining room, and paint for the spacious living room. She'd have to calculate the cost, see if it would make sense to do it.

Her foot landed in cold water, and she froze, her heart thumping frantically again. There shouldn't be any water on the floor. Not unless there was a leak in the ceiling. She turned the foyer light on and looked up, praying that she'd see a big wet blotch on the paint. Nothing. Not even a drop of moisture.

A small chair sat near the door. It hadn't been there earlier.

No!

She checked the dead bolt, fear crawling up her throat. Open.

"Gertrude!" she screamed, loud enough to wake the dead. "Gertrude!"

She dragged the door open, heavy snow flying into the house as the wind gusted again.

"What is it? What's going on?" Gertrude stumbled into view, her nightgown twisted around her legs, her hair standing straight up.

"Alex is gone." She felt sick saying the words. Like she was going to spew what little she had in her stomach, her heart so heavy it felt like lead. "Call the police and get them out here."

"Are you sure?" Gertrude nearly fell in her haste to get down the stairs.

"The bolt was open. There was water on the floor."

"Did you check his bed?"

"I don't want to waste time." She dragged an old brown coat from the closet near the door. There were old galoshes on the floor, and she shoved her feet into them. They were three sizes too big, but she didn't care. "You check the bedroom, but call the police first."

She ran onto the porch, her feet slipping in wet snow.

She could see a trail of footprints leading across the yard. They looked fresh, barely covered by new snow. He must be close. Had he put on a coat? Gloves? Boots? Or was he wandering around in his pajamas?

Dear God, she hoped not.

She followed the trail across the yard. Alex was heading toward the town center. It was a mile to the heart of town, but everything there was closed. With the temperature hovering just above freezing and the ground wet with snow, he'd be hypothermic in no time if he didn't find shelter.

She jogged along the sidewalk, the snow falling faster and heavier.

"Alex!" she called.

The wind howled, and she thought she heard him crying for help beneath its blustering roar. Maybe, though, it was just the leaves rustling.

Oh God! She had to find him, and she had to do it quickly. The stupid boots flopped as she tried to sprint forward, and she fell, her knees skidding through snow and ice, her flannel pajama pants soaked.

She jumped back up, peering into the distance. Was that a little shadow moving along the sidewalk?

"Alex!" Headlights splashed behind her, an engine purring quietly as a car approached.

She just kept running, sure that if she stopped the footprints would disappear, and Alex would be lost for good.

The car pulled up beside her.

No, not a car. An old truck.

The window rolled down, and Cade looked out at her. "Get in the truck."

"We won't be able to see the footprints from there," she said, her teeth chattering, her body shaking from cold and fear.

"You won't be able to follow at all if you're frozen to death." He got out of the truck and dragged her from the sidewalk. "You drive. I'll follow the prints and you follow me."

"I—"

"Only one of us thought to put on cold-weather gear, Tess. Let's not waste time arguing about who should be the one to track Alex."

She nodded and climbed into the truck, her hands almost too cold and numb to grasp the steering wheel.

"Hold on. Let me just grab my flashlight." Cade reached across her and opened the glove compartment, pulling out a large flashlight before running down the sidewalk, the light jumping in front of him.

She put the truck into gear and followed, easing along behind him, her eyes scanning the darkness.

They'd covered nearly the full mile to the town center when Cade sprinted forward. Tess's heart jumped, and she peered through the swirling snow and darkness. She saw a small figure trudging toward them.

She parked the truck and ran, catching up to Cade as he scooped Alex into his arms.

"You okay, sport?" he said, and Alex nodded, his eyes filled with confusion. "Where were you headed?"

"Home," Alex responded simply.

"But what were you doing out in the snow?" Tessa took him from Cade's arms, and Alex wiggled down to stand beside her. He wore a heavy parka, thick gloves, ski pants, snow boots, and a hat. Obviously, he'd prepared for the cold.

"I was looking for my angel, but my legs were getting tired."

"You know someone stole the angel, Alex," Tessa said, her voice sharp with relief and concern. "What in the world were you thinking, coming out on a night like tonight?"

"I was thinking that maybe I could find her."

"But—" she started, but Cade put a hand on her arm and shook his head.

"Let's get in the truck and get back to the house. Then you can say whatever you need to."

She held Alex's hand tight until he was buckled into the middle of the bench seat. Then she crowded in beside him, relief making her weak and dizzy. God, she'd been so scared. More terrified than she'd ever been in her life.

Cade was on his cell phone as he slid behind the wheel. She heard Alex's name, but her teeth were chattering so loudly that she missed the rest.

Apparently she was the only one out of the three

of them who hadn't thought to leave the house prepared for the snow.

"Cold?" Cade asked, flicking up the heater. She held her hands close to the vent, but if there was warm air coming out, she couldn't feel it.

"A little." She made a lie of the words by shivering so violently, she knocked Alex sideways.

"Sorry," she murmured, her hand on his shoulder. His coat was soaked with snow and rain. "Are you cold, buddy?"

"If he is, he'll warm up quick enough when Gertrude tans his hide," Cade muttered.

He pulled into the snow-covered driveway, his headlights slashing across the porch. Gertrude was standing there, a blanket thrown over her shoulders, a hat pulled low over her head, little puffs of hair sticking out from beneath it. She hurried toward them as Tess opened the truck door and helped Alex out.

"My God, son! What were you thinking?" she rasped as she dragged him into her arms. There were tears on her face and a hazy cloud of smoke around her head. She must have tossed the cigarette when she saw them returning.

A patrol car pulled up to the curb, and the officer from the tea climbed out.

"That was quick, Cunningham," he said, eyeing Alex and Gertrude before his gaze shifted to Tess. "Looks like everyone is in good shape. Guess I should go back to the office and write out the report."

"You come in for a cup of coffee first, Max,"

Gertrude called. "Paperwork can wait until after that."

"Don't mind if I do." He smiled into Tessa's eyes.

A few years ago, that kind of smile would have melted Tessa's insides. Now it just made her want to laugh. Guys like him were a dime a dozen. Good looking, charming, arrogant.

"Come on, Alex." She took her nephew's arm and led him into the house, moving to the side as everyone else followed them in. Alex stripped out of his coat and boots as everyone watched. He carefully tucked his gloves into his pocket and walked up the stairs in a long-sleeved flannel shirt and snow pants, dripping water and ice all over the steps.

"Don't you go to that piano, Alex Riley! You hear me?" Gertrude charged up the stairs after him. "You're not playing it for three days after the stunt you just pulled. As a matter of fact, I've a good mind to tan that little hide of yours! You took a year off my life! *Years* off my life!"

Tess sprinted after them both, because she didn't want to be left with the men, and because Alex needed to be made to understand that he could not walk out of the house in the middle of the night ever again.

Her heart couldn't take another scare like the one she'd just had.

Chapter Thirteen

Cade decided to give Tess and Gertrude a few minutes alone with their nephew. It seemed like the right thing to do. Alex had made a big mistake, and he'd be lucky if he got off with the puny three-day sentence Gertrude had threatened. If Cade were his father, he'd have probably grounded Alex from the piano for a month or longer.

"You look done in, Cunningham. Rough night at the house?" Max asked, his shoulder against the wall, his arms crossed at his chest.

"Who says I was home?"

"Me. I drove by your place on patrol and saw the lights on and your truck in the driveway. Sad, really. Guy like you should have—"

"What's your point?" Cade cut him off. "Because, obviously, you have one."

"You seem to have a thing for Tessa. I suggest you act on it before someone else does."

No way would he jump on that bait. "I think we have more important things to discuss."

"Like how we're going to make sure that kid

doesn't freeze to death one night while his family is sleeping?" Max switched gears easily. Not surprising. He loved women, but Cade suspected that he loved his job more.

"They need an alarm system. Something that will go off if he tries to escape again." Cade ran his hand over his hair, wishing Gertrude was around to offer coffee again. He'd been sound asleep when his phone rang, and he still didn't feel wide-awake.

With a police force the size of Apple Valley's, it was protocol to let Cade know when important calls came in. Little things like stolen chickens and broken windows were handled without him, but missing children came under the need-to-know heading.

"Do you think they can afford to get one?" Max glanced around the neglected foyer, probably cataloging every piece of peeling wallpaper and every nick on the wood floor.

"Money might be a little tight, but I'm sure they'll find a way to make it work." He'd make certain they did, because he couldn't stomach the thought of getting another call about Alex in the middle of the night.

Max nodded, running his hand over a tall, narrow table that stood against the wall. Checking for dirt and dust? Knowing him, that's exactly what Max was doing. "If they can't, we can probably get people around town to help out."

"Gertrude isn't the kind to take charity lying down, Max. If she thinks that's what we're offering, she'll fight tooth and nail to keep from accepting it."

"You're smart. You'll figure a way around her."

"Since when is that my responsibility?"

"Since I saw you and Tessa together."

Cade scowled. They were back to that. Of course. Max was like a dog with a bone, and Cade was too damn tired to play a round of fetch. "I think the family has had enough time to discuss things alone. I'm heading upstairs."

He didn't invite Max.

Max followed anyway. Wood stairs creaked under their combined weight, their booted feet adding to the wet mess everyone else had left. There were still piles of things on the landing, still an air of neglect that clung to the house. The apartment was neat as a pin, though. Everything in place, the old floor gleaming with polish, the furniture threadbare but clean.

Alex was sitting at the kitchen table, a cup of what looked like hot chocolate in his hands, Gertrude hovering over him, her face drawn and pale. Years of smoking and worry had carved a road map of lines on her face. They looked deeper, her green eyes shadowed.

"Coffee is ready," she said, not taking her eyes off her nephew. In all the years that Cade had known Gertrude, she'd never been quiet or demure. She didn't know how to hold her tongue, and that had gotten her into plenty of trouble with people in town. Now she was quiet, constrained, every movement carefully plotted as if each one hurt more than the next.

If the stories Ida told were true, and they usually were, Gertrude had lost her parents when she was a teen. A few years later, the bastard she'd married had beaten her senseless. She'd returned the favor and spent two years in jail for it. She'd moved to Apple Valley after that, gotten a job at Walmart and another at the library, living on her own until her younger sister had showed up on her doorstep with Tess and Emily. Despite her gruff exterior, despite her penchant for getting into feuds with neighbors and townspeople, Gertrude had poured everything she had into taking care of the girls. Now she was as much a part of local lore as anyone or anything.

He put a hand on her shoulder, urging her into the seat next to Alex. "Relax for a few minutes, Gertrude."

"I don't think that's possible, Cade. I really don't." She glanced around the room, her hand shaking as she lifted a cookie from a plate and handed it to Alex. "Where is that niece of mine? A time of crisis like this, and she decides to hide in her room?"

"She might be getting out of her wet clothes," Cade suggested, an image of smooth skin and black lace flashing through his mind. His body tightened in response, heat pulsing through him.

Not the time or the place, but, damn, if he didn't suddenly want it to be.

He poured coffee for Max and grabbed a cup for himself, sipping the scalding brew. Something cold might have been better. Like . . . a shower or a snow bath.

"I have to tell you, I feel like just about the worst parent that ever lived," Gertrude said morosely.

"These things happen, Gertrude," Max reassured her before Cade could. "More often than most people think. The important thing is to learn from it, and to make sure it doesn't happen again."

"You don't have to worry about that. Alex won't do such a foolish thing ever again, will you, son?"

He shook his head.

"I want words, young man," Gertrude said gruffly, but she handed him another cookie.

"I won't leave the house without permission ever again," Alex mumbled and dipped his cookie in hot chocolate. He pulled it out, dripping liquid onto the scarred tabletop. He didn't eat the cookie. Just stared at it, watching chocolate pool beneath it.

Gertrude sighed, taking the cookie from his hand and placing it on a small plate. "You know we don't play with food, Alex."

He didn't respond, just tapped his fingers against the table, his knees, the table again, his head nodding slightly to some silent tune.

Poor kid. He'd been through a lot, and losing the angel seemed to be his breaking point. He'd been distraught when he'd realized it was missing, screaming and rocking and putting on a town hall show that the citizens of Apple Valley would never forget.

They wouldn't repeat a word of it, though; wouldn't replay those horrible moments in their conversations. As many faults as the small town had, it was big on compassion.

Cade dropped into the chair beside Alex, touched his shoulder, felt every muscle in the boy's scrawny body tense. "Alex, I'm going to find that angel for you. I promise you that. You don't have to worry. You don't have to keep looking yourself. I'll find it, and I'll bring it home to you."

"I'm tired," he responded, slowly rising, his little body seeming to creak and groan as he shuffled out of the room and disappeared down the hall.

"That poor boy," Gertrude whispered. "That poor, poor boy." A tear dripped down her cheek, meandering through dozens of wrinkles before landing on the table.

"You're going to make yourself sick," Max said gently, meeting Cade's gaze across Gertrude's bowed head. *Now is as good a time as any*, his eyes seemed to say.

"An alarm system will help, Gertrude. You can set it up to go off if anyone is walking through the store or opening doors or windows downstairs," he suggested, and she finally looked up, her eyes hazy and tired.

"It's a sound idea, but I'll have to check with Tessa. It's her house, and she makes all the big decisions." Gertrude walked to the hallway. "Tessa Louise, get out here!" she hollered.

A door opened. Footsteps sounded on hardwood. Seconds later, Tess walked into the kitchen, making a beeline for the coffeemaker. Loose sweats rode low on her narrow hips. A tight-fitting long-sleeved T clung to her flat abs. She'd pulled her hair into a ponytail, the wet ends of it leaving splotches on her shirt as she moved.

She sipped coffee, dropping into the seat across from Cade without ever meeting anyone's eyes.

"Well," she finally said. "This sucks."

"That's an understatement if I ever heard one," Gertrude muttered.

"We were just discussing the possibilities of having an alarm hooked up so Alex can't wander again." Max offered the information as he took the seat next to Tess, somehow managing to move his chair a little closer to hers in the process.

Tess nodded, twisting a strand of her hair around her finger, her brow furrowed. "I was thinking that, too. Is there a good company in town?"

"I have a friend in Spokane who runs a security business. He'll know what you need. I'll be happy to make the call for you."

"Thanks, but I can manage, Max." Tess cut him off at the knees, and Cade didn't even try to hide his smile. "If you give me his name, I'll make the call tomorrow morning."

"Sure." Max dragged a business card from his wallet, scribbled a number on it, and handed it to Tess. "Just tell him you're a friend of mine. He'll make a special effort to get things done quickly. If you think the price is too high or his crew doesn't seem to be working fast enough, just give me a call. I'll handle it for you."

Uh-oh. *This* should be good.

Gertrude's head came up so fast, Cade was surprised it didn't fly off. "What did you just say, young man?"

"I said—"

"It might be best not to repeat it," Cade suggested, because Tess was rubbing her temple like she had one of the migraines she'd suffered from as a kid, and his amusement at the crap Max had just stepped in was outweighed by his concern for her.

"Go ahead," Gertrude dared Max. "Repeat it."

"Well, Ms. Gertrude, I'm thinking it might be better if I didn't."

"Chicken shit," she muttered in reply, shooting him a death glare.

"Gertrude," Tessa interrupted tiredly. "Let it drop."

"Why should I? We've never needed a man to

help us manage things, and we don't need one now!"
Gertrude snapped, her eyes blazing.

Tessa pushed away from the table and pressed her
fingers to the bridge of her nose. "I have a splitting
headache, and your griping is making it worse. How
about we save the arguing for another day?"

"Well," Gertrude huffed, slamming her coffee on
the counter. "If that's the way you feel, then maybe
I'll just go back to bed."

She stomped out of the room and slammed her
door so hard the house shook.

"I'm sorry about that." Tess poured more coffee
into her cup and reached up into a cupboard above
the refrigerator, her bare feet just visible beneath
the long cuffs of her sweats. Her toenails were pink.
A little detail that Cade hadn't noticed before.
"Gertrude is still really shook up. She didn't mean to
take it out on you, Max."

"I think she probably did," Max said, and Tessa
laughed, the sound reminding Cade of long summer
days and late fall evenings, of looking into Tessa's
eyes and feeling like he was looking into her heart.

"Apparently, you've dealt with Gertrude before."
Tess fumbled in the cupboard, finally pulling a
bottle of Tylenol out.

"On a few occasions, so don't worry, I'm just
taking her attitude as a sign that she's recovered from
her scare," Max responded, giving Tess a once-over
that made Cade's fist clench. She seemed oblivious,
her head bent over the Tylenol bottle as she struggled
with the lid.

"Let me." Cade snatched it from her hand, popping the lid easily and handing it back.

Max watched with a slight smile, his hands in his

pockets, his posture relaxed. "Well," he said, "I think I should probably head back to the office and write up a report."

"I'll walk you both down," Tessa said, popping the pills into her mouth and swallowing them down with a gulp of coffee.

Cade hadn't said he was leaving, but he followed Tess and Max outside and stood on the porch as Max said good-bye and drove away.

"Good night, Cade," Tess hinted broadly.

"Are you kicking me out?"

"It's late. We're both tired." But she walked back inside, and he followed, closing the door on the dark cold morning.

"It's as cold in here as it is outside," she said, walking into the front room and flicking on the light.

She sat on a couch near the window, her arms folded around her knees.

"Slippers might help," he suggested.

"I didn't have time to pack any, and it feels wasteful to buy something I already own."

"Are you going to have your stuff shipped from Annapolis?" He opened a couple of trunks and several boxes, finally pulling out a thick blanket.

"Eventually. I need to send in my resignation first, though."

"What's the holdup?" He sat next to her and tucked the blanket around her legs and her arms, his hands lingering a little longer than he'd intended.

"Fear? Anxiety? I don't really know. Gertrude is getting pissy about it, though, and I can't keep putting my boss off when he asks when I'm returning." She sighed, resting her head on her knees, her ponytail sliding across her cheek. He brushed it back and looked into her eyes. They seemed more purple than blue, the shadows under them dark.

"What can I do to help?"

"Be here. Just like you are." She smiled, and his heart responded, jumping toward her with so much force it left him breathless.

He put his arm around her shoulders, and she lifted the blanket so that it covered them both. An invitation to move closer, if he'd ever seen one.

He did, their bodies touching, their heat mingling, and it was like coming home after being away for too long.

Surprised, he touched Tessa's cheek, her skin cool and velvety. They were so close he could see flecks of silver in her eyes and the remnant of pink lipstick on her mouth. Could smell just a hint of her dark perfume.

He bent forward, his lips brushing hers, the heat that zipped through his blood leaving him no choice but to taste her lips again and again.

She moaned softly, her hands sliding up his arms to his shoulders, her fingers weaving through his hair. And then she was up, moving away, her fingers pressed to her lips, her cheeks flushed pink.

He started after her, but she put up a hand, shook her head.

"You'd better go," she said, her voice husky.

"Sure. But not before I say goodnight." He snagged her hand, tugging her in close, because if the night was going to end on a kiss, he wanted to make damn sure it was one she'd remember.

When he broke away, she was breathless, her eyes

hazy with longing. She didn't ask him to leave again but didn't reach for more, either.

Too bad, because he would have been more than happy to give it.

"Goodnight, Tess," he finally managed to say, and then he walked outside, got in his truck, and drove away.

Chapter Fourteen

Alarm system. Done.

Wallpaper. Ordered.

Paint . . .

Yeah. Paint.

Tess glared at five gallons of eggshell white that sat in the foyer. Sunday morning, and Gertrude and Alex were sleeping in. This was as good a time as any to get some work done inside, but she wasn't feeling motivated. She was feeling tired, the remnants of the first migraine she'd suffered in years pulsing behind her left eye.

Stress. That's what the doctor at urgent care had said before he'd shot Tess full of drugs and sent her home with Gertrude. Twelve hours later, and she was feeling almost normal again.

Her cell phone rang, and she dragged it from the back pocket of her oldest pair of jeans. Splotched with paint and scribbled measurements, they were so faded and worn, she was pretty sure they'd give up the ghost soon.

"Hello?" She answered without looking at the caller ID. She knew who it was. She'd sent in her resignation in the wee hours of the morning, right around the time she'd come out of her drug-induced sleep.

"What in the hell are you thinking?" James Winthrop said in his you-really-pissed-me-off voice. She couldn't blame him for using it. He'd hired her right out of college, helped her hone her skills and artistry. Like her, he was passionate about restoration of antiques, and they'd been a good team for seven years; first mentor and student, then peers, sharing ideas about projects and working together on several of James's larger accounts.

It physically hurt to think of breaking away from that.

"I'm thinking that I can't make my nephew leave the only home he's ever had." She sat on a paint can, rubbing a knot from the back of her neck, willing the dull throb in her eye to *not* worsen. "You know I hate to do this—"

"Then don't." He sighed. "We discussed all this when you left for the funeral. We decided you were going to move your nephew and aunt here. I was even going to talk to my kids' school about finding a spot for Alex."

"I can't do that to him, James. He's already been through too much. Tearing him away from his home is just going to make things worse."

"Would telling you that I've been planning to make a special announcement during the company's annual Christmas party convince you to change your mind?" he asked. "I want to make you a partner.

You've worked hard for it, proven yourself. It's time. And not just because I don't want to lose you. I've been planning this for months."

Partnership in one of the East Coast's premier interior design companies? She'd take it. A million times over, she'd take it.

"You're quiet. That must mean you're tempted."

Tempted? She was ready to pack her bags and get on the next plane to Maryland.

"I'd be lying if I said I wasn't," she said, glancing up the stairs.

"Then, come back."

"Is that what you would do if you were in my position?" she asked, because James was a father, his children the absolute loves of his life.

"Don't ask me that, Tess," he growled. She could picture him, sitting in his home office, surrounded by swaths of fabric and cabinet samples, probably staring at a picture of his family.

"I'm asking you because we've been friends for years, and because I trust you to tell me the truth rather than what we both want the truth to be," she pressed, her heart beating heavy and hard. This was why she had postponed sending in her resignation. It was why she'd e-mailed rather than called. James was like a brother to her, his sometimes dramatic and artistic nature tempered by compassion and a true desire to connect with the people in his life.

"Like you trusted me when I told you Kent was a prick?" he responded dryly.

"I trusted you. I just chose not to take your advice."

"Then trust me when I say that you're not a small-town girl."

"That doesn't answer my question, and you know it. What would you do?"

He sighed. "You're like a dog with a bone, kid. That's one of the things I've always liked about you, but right about now, it's annoying the hell out of me."

"Because you'd do exactly what I plan to. You'd sacrifice anything for your kids, James, and you know it. Even a job you love. Even a partnership you've worked seven years to get." Her voice broke, but her eyes were dry.

"Are you crying?"

"No."

"Good, because the damn job isn't worth it." He sighed again, and she knew he was smoothing his black hair, fiddling with the cuffs of his sleeves. "Okay, here's the deal. As unhappy as it makes me, I'll accept your resignation. On one condition."

"What's that?" she said through a mouthful of cotton and unshed tears.

"Knowing you, you're already scoping the area for restoration projects. I want in on that. The market here is picked through and expensive. Out there, you might be able to get some farm-fresh product that the firm can use and that my clients may be interested in."

"I have a few pieces in mind already, but I thought . . ." What had she thought? That James would break his ties with her completely, sever all communication, turn his back on their friendship because she had to stay with her nephew?

"You think too much, Tess. That's your problem. As much as I hate knowing you're going to be three thousand miles away, I don't see why we can't still have some collaboration. I can't offer you partnership, of course, but I can certainly continue to use your pieces in some of my designs and consult with you on some of my bigger projects."

"That means a lot to me, James."

"You mean a lot to me, kid." He cleared his throat. "Do you need me to pack some things up at your apartment and send them your way?"

"I can't ask you—"

"You didn't. I offered."

"It would help. I planned on coming to Annapolis to do it myself, but Alex really needs me here."

"Kids come first. I have your house key, so I'll toss your clothes into a couple of boxes and ship them there. What's the address?"

She rattled it off quickly, her stomach churning.

This was it. The real deal. Knowing James, he'd have the boxes packed and on their way to her by Monday evening.

"Got it," James said. "You're planning to keep the brownstone?"

"I'll probably list it."

"The market isn't good. Why don't you let me find a renter? Maybe someone from the firm? That'll hold you over until you have time to come out and deal with things properly."

"That's fine."

"Great. I'll give you a call once I've sent the boxes. I know you won't be back for Christmas, but think about coming in the spring. Bring your family. You can stay at my place."

"I will."

"Good, and as soon as you have something ready, send me the specs and pictures."

"You can expect something before Christmas."

"Make it in the next two weeks, okay? I'm looking for something special to go in Hinckley Manor. A parlor piece would be really nice, but if you have something for the upstairs lounge, that will work, too. I'll give the kids your love," he said and hung up.

And, damn, if she didn't actually want to cry, because it was over. All those years of hard work, living off of coffee and a couple hours of sleep, so that she could be the best and the brightest in James's company: They didn't mean squat anymore.

Someone knocked on the door, the sound so unexpected Tessa nearly fell off the paint can.

"We're closed," she said as she opened the door.

"That's why I'm here," Cade replied. He looked good, neat and clean shaven, a blue dress shirt visible beneath his coat, dress slacks hugging his firm thighs.

She knew her cheeks were blazing.

She'd been avoiding thinking about him since *the incident*. She preferred to think of the kiss as that rather than the *moment her entire world shifted*.

"Can I come in?" he prodded. "It's ten degrees out here."

"Sure." She moved aside, catching a whiff of soap and winter as he stepped into the room. "What's up?"

"I'm on my way to church—"

"You're kidding." She laughed, the sound spilling out into the foyer and seeming to echo off the walls.

Hysteria? If it was, she was entitled. Her boss had just accepted her resignation, and she was looking into the eyes of the man who'd kissed her senseless

less than forty-eight hours ago. A man that she'd spent ten years trying to forget. Hysteria was as good a response as any.

"Everyone has to believe in something, Tess," he said quietly, and her laughter died.

"I'm sorry. I wasn't laughing about you going to church." She touched his knuckles, fingering the thin scar he'd gotten when he'd freed a cat's head from the inside of a tin can. "It's just been a long weekend, and you surprised me."

He captured her hand before she could pull back, pressing a kiss to her palm and closing her fingers around it.

"Apology accepted," he said. "I heard you were in urgent care yesterday."

"From who?"

"At least ten different people. Ida being one of them. Everything okay?"

"Just a migraine. You know how those go."

"I do." He eyed the paint cans and the plastic drop cloth she'd laid on the foyer floor. "And I'm wondering why you'd think that painting is a good idea after you've been suffering with one."

"I feel a lot better today."

"You're pale as a ghost."

"Spewing my guts up for twenty-four hours because of a migraine tends to do that to me."

"You want to know my opinion?" he asked.

"Not really."

"Tough, because I'm going to give it anyway." He laughed, and she couldn't help smiling. "I think you should lie down for a while longer. Make sure you're feeling a hundred percent before you start filling the house with paint fumes."

"Thanks for sharing, but I'm fine." She popped open a can of paint just to prove her point, gagging when the smell hit her nose.

"Do not spew," Cade warned, setting the lid back on the can and tugging her away. "Because that would be really embarrassing for you and really unfortunate for me."

"Glad your concern is in the right place."

"Sarcasm becomes you, Red," he murmured, his palm sliding against her bare forearm, his fingers caressing her elbow.

"Cade—"

"Tess! Is someone here?" Gertrude called from the top of the steps, interrupting before Tess could say something inane and stupid. Like *please, don't ever stop touching me.*

"Cade stopped by," she called back, slipping away from his touch so that Gertrude wouldn't catch a glimpse of them and start thinking something ridiculous that involved a short engagement and marriage.

"Alex said he heard the sheriff. I thought he was full of sh—stuff." Gertrude walked into view, her hand on Alex's shoulder. She'd been keeping him close, barely letting him out of her sight since he'd wandered off.

He didn't look happy about it, his brow furrowed, his lips pressed together. He'd combed his hair neatly, though, and dressed in a white button-up shirt and dark slacks that were about an inch too short. White socks. Yikes! Shiny black loafers. She needed to get him some new clothes. Boys his age grew like weeds. At least that's what James had said when his son was around Alex's age.

"You look nice, Alex. Where are you heading?"

"Church."

Surprised, Tess met Gertrude's eyes. "Really?"

"Don't act so shocked, Tess. It's not like I'm a heathen or something." Gertrude brushed a hand down black slacks that hung a little too loosely from her scrawny hips. She'd paired them with a muted pink sweater set that only clashed with her hair a little.

She looked almost . . . respectable.

"Besides," she continued, "Emily and Dave brought Alex to church almost every week. He likes the music. Don't you, son?"

Alex nodded, patting his thighs and then his knees, his hands and fingers restless without piano keys beneath them.

"I was heading to church, too, Gertrude," Cade said. "That's one of the reasons I stopped by. On Friday, Reverend Fisher asked me to find out if your family needed anything. I told him that I would, but with everything that's happened, it slipped my mind."

"We are *not* a charity case," Gertrude said with just enough snoot in her voice to make Tess want to giggle. She'd probably laughed more since coming to Apple Valley than she had in years. Which was funny when she thought about it. She'd been happy in Annapolis. Or maybe satisfied was a better word. Content?

"His question didn't imply that you were, Gertrude."

"Humph!" she replied.

"You know Jethro and Natalie. They care about the community and the people in it. They know how difficult losing Emily and Dave was, and they want to make sure that if you need support, they give it."

"Well . . ." Gertrude softened a little. "They are good people, those two. I guess it's fortunate that I'm bringing Alex to church. I can straighten out their thinking while I'm there."

"Gertrude, please don't cause issues," Tessa said, and Gertrude shot her the death glare.

"I am going to church. Church is not a place where people cause *issues*. Not that I *ever* do," she snapped.

"Let's go," Alex said, opening the door. Frigid air blew in, and Tessa shivered.

"It's still a little early, sport," Cade said gently, closing the door again.

"I'm ready," Alex insisted, patting his stomach, his thighs, his stomach again, and it was all Tess could do not to grab his hands and hold them still.

"Not yet. You need black socks," Cade responded, and Alex lifted his foot and frowned.

"Okay," he finally said, trudging up the stairs.

"Good distraction, Cade," Gertrude said. "But Lord help us all if the kid doesn't have black socks. I'd better run up there and make sure he can find some."

"Are you going to come along, Tess?" Cade asked as Gertrude hurried after Alex.

"Dressed like this?" She touched her jeans and the old sweatshirt. "I don't think so."

"You have time to change."

"I know. I just . . . don't know about going to church and seeing everyone." She walked into the front room and pulled back the curtains, letting bright sunlight shine into the room.

"You saw half the town at the tea. That went fine," Cade pointed out reasonably.

"Did you forget my nephew's screaming rage? Or mine?" She sure as heck hadn't. All the pain medicine in the world couldn't knock that one out of her brain.

"He was screaming. You were . . . venting."

"Thanks, but calling it something else doesn't change the fact that I was cursing like a sailor in front of the reverend, his wife, and half the town of Apple Valley."

"So you're embarrassed?" He leaned against the doorjamb, his shoulders fitting snuggly in a brown leather bomber jacket. He looked nearly edible.

"Of course, I'm embarrassed. Who wouldn't be?"

"Probably just about everyone, but no one is judging you, Tess. Except you."

"I'm not—"

"Sure you are. You think you have to act a certain way, be a certain way. You think you have to put on a show, and somehow doing it will make people around town accept you."

"I don't need or want their acceptance! They're just a bunch of judgmental small-town hicks," she snapped, and regretted it immediately, because people in Apple Valley had been nothing but kind since the funeral. They'd bent over backwards to help, and they deserved better than her derision. "I'm sorry, Cade—"

"Forget it," he growled, stalking out of the room and leaving her feeling lower than the lowest kind of scum.

Let it go, her inner voice said. *He's the guy who broke your heart a dozen times, and you're better off without him.*

But she couldn't, because hurting Cade hurt, and because he deserved a lot better.

She followed him into the foyer and put her hand on his arm. His eyes were stony and cold, his expression hard.

"That was one of the stupidest things I've said in a long time," she said, her throat tight and hot, regret jabbing like hard fists behind her eyes.

"*I'm* one of those small-town hicks that you don't want to impress, Tess," he ground out, and she felt like an even bigger loser. "I think you forgot that."

"You know that I don't really—"

"What's going on down here?" Gertrude hurried down the steps, Alex following along behind. Black socks instead of white, and for some reason that made Tessa's eyes fill with tears.

"Nothing," Cade bit out. "You two ready to go?"

"Sure." Gertrude shot Tess a hard look. Assuming, of course, that whatever had happened was her fault.

Which it was.

Because she was an idiot and a fool, and she'd just proven it a hundred times over.

No one said a word as Cade, Gertrude, and Alex left. Not even good-bye. The door closed. A truck engine roared to life, and then silence descended, leaving nothing but the echo of Tessa's stupidity hanging in the dusty air.

Chapter Fifteen

She would not cry.

Would. Not.

Tess sniffed back tears as she poured paint into a pan, nearly puking at the smell of it. Just deserts for what she'd done.

"Idiot," she muttered. "Imbecile."

It didn't help.

The empty house felt lonely, its silence a sad song that she couldn't stop listening to as she rolled paint onto the wall.

After all Cade's kindnesses, after kisses that had curled her toes and made her heart pound hard in her chest, after everything that Cade had done for her family since Emily and Dave's death, *that* was how she'd repaid him. By belittling the townspeople he loved and by belittling him.

"You are a dumb-ass, Tess. That's the problem," she muttered as she swiped more paint onto the wall.

Outside, wind chimes rang, the sound eerie and haunting in the silent house. The stairs creaked, and she swore she heard fabric rustling behind her. Another creak. Another rustle of fabric.

Dear God in heaven! Someone *was* behind her!

She could feel eyes boring into the back of her head. Was it Miriam Riley, coming back from the grave to haunt the woman who'd torn down the wallpaper she'd put up a hundred years ago? Or worse . . . a murderer, stealthily moving toward Tess, a knife clutched in his gloved hand?

Creak!

She swung around, flinging paint across the banister, the stairs, and the huge tabby cat that stood on the third step.

"Margrave! What are you doing in here?" she hollered, her hand shaking as she wiped paint spatter from the woodwork. She tried to wipe specks of cream from Margrave's fur, but he wanted none of it, swatting her hand away and walking past her like he was royalty.

"You're an outdoor cat, remember?" She opened the front door, and he took his good old time walking through it. Either Gertrude or Alex had let him in. She'd have to have a talk with them when they got home. The last thing she wanted was cat hair in the fresh paint or claw marks on the furniture and antiques.

She glanced down the hall at the boxes she and Gertrude had stacked near the kitchen doorway. Keepers. She'd been surprised at how much of the stuff that had been piled into the house was usable. At first, she'd been too blinded by grief to see anything but junk, but days of working through the mess had cleared her vision. Sure, there'd been tons of trash, but there was also a lot of potential.

She liked to think that was Emily's doing. That maybe she and her sister weren't quite as different as she'd always thought.

Thought?

Tess had just *proven* how alike they were. Or at least that they were both really good at hurting people they cared about.

"Idiot," she mumbled one last time.

It took an hour to finish the first coat of paint. When she did, the gloomy hall had been transformed into something that was nearly charming. Another coat of paint and a refinished floor, and she'd be able to hang the artwork she'd salvaged from This-N-That and from the shed behind the house. Price tags in the corners and a streamlined display along each wall. The old church pew that sat in the parlor against one wall and the intricate sideboard she'd found in the kitchen against the other—she could picture it all clearly in her mind, and she couldn't deny the little thrill of excitement it brought.

Her cell phone rang, and she answered. "Hello?"

"Tess?" Cade responded, and her hand tightened on the phone, her stomach churning with a million things she wanted to say. Needed to say.

"I'm glad you called. I still feel—"

"I don't know how else to say this except bluntly. Gertrude's been in an accident."

Her mouth went dry, her ears rang. She needed to sit, but she didn't think she could find the floor.

"Tess? You still there?"

"I . . . yes," she whispered, so, so scared of what he was about to say. "What happened?"

"She fell down the church steps, and it looks like she broke her leg. An ambulance is transporting her to Apple Valley General Hospital."

"Her leg?" she repeated.

"Yes. It was an obvious break, but the EMT doesn't think she broke anything else. They'll be doing X-rays at the hospital, of course. Alex and I are following the ambulance there. Do you want me to swing by and pick you up?"

"No, I'll meet you there." She didn't want Gertrude to be at the hospital alone. Not even for a second.

"Take your time and drive carefully," he said, and she could hear the warmth in his voice, the concern. "The last thing your family needs is another accident." He disconnected, and Tess sprinted upstairs.

She threw on clean jeans and the first clean shirt she could find, ran outside, and realized that she needed car keys.

"Shit! Shit, shit, shit!" she muttered as she raced back into the house and dug through the drawer where Gertrude kept spare keys. She finally snagged the one to the Pontiac, nearly killing herself in her rush to get outside again.

Dying wouldn't do Gertrude any good. It wouldn't do Tess any good, either. She kept her speed to just a little above the limit as she navigated Main Street, turned onto Twelfth Avenue, and made her way to the edge of town. The hospital was there, housed in what had once been an institution for tuberculosis patients. The old building had been expanded in the 1950s when the town had been at the zenith of its population growth, old brick and newer brick merging to create a gothic-looking facade.

Tessa drove to the back and parked near the emergency entrance. Cade's truck was a few spaces away. Thank God he'd been with Gertrude and Alex when the accident happened.

She headed across the parking lot, cold wind biting through her shirt. In her mad dash to get to the hospital, she'd forgotten her coat. Not good when the temperature was hovering just below freezing.

The emergency room lobby was nearly empty, just a few people sitting in chairs, reading newspapers or sipping coffee from carryout cups. Every one of them watched as Tessa made her way to the information desk. She probably knew them all, but she was too worried about Gertrude to stop for chats.

"Can I help you?" The receptionist looked up from her computer and smiled. She looked to be about twenty, her skin flawless, her hair short and trendy.

"My aunt was brought in by ambulance a few minutes ago. Gertrude McKenzie?"

"Hold on." She typed something into the computer. "Let me see if she's in the system yet. Yes. She's in room nine. You can go on back." She gestured to a door behind her desk, and Tessa walked through it.

The hallway split to the left and right, and she pivoted, not sure which way to go until she heard a very loud, very familiar voice.

She couldn't hear the words, but she knew Gertrude's I'm-pissed-off-and-I'm-going-to-kill-someone voice.

She hurried to the right, following the sound

until she reached room nine. She braced herself and opened the door.

Cade was standing next to the hospital bed, his hand on the back of his neck, his back to Tess. He glanced over his shoulder as she walked in, offering a smile that didn't quite make its way to his eyes.

Was he still angry?

Did it matter?

Yes. Damn it! It did. But she had to deal with Gertrude before she could deal with apologies.

"Hey, Gertrude, how are you feeling?" she asked, moving into the room and offering Alex a smile.

He was too busy staring at Gertrude as if she were some strange and exotic creature to notice.

"How does it look like I'm feeling?" Gertrude growled, her eyes flashing with green fire. There was blood on her left cheek and a huge blue lump on her forehead. Her left leg was elevated, but she looked like she was ready to come off the bed swinging.

"You look like you're feeling a lot better than I expected you to be." Tess touched her wrinkled hand.

"I feel like crap, kid. Thanks to that good-for-nothing Zimmerman Beck!" She nearly spat.

"What about Zimmerman?" Tess glanced at Cade, and he shrugged.

"She wants me to arrest him for assault."

"Because he pushed me down the stairs. Devil's spawn!"

"Gertrude," Cade said calmly, "Zim was talking to the reverend when you fell. He was nowhere near you."

"I don't care what he says—"

"It's not just what he's saying. At least a dozen other people told me the same thing."

"Then how did I fall? Explain that to me, young man, because we all know that I have never *ever* fallen in my life!"

"You slipped on some ice."

"If that's what happened, I'd remember it," Gertrude insisted, but she looked a bit confused, her eyes losing some of their fire.

"Do you remember Zim pushing you?"

"I remember him telling me that the building was probably going to fall in on everyone if I walked into the church, and I remember me calling him a jackass."

"That was all before the service began," Cade whispered in Tessa's ear. "They exchanged a few other choice words after it."

"I can hear you, Cade." Gertrude scowled, but her eyelids were drooping and she seemed to have lost most of her fight.

"You bumped your head pretty hard, Gertrude." Tess lifted Gertrude's hand. It was cool and dry, the skin thin and splotched with age. "Your memory may be a little jumbled."

"Go ahead. Take his side." Gertrude yanked her hand away.

"I'm not taking sides. I'm just saying that—"

The door opened and a nurse walked in, her salt-and-pepper hair pulled back from a plain face. "Ms. McKenzie, we're going to wheel you down for an MRI. The doctor wants to make sure that there's nothing going on besides a broken leg."

"Fine." Gertrude closed her eyes as the nurse

rolled her out. Tessa followed them to the door, watching as they made their way down the hall.

"I hope she's okay," she said mostly to herself, and was surprised when Cade's hands slid around her waist, resting low on her stomach, his breath tickling her hair.

"She's too ornery to be anything else," he said, his voice gravely and gruff, and so very nice.

She turned, because she had to, because there was really nothing else she wanted to do. She rested her head against his chest, soaking in his solid warmth. "Thanks for calling me, Cade."

"What else would I have done?"

"Had someone else take care of my crazy family?"

"You know better than that, Tess." His words rumbled under her ear, mixing with the solid thump of his heart.

"I do, and I hope you know that I am so, so sorry for what I said earlier. I am the biggest idiot in the world."

"You're more of a pint-size one." He cupped her face and looked into her eyes, smiling a little. "And I probably overreacted. My ex hated Apple Valley. She loved to call the people who lived in it small-town hicks. Hearing you say that . . . just brought up a lot of old stuff."

"That makes me feel even worse."

"Don't. It's done, and we're both too mature to make it into something bigger than it is." He tucked a strand of hair behind her ear, his hand drifting to the middle of her back, and she thought she'd be happy to stand in his arms forever.

"Can we go find Gertrude?" Alex asked, bumping against Tessa's side as he tried to walk into the hall.

It was enough to break the spell Cade had woven, and she broke away, putting her hand on Alex's shoulder to keep him from walking into the hall. "She'll be back soon. How about we get something to eat while we're waiting?"

"No," Alex said simply, retreating to his seat.

"Aren't you hungry?" she tried again, but he ignored her, his foot tapping the floor, his fingers playing a rhythm on his thigh.

"He'll be fine, Tess. Once they bring Gertrude back, I'll go get him a snack." Cade dropped into one of the chairs, stretching his long legs out and crossing them at the ankles. He looked tired, his eyes shadowed, his hair just a little ruffled. She wanted to smooth it down. She clenched her fists to keep from doing it.

"Did you see her fall?" she asked.

Cade shook his head. "I was still in the church with Alex. We were looking at the piano. It's a nice one. Isn't it, buddy?"

"Yes." Alex's fingers were still tapping his thigh.

"Reverend Fisher is like Ida. Really big into history," Cade continued. "He says the piano has been there since the church was built."

"Hmm-hmmm." Tess glanced into the hall. Were they done with the X-rays? Was there something more serious going on? A brain hemorrhage? Internal bleeding?

"You know," Cade said, snagging her hand and tugging her to his side. "You're not making it easy to distract you."

"Is that what you're trying to do?"

"Have you ever heard me talk town history or antiques before?"

"No." She looked into his dark blue eyes and thought that was really the only distraction she needed. No words. No chatter about antique pianos. Just Cade's eyes, his dimple. *Him.* "I thought maybe my love of all things old was starting to rub off on you."

"There's that, too," he murmured, yanking her into his lap.

"Hey!" she protested, the word dying as his lips covered hers, his hand sliding along her abdomen, his fingers splayed there.

And, God, it felt good.

"There." He set her back on her feet, and she was happy to see that she wasn't the only one breathing hard. "How's that for a distraction?"

"Um . . . wow?"

He laughed, and Alex looked up from the floor just long enough to smile. Had he been watching?

"Knock-knock," someone called from outside the door. Next thing Tessa knew, the room was filled with people. She tried to count heads, but there were too many bodies crowded into too small a space to keep track.

She backed up, tripped over Cade's outstretched legs, and nearly fell into his lap again. Her hand landed on his very firm, very muscular thigh, and heat shot straight into her belly. Oh, man! She was in trouble. Really, really big trouble.

"Careful," he murmured, and she wasn't sure if he was talking about her nearly falling into his lap or the lust that was probably oozing out of every one of her pores.

He stood, tugging her to his side, his hand resting lightly on her waist. At least a dozen pairs of eyes dropped to that hand, and Tessa could almost hear the silent questions.

She scanned the crowd, finally spotting a few familiar faces. "Reverend. Natalie," she said. "It's so nice of you to come check on Gertrude."

"It's the least we could do," the reverend replied. "She fell going down our stairs, after all. I feel terrible about it, Tess. Just terrible. I threw salt down before the service and scraped snow off the stairs, but I should have had someone check again before the service ended. It would have saved your aunt from a lot of pain."

"It was an accident. No one is to blame," she said, trying to reassure him.

"How *is* Gertrude?" Natalie asked.

"They took her to radiology. We'll know more once she's out."

"Hopefully it's only her leg." Jethro worried aloud, his long, narrow face filled with concern. "I've arranged for all her hospital and doctor bills to be sent to me. The church insurance should cover most of the cost of her treatment. Natalie and I will cover the rest."

"Reverend—"

"Jethro," he said.

"That isn't necessary. Gertrude and I can take care of the medical bills and any therapy she needs."

"That could be a pretty penny." Ida Cunningham eased between two rather large blue-haired ladies.

"And your family has already had so many expenses, Tess. This is no time to be stubborn or proud."

"It's also not the time to discuss private matters, Gran," Cade interrupted.

"You're right, of course," Ida replied, her church suit pristine, her hair perfectly in place. She smiled at Tessa. "I'm sorry, Tess. We've overstepped our bounds."

"It's okay," she said, and surprisingly, she meant it. There were a lot of things she didn't like about Apple Valley. Gossips and busybodies and a nightlife about as lively as seniors at home on Saturday night, but the people cared. That was something she hadn't realized as a kid, or something she'd ignored because she'd been too busy wishing she were somewhere else.

"Folks!" someone called from the back of the crowd. "We can only have three people in the room at a time. You're going to have to clear out."

A nurse shoved her way through the group. Wide hipped and broad shouldered, she had silver hair scraped back from a pretty face and a frown that was scary enough to send half the crowd running. The other half trickled out one by one, murmuring good wishes and promises of prayers.

Jethro, Natalie, and Ida walked out last, hovering in the doorway as the nurse glowered.

"Everyone must go," she pronounced, like a queen demanding that heads roll.

"We're leaving. Thank you," Ida responded, more graciously than Tess would have.

"Would you like us to bring Alex home with us, Tess? It might be better for him to be there," Natalie offered, her gaze on Alex. He sat exactly where he'd been since Tess had kept him from leaving the room, his head hanging low as he studied the floor.

"I'm afraid he'll wander off again, and he really prefers familiar places. I'm not sure he'd be comfortable at your house." And she wasn't sure *she'd* be comfortable letting him go.

"We can take him to your place, and we'll watch him every minute," Natalie offered.

"People," the nurse barked. "You can't congregate here to discuss plans. Three people. That is all we allow. Three of you need to leave. Now!"

"Okay." Alex stood, brushing his hands up and down his coat sleeves.

"Alex, not you." Tess grabbed his arm before he could walk out the door.

"Nat," Jethro said, "why don't you and Ida take Alex to get a little snack in the cafeteria? Tess, Cade, and I can discuss plans while you're gone. Is that okay with you, Tessa?"

"Sure. Just . . . keep an eye on him."

"We will." Natalie smiled like she'd just won the lottery and took Alex's hand, talking to him quietly as she and Ida headed down the hall.

"Well, that's better," the nurse said. "Ms. McKenzie should be back from radiology shortly. Make sure the room is still quiet when she gets here."

She bustled away, and Jethro turned to Tessa with a smile. "Well, now that Nurse Ratched is gone, why don't you tell me what you want Alex to do, Tess?"

"I think it's probably best if he stays here. It's not that I don't trust you and Natalie. It's just that he got out the other night, and I'm worried—"

"You don't have to explain. I'd feel the same if he were mine. The thing is"—Jethro shoved his hands deep into his coat pockets, his smile gone—"Natalie and I have had a lot of losses in the time we've been married. Three babies. Each of them born too early to survive. After the third one, we didn't have the heart to try again."

"I'm sorry." She was shocked by the story, surprised that she hadn't heard even a whisper of a rumor about the couple's loss.

"It's been hard. One of the reasons we moved here was to put that part of our lives behind us." He shrugged. "Four years ago today, we lost our last baby. I think Natalie would really like to have something to occupy her time. Just to get her mind off of that."

"I see." She shifted uncomfortably. She'd never wanted children, and she felt almost guilty that she had Alex while a woman who was desperate to parent had no one.

"It would really help her . . . help us both . . . if you'd let us take care of Alex this afternoon. We don't have church service until seven, and if you need Natalie to stay longer than that, she can." He cleared his throat, and she was sure there were tears in his eyes.

Which made her feel like crying, because she hadn't really mourned Emily and Dave, and all that sorrow was still lodged deep in her heart.

"Okay," she conceded, because how could she not? "But you have to be careful that he doesn't leave the house."

"He won't be out of our sight. I can promise you

that," Jethro boomed happily. "I'll head down to the cafeteria. We'll just leave from there, if that's okay with you? And I may stop by the church. Alex really wanted to play our piano. It might be a nice way to help him focus on something other than Gertrude's accident. Here's my cell phone number. Call and check as much as you'd like." He scribbled the number on a business card and handed it to her.

"Thanks." She bit her lip. Reminding Jethro to be careful again seemed like overkill, but she really wanted to do it anyway.

"Call as soon as you know something. Hopefully, she won't have to stay the night, but if she does, and you want to stay with her—"

"I'll come home as soon as the doctors figure out what's going on." Because, as much as she trusted the Fishers, she had no intention of leaving Alex with anyone overnight. She dug keys out of her purse and handed them to Jethro. "I didn't turn the alarm on when I left. I'm not even sure I locked the door, but you'd better take these. Just in case."

"Don't worry about a thing, dear." He patted her arm in that age-old reverend way that conveyed warmth and compassion all at the same time. "The church is praying for Gertrude and your family. I have no doubt that all will be well."

It was good that *someone* didn't doubt it. The way things were falling apart, Tess was about as confident in things turning out okay as she was that Gertrude would come back from radiology with a smile on her face.

She watched the reverend walk down the hall, still not all that sure about her decision. Alex had issues, and the Fishers hadn't even parented before.

Then again, neither had she.

She sighed, turning away from the hall, her stomach churning with worry and fear, her nose coming within a quarter inch of Cade's hard chest.

That's when she realized they were alone. Just the two of them standing a quarter of an inch from each other, the memory of Cade's toe-curling, soul-searing kiss suddenly filling the air with an electric charge that threatened to short-circuit medical equipment from there to the Atlantic Ocean.

Chapter Sixteen

Alone at last. Unfortunately for Cade, now wasn't the time to take advantage of it. His hands had a mind of their own, though. They glided up Tessa's arms, sliding over the smooth skin revealed by her blue tank top. Not the best choice for winter wear, but Cade could sure appreciate it.

"You forgot your coat," he murmured, taking his off and dropping it around her shoulders, hiding a little of the creamy flesh her tank top revealed.

"I was so scared after you called that I didn't think about the weather." She slid her arms through his coat sleeves, her hands not even peeking out from beneath the cuffs, her hair falling out of a high pony-tail that listed to the right. Her face was speckled with cream-colored paint. Not a lick of makeup, but her lips were deep pink, her lashes dark red. God, she was cute! Gorgeous. Cade could probably think of a dozen more descriptive words, but it wasn't the time for that, either.

"I really hope I made the right decision about Alex," she said as she dropped into a chair, then jumped up again, pacing to the door. "He's not a typical kid, and I'm not sure the Fishers realize that."

"I've known Jethro and Natalie since they moved to town. They're good people, and if they make a promise, they keep it."

"I'm sure that's true, but Alex—"

"Don't borrow trouble, okay?" he replied, cutting her off. "You have enough on your plate without adding to it."

"But—"

"Tess." He moved in close, leaning down so that their breath mingled. She smelled like summer sunshine and paint, and he thought he would never whitewash his fence again without thinking of her. "Alex is going to be fine."

"It's not just Alex." She sighed, running a hand over her hair, her palm stopping at the tilted ponytail. She frowned, pulling it from its elastic band and scraping it back into a messy bun. "Gertrude has a broken leg, and that could be the least of her problems. Did you see the goose egg on her head?"

See it? He'd pressed ice to it while they waited for the ambulance, looking into Gertrude's dazed eyes and listening as words that would have made a sailor blush poured from her mouth. "It's a good-sized knot."

"That's an understatement, and you know it. What if she has a cerebral hemorrhage? What if she falls into a coma and never comes out? What—"

"How is worrying about any of those things going to change what's going to happen?"

"It won't, but it sure is making me feel better to just . . . say them." She dropped into the chair again,

brushing lint from dark blue jeans and frowning.
"Man, I'm a mess."

"You look pretty damn good to me," he responded,
sitting in the chair beside her.

"I bet you say that to all the single ladies."

"Not even close, Red." He took her hand, rubbing
a fleck of paint from her knuckle, his thumb skimming along work-rough skin that was a hell of a lot
sexier than a soft, smooth hand could ever be.

She shuddered, snatching her hand away. "You
really should stop doing that."

"What?"

"Touching me all the time. It's not—"

"Pleasurable?" He slid a finger across her lips just
so he could watch her eyes dilate.

"I didn't say that," she murmured, jumping up
from the chair and taking a step into the hall.

She'd pissed him off royally with her comment
about small-town hicks, but she wasn't anything like
Darla. Not in the way she thought or the way she in-
teracted with the community. She'd been gracious
to the Fishers, forgiving of Ida's nosiness, accepting
of the crowd that had shoved its way into the room.

She understood Apple Valley life, and she fit
there.

Even if she didn't quite believe it.

"Then why do you keep moving away?" He
crossed his legs at the ankles, not bothering to chase
her down. She wouldn't leave. Not until Gertrude
returned.

"Truth?" she asked, glancing over her shoulder,
her eyes deep purple-blue in her pale face. "I'm not
into games. Even if I were, I'm not in the mood to
play one."

"Who said we were playing?"

"What else could it be? We barely know each other."

"Funny, Tess, I was just thinking that we probably know each other better than we know ourselves."

"*Used to* know each other that well. You keep forgetting that up until two weeks ago, we hadn't seen each other in ten years."

"Trust me. I haven't forgotten." He walked across the room, smiling a little as she stepped back. "And I haven't stopped asking myself how I could have been so blind as a kid that I didn't see what was right in front of me."

"You weren't blind. You were just looking in a different direction." She shifted uncomfortably, her gaze jerking away.

If he didn't know better, he'd think she was hiding something. Maybe she was. Ten years *was* a long time, but he still felt like he knew Tess.

Though, not nearly as well as he wanted to.

"Did it bother you that I dated Emily?"

"Why would it have?"

"I don't know, but you look like you just bit into a lemon, so I'm thinking maybe it did."

"You have an overblown ego, Cade. You know that?"

"I don't think I do." He cupped her face, looked into her eyes. There was sadness there and a wariness that he didn't want her to feel. Not around him.

"I'll never hurt you like that again, Tess," he said, brushing a gentle kiss across her lips.

He wanted so much more than that, but she jerked back, her cheeks bright pink. "Cade—"

"Watch what you're doing, lady! This leg is killing

me!" Gertrude's shouted warning echoed down the hallway, the words cutting off whatever Tess might have said.

Cade glanced out the door. No sign of Gertrude yet, but her voice alone was enough to draw the attention of a few nurses who were walking through the corridor.

"That's Gertrude," Tess said, as if Cade wouldn't have recognized her cantankerous aunt's voice.

How could he not? The woman was shouting loudly enough to wake the dead.

"I said, be careful! You're about to ram me into the wall! Do you want to break my other leg?"

"We'll get you back to your room without breaking any more of your bones, Ms. McKenzie." A nurse pushed Gertrude's gurney around the corner, a smile hovering at the corner of her lips.

Obviously, the woman had the patience of a saint.

"Let's get out of the way," Cade said, pulling Tessa back into the room and holding her arm as Gertrude was wheeled in.

"Here you are, Ms. McKenzie," the nurse said, patting Gertrude's limp hand. "We've made it back without bumping one wall."

"Good job. I'll send you a medal for it. Now, get me a wheelchair, because I'm outta here."

"I think the doctor is going to want to keep you for at least a night."

"I'm not staying the night. I don't care what that dingbat of a doctor says," she nearly shouted.

Tess moved closer. "Calm down, Gertrude."

"I'll calm down when I'm damn good and ready to do it," Gertrude muttered, but she subsided, apparently having used up what little energy she had.

"The doctor will be in once she reads the scans. I can bring you something for the pain while you're waiting. How would that be?" the nurse asked.

"A fifth of scotch would be good," Gertrude mumbled, her eyes closed.

"Not with your head injury." The nurse laughed. "I'll bring you what I can. I'll be back in a few minutes."

"I could be dead by then," Gertrude groaned.

"You're not going to die." Tess brushed a strand of frizzy orange hair from Gertrude's cheek. "How are you feeling?"

"Like I fell down ten steps and landed on cement." Gertrude didn't open her eyes, but she snagged Tessa's hand and patted it. "Don't worry, kid. I'm going to be fine. I just have a killer headache and enough pain in my leg for me to want to gnaw it off."

"Once you get some pain medicine, it won't be so bad."

"Humph!"

"It won't!"

"That's exactly what I told you when you broke your arm in fifth grade." Gertrude finally opened her eyes. "After you took the medicine, you said that I'd lied. As a matter of fact, you spent nearly a week complaining about how much pain you were in!"

"I was a kid."

"And I'm an old woman!" Gertrude retorted. "With bones as ancient as mine, I'll probably be in pain for the rest of my life. I'll probably spend the rest of my days hobbling around with a walker."

"Obviously, she's going to be just fine," Cade said dryly.

"Who asked you?" Gertrude retorted, but there wasn't a whole lot of strength in her words. She glanced around the room, her brow furrowing. "Where's Alex?"

"Reverend and Mrs. Fisher took him home."

Gertrude nodded and closed her eyes again. No comment about Tess making the wrong decision. No questions. Not even the hint of a fight.

Tess hovered over her, touching her forehead and then her hand, pulling the blanket up around her.

Cade wanted to pull her hand away, hold it still, remind her that Gertrude was going to be fine, but he thought that what she needed more than that was his presence and his silence.

He put a hand on her back, cool leather beneath his palm.

She glanced his way, smiling into his eyes, the sweet curve of her lips intoxicating. "Thanks for being here, Cade."

"Where else would I be?"

"Home? Enjoying your Sunday off?" She turned her attention back to Gertrude, a small frown line appearing between her brows. "She's pale."

"You would be, too, if you just fell down a flight of steps and broke your leg," Gertrude muttered.

"Good afternoon." A striking woman walked into the room, her hair white-blond, her eyes pale amber. She looked at Gertrude, then Tessa and Cade. "You two must be Gertrude's family. I'm Dr. Elizabeth Sheffield. I've looked at Gertrude's scans, and we should be able to keep her—"

"Keep me?" Gertrude levered up on her elbows, suddenly wide-awake and apparently raring for a fight. "Wrap up my leg and get me out of here, because I'm not staying in this joint a minute longer than I have to."

"I understand how you feel, Gertrude—"

"Bullshit!" Gertrude proclaimed so loudly that the bed shook.

"Gertrude, you need to calm down." Tess tried to intercede.

Cade could have told her the effort was going to prove futile. Gertrude on a rant was a sight to behold, and that was exactly where she was heading.

"Why should I?" Gertrude snapped.

"Because you have a mild cerebral hemorrhage," Dr. Sheffield cut in calmly. "And you probably have a heck of a headache. Being upset is only going to make it worse."

"I have a *what*? Explain it to me in English, Doc. If I'm not going to make it, I want to know it now so I can prepare myself." Gertrude collapsed onto the pillows again.

Tess wasn't sure if her aunt's sudden weakness was an act or a result of her injuries. She touched Gertrude's shoulder and was relieved when her hand was swatted away.

"Give me some space, Tess. I'm trying to breathe my last."

Dr. Sheffield laughed, patting Gertrude's good leg. "I'm afraid that I can't let you do that, Gertrude. Not on my shift, anyway."

Tess wasn't quite as amused as the doctor seemed to be. As a matter of fact, she was about ready to tell Gertrude to knock it off. She sympathized with her aunt's pain, but enough was enough already!

"What we discovered, Gertrude," the doctor said with a lot more patience than Tessa was feeling, "is a tiny bleed in your brain. Not something that is terribly worrisome, but we need to keep an eye on it for the next twenty-four hours."

"A brain bleed, huh?" Gertrude closed her eyes, seemed to sink into herself a little. "That explains this damn headache, then."

"We'll bring you something for that shortly. The good news is that it should heal up just fine. In a week or so, you'll be almost as good as new."

"What about her leg?" Tess asked.

"A clean break. We'll cast it before she leaves tomorrow. For tonight, we'll just keep it wrapped and elevated. She really is going to be fine." The doctor smiled and patted Tessa's shoulder. "The nurse will be in shortly to move her to her room. You're welcome to stay with her tonight if you'd like. We can have a cot brought in."

"I don't need a baby-sitter," Gertrude mumbled as Dr. Sheffield left the room. "*I don't,*" she repeated, opening her eyes and glaring at Tess. "But I *do* need a cigarette."

"You can't smoke in here, Gertrude. You know that," Tess said wearily. Sometimes her aunt was worse than a two-year-old.

"How about a Pepsi, then?"

"I don't know. . . ."

"It probably wouldn't hurt," Cade said. Then he leaned close to Tessa's ear and whispered, "Even if it would, she'll be asleep before you bring it back."

Her insides melted and her toes curled, because his lips were so close to her ear, so close to her skin, and she seriously wanted them to be closer than just close. She wanted them pressed to naked flesh, trailing along her neck and . . .

Oh. Dear. God!

She really must be exhausted. Emotionally drained. Out of her mind!

She jumped away, running to the door and calling over her shoulder as she went, "I'll get you one, Gertrude. Be back in a minute."

"Tess!" Cade called from the doorway of the room.

She pretended she didn't hear and kept running like the chicken she was.

How in the world had this happened?

How had she gone from living a Cade-free life in Annapolis to wanting him so desperately she was prepared to jump his bones in the emergency room of Apple Valley General!

In front of Gertrude!

She had to get this under control. Had to. Because if she didn't, she'd . . .

What?

Fall into Cade's arms and live out every fantasy she'd ever had? Find out that the guy she'd mooned over and lusted after and loved with every bit of her adolescent heart was still worth mooning over and lusting after, and even loving?

Would that be so bad?

She didn't know, but she had a feeling she was going to find out, because in a town the size of Apple Valley, avoiding someone was about as easy as forcing the sun to stand still in the sky.

She walked into the emergency room lobby and shoved some quarters into a vending machine. Somewhere in the distance she was sure she could hear Gertrude cursing a blue streak.

They must be moving her to her room.

Good, because Tess needed to make sure her

aunt was settled and comfortable, and then she needed to head home to Alex. Everything else—the store, the furniture she needed to refinish, *Cade*—could wait. But Alex? He needed her. And Tess? She needed to do this one last thing for Emily.

Because, despite all her sister's faults, Tessa really had loved her.

Chapter Seventeen

"My leg hurts," Gertrude groused, plucking at the thick blanket that Tess had dropped over her lap.

Tess ignored her. It was that or completely lose her mind. The woman had been home from the hospital for twenty-four hours, and she'd spent at least twenty of them complaining.

"Did you hear me, Tess? My leg hurts."

"I heard you." She pulled a strip of faded wallpaper from the parlor wall and dropped it into the trash can. She'd made no progress on the store in the past two days. Between Gertrude's accident, Alex's obvious distress, and the people who'd stopped by to see how Gertrude was doing, there hadn't been time.

Now she needed to focus, because at some point, they had to reopen This-N-That and make some money from it.

"If you heard me, then why didn't you answer?"

"Because it wasn't a question, Gertrude. It was another complaint."

"You'd be complaining, too, if your leg had snapped in half."

"Do you want me to get you some pain medicine?" she offered.

"You know I hate that stuff."

"Then what do you want me to do?"

"Kill Zim Beck. My leg will feel a hell of a lot better if I know he's dead."

"Gertrude!" Tess hissed, glancing toward the foyer. Alex had come home from school and gone straight to his room, but that didn't mean he'd stayed there. She'd found him silently walking through the house a few times, touching items that she'd cleaned and put out for display. He seemed . . . discontent, even his music somehow riotous rather than restful.

"Alex is upstairs with his headset plugged in to the keyboard. He can't hear a thing. Besides, the man is an ass and a murderer, and he deserves to die."

"Zim didn't murder anyone."

"He tried."

"Are we back to that again? Reverend Fisher told you that he and Zim were talking when you fell." She yanked at another piece of wallpaper. They'd had this conversation a dozen times in a dozen different ways, and she was tired of it.

"It's a conspiracy. That's what it is."

"So you're saying the reverend, Zim, and a half a dozen other people are all conspiring against you?"

"I'm saying that Zim wants us out of this house. Getting rid of me is the perfect way to accomplish that."

"Oh, come on, Gertrude. Do you really think he'd murder you to get the house? Why not go after me? I'm the one who inherited it."

"But it's Alex's place, and I'm the one who has the most interest in keeping it for him. Zim knows that."

"Don't worry, Gertrude. If you die, I'll stay here just to piss Zim off." Tess yanked a three-foot strip of paper down and shoved it into the trash bag, trying really hard to keep a lid on her temper.

"Are you being smart with me?"

"Yes, as a matter of fact, I am." She whirled, looking into Gertrude's pale, lined face, all her irritation slipping away. "Sorry, Gert. I'm stressed, and it's getting the best of me."

"I can't say I blame you," Gertrude conceded, surprising Tess with her acquiescence. "This whole thing has been a mess. Thing is, I know it's my fault. If I hadn't—"

The stairs creaked, cutting off her words. She glanced at the foyer. "Is that you, Alex?"

"Yes," he responded, appearing on the threshold. He wore his thick coat, snow boots, and gloves. A bright blue knit hat was pulled down over his ears, and bits of reddish-blond hair peeked out from under it.

He looked adorable. So seriously cute that Tessa's heart melted.

"What are you doing, Alex?" she asked softly, wishing she could just tug him into her arms for a hug without worrying that he would push her away.

"I am going to the park."

"Son." Gertrude sounded as soft as Tessa felt. "Just because I'm laid up doesn't mean you get to go wandering around town on your own. You'll have to wait to go to the park until I'm feeling better."

"Tessa will take me," he said simply.

"Alex—" She was going to tell him that she had

too many things to do and didn't have time for jaunts through Riley Park, but he'd never asked her for anything before, and she couldn't deny him this one request.

She sighed, dropping another piece of old wallpaper into the trash. "All right, but just for a little while, okay?"

"Okay." He nodded, and for the first time ever, he smiled straight into her eyes. He had a dimple in each cheek that she'd never seen before, and she felt a hot wash of emotion so intense that she could only call it love.

She bundled up. Coat. Hat, gloves, and scarf that she'd found in Emily's things. James had assured her that her belongings were on the way, but she needed to be warm *now.* Still, wearing Emily's clothes felt like moving on. She wasn't sure she was ready to do that yet. In the farthest recesses of her mind, she kept thinking that Emily and Dave were going to walk through the front door and take over their lives again.

"Do you want me to bring anything back for you, Gertrude?" she asked, her hand on the front doorknob.

"Seeing as how you can't bring me a new leg, how about one of those doughnuts from Murphy's? Pumpkin would be nice. Maybe a chocolate-covered, too. They'll be closed by now, but if you knock, Murphy will give you what he has left from the day."

"All right."

"And a sandwich from the diner. I've got a hankering for a hot turkey. Nice as all the church-lady casseroles are, they all taste the same, and none of them taste good."

"I couldn't agree more," Tess said with a laugh, ushering Alex outside, shivering as they stepped onto the porch. God, it was cold. Her teeth were already chattering and they hadn't even left the yard. "How about we drive to the park, Alex? That way we won't freeze."

"What about the lights?" he asked.

"What lights?" she responded, but he grabbed her hand and pulled her across the yard, tugging her to the sidewalk.

He didn't speak, but maybe she didn't need him to. The sun had nearly set, and the sky was deep azure blue, the moon rising above distant mountains. Christmas lights sparkled from every house on the street. Nearly every tree and every bush had the same: white, blue, green, red, they glistened in the purplish twilight.

She tightened her grip on Alex's hand, struck by the beauty of the scene, the simplicity of walking with her nephew.

"Hello, Alex and Tessa!" Charlotte called, waving from her front porch. Old Mrs. Landry on the corner called out, too. It was like walking through Mayberry, everyone knowing everyone, and all of them willing to say hello. Tess had hated that when she was a kid. Now it was like coming home—warm, welcoming, comfortable.

Alex held her hand for the entire mile into town, and Tess didn't feel nearly as cold as she'd thought she would.

"You tired, buddy?" she asked as they neared the town center. "How about a hot chocolate?"

"The park first," Alex responded, pulling her across the street.

The entrance to the park was just ahead, the wrought-iron gate open just like it always was. White lights sparkled in all the trees. Had it been this beautiful when Tess was a kid?

"Tess! Wait up!"

She knew the voice.

How could she not know Cade?

The best thing, she thought, was to ignore him, because standing in the dusky evening, Christmas lights sparkling all around, the night air cold and crisp . . . that was asking for trouble.

Alex had other ideas. He stopped short, swinging around and holding tight to Tessa's hand as Cade approached.

Still in his uniform, his bomber jacket hanging open, leather gloves on his hands, Cade looked tough and rugged. Outdoorsy and strong. So different from the guys Tess had dated, so different from Kent. After leaving Apple Valley, she'd gone for the more anemic type.

Not anemic.

Academic.

"Where is my angel?" Alex demanded, patting his thighs. Once, twice, three times.

"I'm afraid I haven't found her yet." Cade crouched in front of him. "But I'm still looking, and I won't stop until I do. As a matter of fact, that's what I wanted to talk to your aunt about."

"Okay. Good. Okay." Alex started walking again.

"Wait, *Alex.* The sheriff isn't done." Tess tried to pull Alex to a stop, but he was strong for his size and more than a little determined.

"It's okay." Cade fell into step beside her. "I just

finished my shift. I was planning to stop by your place on the way home, but this will work just as well."

"Are you sure? I don't mind coming into your office or—"

"What's the matter, Red? Are you afraid that people will see us walking under the Christmas lights and assume we're an item?" He smiled to take any sting out of the words, and she couldn't *not* smile in return.

"No, I'm worried that *I'll* start thinking we're an item," she said truthfully.

"Would that be such a bad thing?" he asked, snagging her free hand.

"I haven't decided yet." She looked up at the deep blue sky, the tall spruce trees, anywhere but in Cade's eyes.

"Liar," he whispered, his breath warm near her ear, and she felt herself melting into the moment.

"What did you want to talk to me about?" she asked, because if the subject didn't change, she'd turn into a quivering puddle of longing, and then where would she be?

Right back where she'd been that night ten years ago when he'd told her he planned to marry Emily.

"We found more than a dozen individual prints on the display case the angel was in. None of them match anything we have in our system." He switched gears easily but didn't release her hand.

She couldn't say that she was sorry.

"Which means what?"

"That we can't name a suspect, yet. We are narrowing things down, though. A couple of people mentioned someone being at the tea and leaving right before the angel went missing."

"Who?"

"I'm not at liberty to say, Tess. We need to do a little more digging, verify things. Even in Apple Valley there are procedures that have to be followed before we release a name to the public."

"You love what you do, don't you?" She hadn't ever thought of what Cade would be like as sheriff of Apple Valley, but she'd never doubted that that's what he'd be. He'd talked about it the first day they'd met, introducing himself as Cade Cunningham, future sheriff of Apple Valley. Thinking about it made her smile.

"You should do that more often, Tess," he said quietly, his hand tightening around hers.

"What?"

"Smile. You're always beautiful, but when you smile you take my breath away."

"Yes," Alex said and broke away from Tess, shuffling off the path that wound its way around Riley Pond and heading in toward a thick copse of trees.

"Where are you going, Alex?" Tess grabbed his arm, pulling him up short.

"To church." He pointed at the well-lit church that stood on a hill overlooking the park. Even from a distance the old nativity scene was visible, small spotlights shining on the wooden figures that had been around for as long as Tess could remember.

"That hill is really steep, Alex. We need to drive. Not walk."

"Okay." Alex turned back the way they'd come, apparently thinking that her comment was a form of consent and that they were going to find a ride.

"We left the car at home, remember? We'll have to go another day."

"I don't mind driving you," Cade offered.

"I doubt Jethro and Natalie would want us hanging out there on a Tuesday evening."

"You've met them. I think you know that they won't mind."

"But—"

"How about you just go with the flow for a change, Tess? Let me give you and Alex a ride, see what happens after that." He touched her cheek, his glove cold against her already frigid skin.

And how could she possibly say no?

"All right, but we can't stay too long, Alex. Okay?"

"Okay," he responded, taking her hand again.

They walked back through the park, Cade leading the way to his truck. He opened the door and helped Alex in.

"Seat belt on, sport," he said. Then he turned to Tess. "Your turn."

"I can mana—"

Too late. She was up and in the truck cab so quickly she barely knew how it had happened.

"I'm perfectly capable of getting in a truck by myself, Cade," she sputtered.

"Sorry." He leaned into the cab, tucking a strand of hair behind her ear. "Old habits."

"What habits? You didn't have a truck when we were kids."

"I always used to help you onto the swings in the park. Remember?"

She did. Even when she'd been tall enough to get on those swings by herself, she'd pretended she couldn't. Her little tomboy heart must have known what her head hadn't. By the time the two had decided to consult with each other, her days in the park with Cade were over, and he'd been too busy helping Emily into his 1967 Ford Mustang to notice Tessa.

"That was a long time ago."

"I know. I thought it was time we revisited it." He climbed into the driver's seat. "Seat belt on, Alex?" he asked.

"Yes."

"Then let's go."

He turned the heater on full blast, classical music playing on the radio. It wasn't something that Tessa recognized, but Alex hummed softly.

The moon had risen above the mountains, full and deep orange. A few clouds dotted the horizon, but closer in, stars twinkled in the deep blue sky. Against that backdrop, Apple Valley looked like a fairy-tale village.

"God, it's beautiful," she whispered.

"That's one of the reasons why I love it."

"What are your other reasons?"

For a moment he was silent. "Just one other reason," he finally responded. "It's home."

He said it like a promise and a benediction. As if the words held the secret to everything he'd ever wanted or needed.

"I'm not sure I even know what that means," she murmured.

"What?"

"Home."

"I think if you stick around here long enough, you'll find out." He stretched his right arm along the back of the bucket seat, his fingers just skimming the side of her neck.

"I've been thinking," he said. "The historical

society's Christmas dance is this Friday. I'd love to take you."

"Why?"

What a stupid, stupid question.

"Why not?" he responded, his thumb running along the tender flesh behind her ear. She couldn't think straight when he was doing that, but she didn't want him to stop. As a matter of fact, she could think of about a dozen other things she'd like him to do.

"I . . . can't think of one good reason, but I'm sure I should."

He laughed, and the sound lodged somewhere in the region of Tessa's heart. "You don't have to give me an answer yet. But just so you know, it's a costume party. Everyone has to wear clothes like what the Rileys might have worn. I figure that's right up your alley."

She had to admit, the idea of a Victorian Christmas party appealed to her. People dressed in period costume, dancing the waltz to Christmas carols. What wasn't to love about that? There were probably boxes of old clothes up in the attic. The Rileys hadn't been the kind of people to throw things away. She could go up there—

"We're here," Alex announced loudly, leaning forward and pointing at the church as Cade pulled into the parking area. It was a gorgeous little building, the white steeple spearing up toward the sky, a wrought-iron cross at the top. A wide stairway led to curved double doors, lights spilling from windows on either side of it.

Alex barely waited for the truck to stop before he was scrambling out, reaching for Tessa's hand and dragging her toward the building.

"Let's go," he commanded, and she picked up the pace, jogging up the stairs that Gertrude had fallen down.

"Maybe we should try to find the reverend before we go in, Alex," Tessa cautioned, but Alex didn't seem to hear. He pulled open the doors and barreled inside.

She hoped the Fishers wouldn't mind.

Tess followed more slowly. She'd been in the church a few times when she was a kid. Christmas. Easter. Not consistently, but enough that the smell of the place was familiar. Wood polish and old books.

A small vestibule opened into a simple chapel. Dark floors and two rows of pews led the way to a wide platform and a podium that had probably been standing there for as long as the church had existed.

Alex broke away, moving faster than Tessa had ever seen him go, taking a seat in front of an old baby grand piano. Cade had been right. It was gorgeous, hand-carved scrolled vines and flowers spinning up the legs, the wood deep mahogany.

If it had been there when she was a kid, Tess hadn't noticed it. She'd been too busy studying the old stained-glass windows that ran along each side-wall. Unlike most churches, these windows didn't depict biblical scenes. Instead, each one showcased local flora and fauna. Flowers. Trees. Birds. Animals. Local legend had it that Miriam Riley had designed and commissioned the pieces. If it was true, it was possible she'd also designed and commissioned the piano.

Alex set his hands on the keys, his eyes closed.

The silence seemed heavier, the stillness of the room thick and expectant. He could have been sitting in Carnegie Hall, an audience of thousands waiting for him to begin.

Tess took a step toward him, worried that he shouldn't be playing the piano without permission, wondering what the congregation would think if they found out that she'd allowed him to enter the chapel uninvited.

"Don't." Cade put a hand on her shoulder, holding her in place as Alex opened his eyes and began to play.

Chapter Eighteen

Music poured into the room. Not the somber song that Tessa had expected. A quick burst of notes and chords that fell into the silence and filled it up. Not happy exactly, but not sad like Alex's angel song. This song had life and energy and a mystery that made Tess want to keep listening.

Cade pulled her to a pew and sat, tugging her down with him. His arm wrapped around her shoulders, his fingers playing in the ends of her hair.

She didn't know if it was the song or the man that kept her in place, but she found herself leaning against Cade, her gaze on Alex and his flying fingers, his enraptured expression. He seemed to be saying something to her, and she wanted to grab the message from the song, learn what it was he needed her to know.

The door opened and cold air blew in, but Alex didn't stop playing, and Tessa couldn't stop watching. Jethro Fisher sat in the pew across from theirs, and Tessa glanced his way just long enough to see the contented look on his face.

She didn't know how long the song lasted.

When it ended, Alex sat for a moment, his head down, his fingers lax on the keys.

Jethro clapped, and Alex finally moved away from the piano.

"Thank you," he said to Jethro, and the reverend touched his head.

"Thank *you*. Does your song have a name?"

Alex nodded, tapping his fingers together rapidly. "'Tessa's Song,'" he said, looking straight into her eyes, and she knew the gift she'd been given, the weight of it so heavy and yet so wonderful she wasn't sure how to respond.

"Thank you, Alex," she finally managed, but he'd already moved away.

"I'm sorry for interrupting your time together," Jethro said softly, his eyes warm, chocolaty brown. "I saw the truck from the parsonage and thought I'd come over to see if everything was okay."

"We should have asked permission before using your church. I'm sorry we interrupted your evening."

"Oh, it's not my church, Tess. It belongs to Apple Valley. I'm just the caretaker of it. As for interrupting, I think of it more as a pleasant distraction from dish duty."

"I'm not sure Natalie will be happy about that," Cade said.

Jethro chuckled. "Actually, I'm hoping she'll take pity on me and do them while I'm gone." He glanced at Alex. "He's very talented, Tess. You know that, right?"

"Yes."

"I was wondering . . . would you be willing to allow him to play at the Christmas Eve service?"

"I don't think he'd be comfortable with that."

"He played at the tea," Cade pointed out, choosing exactly the wrong moment to rejoin the conversation.

"That was different."

Neither man asked her how playing piano in front of a hundred people was different from playing in front of a church congregation. Thank goodness.

"Well, if you change your mind, let me know. Our choir director would love to include your nephew in our program."

"I will. Thank you again for letting Alex play the piano tonight."

"Don't mention it, my dear." Jethro smiled and then turned his attention to Cade. "Cade, if you have a moment, I wanted to talk to you about a workday we're planning here at the church. We need to clean up the yard. Would it be possible to get the boys' club to help? If so, I need your input on dates. It will only take a minute."

"Do you mind, Tess?" Cade asked.

She didn't, but she was pleased that he cared enough to ask. "Of course not. We'll wait outside. Come on, Alex, it's time to go."

Alex shuffled to the door, his old-man gait more pronounced. He seemed reluctant to leave, but it was time. She urged him outside, shivering as a frigid breeze blew through the trees and rustled the grass.

The truck was straight ahead, but Alex veered to the right.

"Alex! Where are you going?" She grabbed his arm, but he shrugged away, continuing around the side of the building. She knew where he was going, of course. She probably should have realized that he'd want to go there, long before they'd arrived at the church.

Maybe she had. Maybe she just hadn't wanted to think about it. They hadn't been back to the grave sites since Emily and Dave's burial. *She* hadn't, anyway. It was possible Gertrude had taken Alex when they'd attended church.

"It's late, Alex. We should come back when it's light. Maybe after school tomorrow," she said, but he just kept walking.

The graveyard was behind the church. Spread out over a dozen acres, it had served as the cemetery for congregation members for over a century. Tess and her friends used to visit it every Halloween, sitting under gravestones and calling to spirits. They'd never gotten a response, but they sure had scared the hell out of each other with ghost stories.

The Riley section of the graveyard was easy to find. A huge marble statue stood in the center of it. A woman holding a baby, her face serene. Daniel Riley had commissioned it after Miriam died, and it had been placed over her grave a year later.

Some people said the statue cried every Christmas Eve. Others said that she sang to her baby when the moon was full. Even as a kid, Tess had scoffed at the idea. Right now, with the moon full and deep orange, she couldn't help shivering a little.

Emily and Dave's graves were a few yards away.

Alex didn't hesitate. He knew exactly where they were, and he walked over to the slightly mounded earth. Dark against the grass, the graves were like blemishes on the otherwise pristine lawn.

Alex knelt between the two, stretching his arms out and laying his hands flat on the dirt. He hummed quietly, looking up at the moon and the stars as if he might see his parents there.

And for the first time since her mother had driven away in her grumbling station wagon, a tear slipped down Tessa's cheek. It hurt that much to see Alex kneeling there.

She wiped it away, her hand shaking, her heart heavy. She wanted so badly to give him back what he'd lost, but all she could do was stand and watch while he grieved. The breeze picked up, blowing dry leaves across the grass, the sound like dry bones. She should tell Alex to get up, tell him it was time to go home. She didn't have the heart to pull him away.

Another tear slipped down her cheek. This time, she didn't bother wiping it away.

Cade knew that he would find Tessa and Alex in the graveyard, but he took his time walking around the church, wanting to give them space. Moonlight illuminated the path, its soft yellow glow painting the world in shades of gold and gray. White head-stones jutted up from the ground. Some new. Some crumbling. Cade found the Riley plot easily, the marble statue of Miriam Riley still beautiful after nearly a hundred years.

Tess stood with her back to Cade. Alex knelt a few feet away, his hands on his parents' graves, his face turned up to the sky.

Their grief was palpable, and he felt like an inter-loper. He would have probably walked away if Tess hadn't glanced over her shoulder.

She'd been crying, her lashes clumped together. "It's okay. We're almost finished," she said.

He took it as an invitation and walked to her side, took her hand. Stood there with her in the moonlight, thinking about Dave and Emily, and how they'd all been friends for a while. Dave's betrayal had cut deep. Probably deeper than Emily's. She'd always been flighty, unfocused and scattered, her emotions running the gamut from sweet to bitchy in about the time it took to take a breath.

When he was young, he hadn't cared. He'd liked the drama and the passion that went with it. It would have worn thin, though. By the time Emily had announced her pregnancy, it probably already had.

Alex started singing, his voice husky and low, the words barely audible. Something about sleeping and good-bye and tomorrow. Cade didn't find much to cry about in life, but, damn, if that kid's song didn't touch something deep inside. His chest tightened, and he looked away, took a couple of deep breaths as Tessa let out a soft hiccup.

"Shhhhhh," he said, pulling her into his arms and pressing her head to his chest, because she hated to cry, and he knew it. "It's okay."

She nodded but didn't speak, her arms sliding around his waist, her hands clutching his shirt. She smelled like sunshine and flowers, and he couldn't help himself, he inhaled a little more of her, his hands finding their way under her thick coat. She wore a soft sweater that had hitched up on one side, and his right palm landed on her warm flesh. Satiny skin and heat, and if they'd been standing anywhere else, if she'd been anyone else, he'd have let his hand wander. Pulled her a little closer. Tasted her lips again, because he didn't think he could ever have enough of Tess.

He kept his hand right where it was, then tilted her chin so he could see her face.

"It's okay, Red," he murmured, even though they both knew it wasn't and it wouldn't ever be again. Not for Alex, anyway. Not for Gertrude or Tess. They'd make it through, they'd go on, but losing Emily and Dave would never be okay.

"No." She hiccuped. "It's really not. My sister is dead. Her husband is dead. And I am completely messing up the only really important job I've ever had. Look at him," she said as she gestured to Alex. "Sitting between his parents' graves singing, and I'm just letting him."

"If it's what he needs, there's no harm in it. Give yourself a little credit and trust that you know what's best for him."

"Thanks." She offered a watery smile. "But I *don't* trust that I know anything about raising a child. My genetic pool doesn't come with very strong maternal instincts."

"You're selling yourself short, Tess."

"Just being honest. It's not like my mother knew what the hell *she* was doing. It's only natural that I'd be an abysmal failure at parenting."

"Your mother was a loser, but Gertrude did a good job of raising you and Emily."

"She tried," she said, sighing. "She is also going to try to kill me when she finds out that I let Alex do this."

"She'll have to catch you first, and she's not all that fast right now."

That got a shaky laugh out of her.

"She's also not here, so I guess as long as we keep quiet, I don't have to fear for my life."

"Are you asking me to keep this to myself?" he teased, hooking his arm through hers and tugging her close to his side. Damn, it felt good to have her there.

"Of course." She glanced at Alex. "It's not like he'll say anything."

"I won't, either. *If* you come to the Christmas dance with me." He tossed the invitation out again, because Ida had been nagging him about attending, reminding him daily that if he didn't bring a date, he'd be hounded by every unattached woman in Apple Valley.

She hadn't suggested that he bring Tessa.

As a matter of fact, she'd hinted broadly that Charlotte would be a good choice. She would have been, but Cade figured that if he was going to put on fancy old-fashioned clothes and waltz around town hall, he'd much rather do it with Tessa.

"That's blackmail." She laughed again, and Cade wanted to press his lips to hers, taste the laughter that spilled into the cold night air.

"Guilty as charged," he responded, his body tight with need, his heart thumping hard for Tessa.

"You won't tell her," Tess responded. "You kept way too many of my childhood secrets for me to think you'd do anything different now."

"What if you're wrong?"

"Gertrude wouldn't really kill me, and I'm not really afraid of her, so I guess your blackmail is useless."

"Too bad. I really wanted to see you in one of

those old-fashioned corsets." He also really wanted to figure out how to get her out of one.

"You're going to be disappointed, then. Victorian misses didn't wear corsets as shirts, the way women do today. They wore them under layers. Lots and lots of layers." She turned her attention back to Alex, her amusement falling away. "Alex, we need to go home."

"Okay." Alex didn't seem upset about leaving. He was humming as they walked away. The same tune he'd been singing at the grave sites.

Poor kid. He'd been through the wringer, and it showed. His skin pale, his cheeks hollow. He looked thinner, more fragile than he had before Emily and Dave died. Cade helped him into the truck, more concerned for the young boy than he probably should have been. Alex wasn't his, after all.

He could have been, though.

That was one of the things Cade had never been able to forget, that if things had been different, Alex would have been his child.

He and Emily would have been miserable together. He knew that now. Maybe they'd have lasted a couple of years. Maybe they would have muddled through for longer. A kid, though? That would have been nice.

Tess climbed into his truck, and Cade walked around to the driver's seat, light spilling from the church windows and illuminating the parking lot. The night was quiet, just a few cars on the road back to the town center. Cade drove Tess to Murphy's for doughnuts and to the diner for a sandwich that she said Gertrude wanted. She asked about Cade's family and his job. He asked about her job and her life in Annapolis. Mundane stuff, but it felt good. As if they'd come full circle, from their years of wandering around town together on bikes to driving around it in his old truck. As if all the years that they *hadn't* spent together had never been and all that existed was one long expanse of time that stretched unbroken between them.

He drove slowly on his way back to the Riley place, not quite ready to say good night. It was early, and aside from microwaving a frozen meal, he didn't have plans.

He pulled into the driveway, and Tess got out before he could round the truck and open the door for her. Alex followed, walking slowly behind her.

Cade followed them up the porch stairs, hovering behind Tess as she unlocked the door.

Alex walked into the foyer, disappearing without a good-night or even a glance over his shoulder.

And Cade and Tess were alone, standing in the light spilling from the open door. Not kids anymore, but he felt like a teenager, anticipating that final good-night, that last kiss. Wanting it more than he thought he'd wanted anything in a very long time.

"Okay," she said, and he frowned, not sure what she was talking about.

"Okay what?"

"I'll go to the Christmas dance with you."

Gertrude yelled something from inside the house, and Tessa glanced over her shoulder.

"I'll be right there," she shouted back, before meeting Cade's eyes again. "Thanks for the ride. I owe you one."

He snagged her hand before she could disappear

inside. "Is that why you agreed to come to the dance with me? A sense of obligation?"

"*You're* why I agreed, Cade," she said simply.

"Good," he whispered, kissing her gently, tenderly, keeping it light and easy, because there'd be time for more later, and because, with Tess, he wanted to take his time.

"I'm starving in here!" Gertrude shouted, and Tess jerked back.

"I'd better go. Thanks again."

She shut the door, and Cade was left standing in the cold, smiling like a fool because of a Christmas dance and a woman he should have noticed a lifetime ago.

Across the street, Charlotte's door opened. She stepped outside, waving him over.

"What's up, Charlotte?" he asked as he approached her.

"I baked banana bread today. I thought you might like a loaf." She thrust a foil-wrapped package toward him, but he didn't think that was all she wanted to say. She seemed nervous, her gaze skittering away, her fingers fiddling with the buttons on her coat.

"What's wrong?"

"I . . ." She sighed, running her hand over her hair and shifting from foot to foot. "Look, I'm really uncomfortable with this, but there's something I think I should tell you. I just don't want to get anyone in trouble."

"If the person didn't do anything he should get in trouble for, then there's nothing to worry about. If he did, you have an obligation to let me know what it was. What's going on?"

"I saw Zimmerman Beck come out of the Riley place Sunday afternoon," she said quickly, and then pressed her lips together. "I probably shouldn't have said anything. I'm sure he had a reason for being there."

"Probably," Cade said just to make her feel better. There was no way Zim had a reason to be in his neighbor's house. At least none that Cade could think of. "I'll go have a talk with him. See what he has to say about it."

"You're not going to tell him I was the one who said he was there, are you? I've always gotten along well with Zim, and I don't want that to change."

"I'll just tell him that someone mentioned seeing him."

"Thanks, Cade." She smiled, but she still looked worried. "I'm sure it's nothing."

"I'll let you know what I find out." He waved and headed back across the street, bypassing his truck and walking to Zim's place. The lights were on, the curtains open to reveal a decorated Christmas tree. Zim might be difficult, but he loved holidays.

Cade rang the doorbell and heard Zim call from inside, "Hold on! I'm coming!"

Seconds later, something bumped the door. Probably Zim's head as he leaned in to look through the peephole.

The door opened, and Zim stood on the threshold, scowling. "What do you need, Sheriff? I'm right in the middle of my show, and I don't have a lot of time."

"What show is that?"

"What's it to you?"

"Just making small talk, Zim," Cade responded. "Mind if I come in?"

"I told you—"

"You're watching your show. Yeah, I know, but I have a couple of questions I need to ask you, and it's cold out here."

"Fine." Zim stepped aside, allowing Cade to enter the small foyer.

That was as far as they went, but Cade could see into the living room from there. A large-screen television hung on the wall, tuned to some show about real housewives.

"You said you had questions?" Zim prodded.

"Were you in Gertrude's place Sunday afternoon?"

"That's an idiotic question," Zim growled. "She was in the hospital, so why would I be there?"

"I don't know, but I have it on good authority that you were."

"What authority? That sniveling Gertrude woman? The one who accused me of pushing her down the steps even though half the town clearly saw her fall without any help from me?"

"Someone saw you leave the house, Zim," Cade revealed.

Zim blanched. "Let me tell you something, Sheriff. That place is a junk pit. I wouldn't set foot in there for a million dollars. Not to mention the fact that the woman who lives there is a pain in the butt."

"You're sidestepping my question, Zim. Which makes me think that you actually *were* in the Riley place. Seeing as how I have a witness, you may as well just admit it."

"I'm not sidestepping anything. I'm stating the facts. Pure and simple. Gertrude McKenzie is a witch. An ogre. She's the nastiest piece of garbage in the entire junk-pit of a house."

"Is that why you were in her house? Because you despise her?"

"It's not her house. It belongs to that niece of hers. That Tessa girl. Now, *she* is hardworking and polite." Zim nodded in agreement with himself, the way he always did when he had an opinion.

"Someone saw you coming out of the Riley place, Zim," Cade said again.

"Who? Because whoever told you that is lying!" Zim's face went from pale to purple.

"I don't think so. This person knows you well and is a trustworthy witness."

"And I'm not? You've known me your whole life, Sheriff. Since when have I ever gotten into trouble? Since when have I ever been underhanded or untrustworthy?"

"There's a first time for everything." Cade stared Zim down.

"Not with me. I'm not into breaking the law. Never have been. Never will be. As a matter of fact, I say my record stands for itself. I say that if I stood before a jury of my peers—"

"Zim." Cade cut him off. "I don't want to keep arguing about this, so I'm just going to cut to the chase. Since you've said you don't make a habit of going into This-N-That, I shouldn't find any of your fingerprints there when I go dust for them."

Zim looked away.

"Come on, Zim. Make this easy for both of us. We both know you were in there. Why?"

"You want to know the truth?"

"That's why I'm here," Cade said, trying for patience.

"I did go in there Sunday." Zim smoothed his hair, his eyes shadowed. "Not to cause any trouble. I . . . just felt bad about what happened to Gertrude. I can't stand the old biddy, but I don't wish her ill."

That Cade could believe. As grumpy and belligerent as Zim was, when push came to shove, he had a good heart. "If you weren't there to cause trouble, what were you there for?"

"Well . . . I . . . I thought I could help do some of the work around the place. Make things look a little better for when Gertrude got back, but it was too big a job for one person, so I left."

It could have been true, but Zim's hesitation said different.

"Until I hear that something is missing or that damage has been done to the place, I'm going to have to take your word for it. But stay out of the Riley house from now on. The antique store—"

"Antique. Ha! You mean trash dump."

"Stay away until Tess reopens the store. After that, you can shop there all you want, as long as you don't cause the family any trouble. They've had enough of that to last awhile."

He said good night, ending the conversation because continuing it wouldn't do any good, and because a glimmer of an idea was forming in his mind and he wanted to think on it a little more.

Up until a week ago, there hadn't been a theft in town for over a year. Then the angel was taken out from under the noses of half the population of Apple Valley. Now, Zim Beck, a man who couldn't stand his neighbors, was claiming he'd wanted to help them.

Maybe Zim wasn't quite the upright citizen he

pretended to be. An interesting idea, seeing as how he was on the town council, volunteered at the local food bank, and had never even gotten a parking ticket in the time Cade had been working for the sheriff's department.

Interesting, and an idea worth pursuing, Cade thought as he drove down Main Street and headed home.

Chapter Nineteen

"It's probably been fifty years since anyone has been in there, Tess. Are you sure you want to do this?" Gertrude asked, her scrawny behind perched on a beautiful chaise lounge Tessa had dragged from the shed.

"It's an attic, Gertrude. Not a tomb. Stop acting so scared," she chided, wondering if Gertrude would take offense if she was asked to move from the chaise to a chair.

Probably, but Tess still wanted to do it. Dating from the early 1900s, the piece had beautiful lines and a stately presence that would be perfect in a project James was working on. Tess had already stripped the wood and restained it. All she had to do was reupholster the cushions and polish it up. James had seen photos and approved the price; all Tess had to do was finish the restoration and ship it to Annapolis.

One thing at a time. She mentally rehearsed her new mantra.

With her to-do list growing longer every day, she had no choice but to follow through on the idea.

Right now, the one thing she *had* to do was find something to wear to the costume party, which was less than twenty-four hours away.

Nothing like putting things off until the last minute.

"Not a tomb? I bet there are hundreds of bodies in there. Mice. Rats. Spider carcasses. Not to mention all the critters that are still alive and kicking," Gertrude intoned, lifting her casted leg and setting it on the chaise.

Tess winced and turned her attention back to the door that stood at the end of the upstairs hallway. It was locked, and she tried the first of several dozen keys that she'd found in one of Emily's drawers. "It's too cold for critters, Gertrude."

"Humph. What do you know? There are probably thousands of creepy crawlies up in that attic. Right, Alex?"

"No," Alex answered emphatically, patting his thighs, his legs swinging beneath the high-backed chair he was perched on.

"What to do you know, anyway?" Gertrude griped.

Tess smiled, enjoying the exchange and the sense of routine that they were building together. Slowly, almost imperceptibly, things had been changing, the three of them becoming what Tess could only think of as a real family.

The first key didn't fit in the old pine door's lock. Neither did the second. She hit pay dirt with the third, the old skeleton key sliding in and the lock turning.

The door creaked open, revealing a narrow stairway that led to the attic.

"Tess, I'm really not sure you should go up there," Gertrude fretted, her nervousness making Tess suddenly nervous.

"What are you so worried about, Gertrude?" she asked.

"Whatever is up there!" She pointed toward the ceiling. "You know how these things always work. The woman goes up into the attic alone or down into the basement alone. Next thing she knows . . ." Gertrude slid her finger across her throat. "The end."

"We're not living in a horror movie."

"No, but . . ." Gertrude glanced at Alex and pressed her lips together.

"What? Spit it out, will you? I have a million things on my to-do list, and I don't have time to try to guess what's going on in your head."

"This is all because of the A-N-G-E-L," Gertrude whispered, and Alex's head popped up.

"My angel?" he asked.

"When did you learn how to spell that?" Gertrude snapped.

"First grade." He kicked at the wood floor, his bare feet small and pale. *Go put socks on*, Tessa almost said, but he seemed content, and she was happy just to have him sitting there trying to be part of what she was doing.

"Damn the school system for being so efficient, then," Gertrude muttered.

"Gertrude, in about three seconds I'm going up in the attic. So, either say what's on your mind or don't."

"We're cursed," Gertrude announced, plucking a cigarette from her shirt pocket.

Tess couldn't help it. She laughed. "You're kidding me."

"Do I look like I'm kidding?" Gertrude tapped the cigarette against her thigh but didn't light up. She'd been trying hard to quit smoking. She'd slipped up a few times but had only smoked outside.

Maybe that was why she was talking about curses. She was going crazy from nicotine withdrawal.

"Explain. Quickly." Tess glanced at her watch. Time was ticking, and she wanted to finish reupholstering the chaise lounge before morning. Then she could crate the piece and send it. The sooner she did, the sooner she could start getting some cash flow. The store would be open Monday, but she needed more than a few Christmas sales to keep Emily and Dave's creditors away.

One thing at a time.

"That angel was never supposed to leave this house. Not as long as a Riley was in it." The words seemed to burst out of Gertrude, jumbled together and barely intelligible. "I didn't know it. If I had, I never would have handed it over to Ida. Now it's lost, and we're all doomed."

"Doomed? That's a little melodramatic, don't you think?"

"My leg is broke, isn't it? And Alex nearly died out in that snowstorm."

"He wasn't even close to dying, and you broke your leg falling down icy stairs. It could have happened to anyone." Tess sighed. Gertrude really *had* gone off the deep end.

"Mock all you want, but we're cursed. Cursed!"

"I don't suppose you want to tell me where you got that idea?"

"This." She fished in her pocket and pulled out a folded piece of paper. "Ida asked me to read it during the tea, but we never got around to it. Miriam's great-great-grandniece remembered hearing stories about the angel when she was a kid, and she told Ida all about it."

Curious, Tessa unfolded the page, smoothing the creases and wrinkles. It looked like Gertrude had folded and unfolded it more than a few times. Apparently, she'd been reading the paragraph over and over again since the tea.

Miriam's Angel

As Told to the Green Bluff Historical Society by Her Great-Great-Grandniece, Alta Riley Morrow

She crafted the angel with her own hands, smoothing it out of clay and firing it in the kiln Daniel had built for her. It pulsed with the life she was losing, and some say she meant her spirit to be captured in it. She knew she was dying, you see, and she worried for her husband and son. She painted her heart into that angel. Every stroke of her brush was a prayer that her family would be prosperous and well. On Christmas Eve, she pulled her frail body from her sick bed and wrapped the finished angel in shiny silver paper. She died with it in her hands, her last gift to Daniel and their son. The angel was meant to be a constant reminder of her love for them, but Daniel couldn't bear to look at it. He put it in Miriam's china cupboard and left it there to gather dust. Still, it had the power of love in it. Legend has it that as long as the angel remains in the house, the Rileys who live there will be safe and happy. It's the way that Miriam meant things, and it's the way it will always be. But that isn't all there is to the angel. See, my grandma said that if a person looked long enough, she might see the angel unfurl its folded wings. Me? I never did, but that doesn't mean it doesn't happen. Miracles are all around us if we take the time to look for them.

The hair on the back of Tess's neck rose as she read. The story had the kind of power most oral tradition did. It rang of truth and of myth, and Tessa could almost see the porcelain angel in the frail hands of its maker.

"See?" Gertrude broke into her thoughts. "We're doomed because of what I did. From now until that angel is returned, there will never be a bit of happiness in this house."

"That's bull, Gertrude," Tess said sharply, because she didn't want Alex to think there was any truth to what Gertrude was saying. "There's not one word about a curse here."

"Read between the lines, girl. If the angel is here, we're going to be happy. That means if it isn't, then we won't be."

"Seriously, Gertrude." Tess thrust the paper into her aunt's hands. "I don't have time for this. I'm going to look for something to wear to the party. I'll be down in a minute."

"You hold on there, girly! I'm telling you, there's a curse, and it's all my fault. I'm telling you—"

Tess walked into the attic and closed the door on her aunt's tirade.

Enough was enough!

She did not have the patience for this kind of crap. She walked up the dusty stairs, searching the gloom for a light switch. A chain hung from a lone bulb, and she tugged it, surprised when it actually turned on.

Unlike the rest of the house, the attic hadn't been filled with Emily and Dave's stuff. Maybe they'd just never gotten around to it. Several dozen ancient trunks lay on the floor, all of them coated with thick layers of dust. A few boxes were piled near a small window. A child's rocking chair sat abandoned near a beautiful dollhouse, and a battered rocking horse stood beside it. They were toys that a child would have played with at the turn of the last century, and Tessa shivered with excitement as she touched one item after another.

She wouldn't sell any of the items. They belonged to Alex, but they deserved to be displayed and enjoyed rather than hidden away.

She ran her hand over a Victorian couch, its cushions almost pristine, the velvety fabric still bright peacock blue. A chair sat behind it. Tall backed and austere. An older piece, it dated from a time before the house existed. There was more. Way more than she could take in. She'd have to go through everything, catalog it, decide which pieces should stay in the attic, which could be used in the house, and which, if any, could be sold.

Her fingers itched to go through every trunk and every box. She could have spent hours discovering what was in each one, but she didn't have hours, so she went to the closest trunk and opened the lid. There were several patchwork quilts, a few old books, and a rag doll. She left them in the trunk. They were salable, but she'd have to look at them more closely later.

The second trunk contained a black flapper dress with crystal fringe, an old pair of Levi's that was probably worth a pretty penny, and three 1950s dresses that she wouldn't have minded trying on. She lifted one out, a pale blue swing skirt and fitted bodice. The crinoline beneath was intact and nearly spotless.

She held it up to herself. A perfect length, but not quite what she wanted for the party. She set it aside. Opened another trunk. A wedding dress lay on top, folded neatly, its ivory lace soft with age.

"Gorgeous," she murmured, pulling it out and letting it unfold. Silk-covered buttons ran from the high neck to the base of the spine. The long sleeves were fine, unlined lace. There was even a train, narrow in the style of the day.

The door opened and the stairs creaked, and she thought that Gertrude must have decided to brave the curse just so that she could harass Tess with more tales of their apparent woe.

"Take a look at this," she said, swinging toward the stairs.

Not Gertrude.

Cade. Standing there in all his glorious masculinity, eyeing the dress and her.

"Beautiful," he agreed.

Her pulse jumped, her cheeks heated, but she didn't look away from his searching gaze. "Isn't it? I wonder if this is Miriam's dress. I'll have to see if I can find a wedding photo."

He nodded, but she didn't think he'd heard a

word she said. His gaze drifted from her eyes, to her lips, to the hollow of her throat, and her mouth went dry, her heart skipping and stuttering.

"I wasn't talking about the dress, Tess," he said, taking it from her hands and carefully setting it back in the trunk.

"No?"

"No," he murmured, his hands cupping her face, his palms cool. "I've missed you the last few days."

"I—" Missed you, too? That sounded too needy. Too much like she'd been twiddling her thumbs hoping and praying he'd come for a visit. She hadn't been, but she *had* been wondering when she'd see him again. "Wasn't expecting you today."

He smiled, flashing the dimple that always made her heart jump. "I would have called first, but things have been hectic, and I didn't get a chance."

"Hectic? Has there been a crime wave in Apple Valley?" she asked. "If so, I'm surprised the phone hasn't been ringing off the hook all day with news of it."

"No crime wave. Just preparation for the party. I had to corral a dozen wily teenage boys to get them to help with the setup."

"I'd have liked to see that."

"I doubt they would have gotten anything done if you'd been around. A beautiful woman has a way of messing with the heads of impressionable young men."

"Stop calling me beautiful, Cade. It might go to my head." She lifted the wedding dress out of the trunk, giving her hands something to do so that they wouldn't reach for Cade.

"I call it like I see it, but let's not argue the point. We have more important things to discuss." The

serious edge to his voice made her look up from the
trunk into his dark blue eyes. They were solemn.
Worried even.

"What's wrong?"

"We have a lead in the missing angel case."

"What?"

"A few days ago, a witness said she observed
Zimmerman Beck leaving This-N-That on Sunday
afternoon. He admitted to being here."

"Sunday? The store was closed. We were at the
hospital."

"I know. Did you lock the door when you left? Set
the alarm?"

"Probably not. I was in a hurry, and I didn't think
about doing either."

"Then Zim would have had easy access."

"Sure, but why would he want it? That doesn't
sound anything like Zim. He's been avoiding us like
the plague since . . ."

The tea.

Up until then, he'd been vocal, standing on his
front porch and trading barbs with Gertrude every
time he saw her. After the tea, he'd gone quiet. As a
matter of fact, Tess couldn't remember the last time
she'd seen him.

"What are you thinking, Tess?" Cade prodded.

"That he's been awfully quiet since the angel disappeared."

"That's what a few other people have said. I've
been checking around. He's one of ten people who
were at the tea and disappeared around the time the
angel went missing."

"You don't think he could really have taken it?
And if he did, why come into the house while we

were gone? I can't imagine that there's anything in here that he's desperate to have."

"You have a lot of nice antiques, Tess. Maybe he took a few. Would you have noticed if he did?"

"Probably not. I haven't finished cataloging everything." She carefully folded the wedding dress and set it in the trunk with the quilts, uneasy with the story Cade was telling. Zim was a pain in the ass, but she couldn't, even in her wildest imagination, picture him stealing. "Why would he steal from us, Cade? Everyone knows he's got money. Wasn't he in real estate or something before he retired?"

"He's had it in for your family for years. Maybe this is his way of getting back at you." Cade rubbed his neck, and she thought that he looked weary, as if naming Zim prime suspect bothered him as much as hearing him do it bothered Tess. "I can't tell you how many times I've arrested good people who did really stupid things."

"I'm sorry, Cade."

"It's not your fault. Or your family's. *If* Zim took the angel, *if* he came into This-N-That to take something else, it has nothing to do with any of you and everything to do with him."

"So, what are you going to do? Arrest him?"

"I need proof first. I think I have enough evidence to convince him to confess. I'm going to bring him in for questioning tonight. I wanted to let you know what was happening, so you'd be prepared if the story starts circulating."

"It will. Poor Zim." She sighed, lifting a second dress from the trunk.

"If Zim is guilty, he doesn't deserve your sympathy, Tess."

"I don't know. Living next to my family would drive anyone to desperation." She unfolded the dress, letting deep violet fabric ripple to the ground. An evening dress with a low neckline edged with creamy lace, it had belonged to someone with money, the velvet rich and luxurious, the bodice sparkling with crystals and beads.

"Wow!" Cade said. "Is *that* what you're wearing to the dance?"

"Maybe." She held it up, trying to measure the waist against hers. The skirt was several layers. Velvet over a silk lining and netting. Beautiful, but heavy. "It might be too small. Whoever wore it had a tiny waist."

"You have a tiny waist, too." He took the dress from her hands, set it on the trunk. "You know what I've been thinking, Tess?" he said quietly.

No, and I don't want to, because if I did, I could not be responsible for my actions. Most of which would involve stripping every bit of clothes off your body.

Thank God, he couldn't hear her thoughts.

"I've been thinking that I made a mistake when we were kids," he murmured, his palms sweeping across her shoulders and down her arms until their hands were linked. "And I'm not going to make another one. This time around, I'm not going to miss what's right in front of my face."

"Cade—"

He brushed her lips with a kiss so light she barely felt it, but her heart thundered, her pulse racing so fast, she felt breathless. Dizzy with need.

"I'll stop if you want me to," he murmured, but she didn't want him to, and she dragged his head down for a kiss that she hoped would leave him as breathless as she was.

He moaned, pulling her closer, his hand sliding under her shirt, his hand hot on her cool skin.

She wanted this. Wanted it more than she wanted her next breath. Wanted him, because he was her childhood dream, her best friend. Because it had been too long since she'd been skin to skin, heart-beat to heartbeat with someone.

He deepened the kiss, his hand sliding up her ribs and down to her hips, his restlessness matching her own.

She barely noticed when he lifted her, didn't care when he laid her on the old dusty sofa. His fingers brushed her collarbone, and he pressed a kiss to the tender flesh there.

"Tessa! Did you find anything?" Gertrude called, her voice a splash of ice water that brought Tessa back to her senses.

Almost.

She lay still, staring into Cade's eyes, both of them breathing heavily.

"You should answer her," he said, his voice gruff and gritty with desire.

"I know." She ran her palm along his jaw, loving the bristles of his five o'clock shadow.

He shuddered, pressing her hand to his jaw, still-ing the movement. "*Now*, before I completely lose control, and your aunt comes up here and sees more than any of us want her to."

She kind of liked the idea of him losing control.

She wasn't so keen on having her aunt there when it happened.

"Tess? What's going on up there?" Gertrude yelled, her crutches tapping the floor below the stairs.

"Just trying to decide which dress to bring down," she responded, hoping Gertrude couldn't hear the wanton lust in her voice.

"Bring what you have down here. I want to help you choose. And tell that boy to get his hands off you. I don't want another of my nieces pregnant and unwed."

"Good grief," Tess muttered.

Cade chuckled, standing up and pulling her to her feet. "She's a piece of work."

"She's a pain in the ass. Now I have to find another dress. Otherwise she'll be sure we were up here making out."

"Weren't we?"

"Yes," she said, blushing. "But that doesn't mean I want my aunt to know." She lifted another dress from the trunk, her heart still beating too fast. She didn't dare look at Cade. If she did, she was afraid she'd throw herself into his arms again. "This one will be fine."

"What is it?"

His question was enough to make her look at the thin silky material. An ivory negligee with a low neck and low back. Not from the same time period as the dress. More like the 1930s. She refolded it and placed it into the trunk.

"Too bad," Cade murmured. "That would have been my choice."

"If I showed up in that, you'd have to arrest me." She pulled out two other dresses. One a wool day dress with buttons down the front and a skirt that fell straight to the floor. The other a dark blue ball gown from the Edwardian era, the neckline matching back to front, the cap sleeves jeweled and sweet.

"Okay. We're good." She lifted all three of her finds, avoiding contact with any part of Cade's body because she could not be held responsible for her actions if they touched again.

"Let me," he offered, taking the dresses from her arms, his knuckles brushing her abdomen. Her breath caught, and he smirked.

"Bastard," she muttered, and he laughed, gesturing for her to precede him down the stairs.

Gertrude was waiting at the bottom, her lined face set in a scowl so deep her mouth was nearly lost in it.

"It's about time," she snapped, the crutches under her arms nearly slipping as she pivoted and headed out of the tiny entryway. "What'd you find? Anything that will fit an old lady like me?"

"I didn't get a chance to go through everything." *Because I got distracted by the very hot sheriff.* She shot a look in Cade's direction, and he offered a slow, easy grin that made a thousand butterflies take flight in her stomach. "I can go back up and look for something for you, though."

"Don't bother. I guess it would be a little hard for me to go to the party with my leg in a cast." Gertrude sighed. "Besides, I really need to be here with Alex. A baby-sitter isn't going to cut it. If he got outside again that would be it. What with the curse and all, we just can't take a chance." She shook her head, her hair puffing wildly around her head.

"Curse?" Cade asked, raising a dark eyebrow.

"It's a long story." Gertrude sighed dramatically, plopping down on the chaise lounge and settling in for what looked like a long stay.

"And you are not going to tell it again," Tess interrupted. "Cade, you can put the dresses in Gertrude's room. We can look at them there."

"Are you trying to distract me?" Gertrude griped.

"Yes, as a matter of fact, I am."

"Well, you're lucky, because I'm in the mood for a distraction. Let's go."

Gertrude led the way into her cluttered room and pointed to her bed. The one spot that was not covered with stuff. Another item for the to-do list.

"Lay them out on the bed, Cade. Maybe Tess can do a little fashion show for us."

"No." A thousand times, no! She was not going to slip into Victorian or Edwardian or any kind of clothes and prance around in front of Cade while Gertrude watched!

"Maybe you should give it a little more thought," Cade said. "It sounds like fun to me."

"Do you know how long it takes to put on dresses like those?"

"No." *But I'd like to know how long it would take to get you out of one of them,* his eyes said.

She blushed. "A long time."

"Too bad. I'm working the night shift and have to be at work in ten minutes. I guess we won't have time for the fashion show after all." He spread the dresses out on the bed, smoothing his hand down the bodice of the velvet Victorian.

Tess shivered.

"Yeah. Too bad," she said, her voice husky.

"Wow! Those are gorgeous, Tess!" Gertrude exclaimed, completely oblivious to the electricity in the air.

Thank God!

"There are more up there. Lots more, but these were too beautiful to pass up."

"That's for sure." Gertrude whistled softly. "Wait until the men of Apple Valley get a load of you wearing this stuff."

"Should be interesting," Cade said. "Seeing as how she's going with me."

"I didn't mean anything, Cade. It's just, you and Tess are old friends. That's all you've ever been," Gertrude said as she touched the rich velvet. "And Tess is getting up there in years. She needs to find herself a man before it's too late."

"What? I'm twenty-eight!"

"That's an old maid in most parts of the world," Gertrude huffed.

"I hate to interrupt the argument, but I need to head into the office," Cade cut in. "I'll give you a call after I talk to Zim, Tess."

"Talk to Zim about what?" Gertrude barked, her focus turned from Tessa's old-maid status to her least favorite neighbor.

Cade had planned it that way. Tess could see the gleam in his eyes, the smile he wasn't quite hiding. "Tess will explain."

"No, she won't. She's about as tight-lipped as a toddler with a penny in his mouth."

"What does that even mean?" Tess asked, exasperated and frustrated.

"You'd know if you'd had any children, but at the rate you're going your ovaries are going to shrivel—"

"I think that's my cue to get out of here. I'll call later." Cade walked out of the room.

Tess followed. Anything to keep from hearing the rest of what Gertrude had to say about her shriveled ovaries.

"Thanks for stopping by," she said as Cade opened the front door. *Please, come again when we have a little more privacy and a lot more time.*

She managed to keep the thought to herself. Barely.

He smiled, and she was nearly certain he knew exactly what she was thinking.

"Do me a favor, Red. Don't tell Gertrude that Zim was in here Sunday. I don't want her going over and confronting him."

"I won't." The last thing she wanted to do was bail her aunt out of prison.

"And one more thing." He pulled her close, his lips brushing her temple, his words tickling the fine hair there. "Wear the purple dress. I like the way it feels."

He gave her a leisurely kiss that made her toes curl and her heart race, and then he left.

She stood on the threshold long after he drove away, cold winter air sweeping into the foyer, the leaves rustling in the trees outside; and just below the sound of wind and leaves, a soft sigh of sound that could have been anything, but sounded just exactly like her sister laughing.

Chapter Twenty

Cade could still smell Tessa's perfume as he pulled up to the station, and he was half tempted to turn around and go back to her place. He jumped out of the truck to keep himself from doing it. He had to work. Even if he didn't, he wouldn't rush things with Tess. He'd been given a second chance, a golden opportunity. He wasn't going to screw it up.

He walked into the building, waving to Emma and snagging a cookie from her desk. "Anything I need to know about?"

"Harrison Sheffield's prize goose is missing. He said it's the best he's ever raised, and he planned on serving it to a party of twenty on Christmas day."

"Doesn't this happen every year?"

"It does." She glanced at a printout that lay on her desk. "At least it has every year since 2005."

"That was about the time he was diagnosed with dementia, right?" Harrison had been a teacher for forty years. A well-loved member of the community, he'd retired ten years ago but still volunteered as a teacher's aide at the middle school. Sure, he had moments of forgetfulness, but the kids and staff at the school helped him through it.

"Right."

"Did you talk to his wife?"

"Not yet. Harrison called it in. He said his wife was in town having dinner with friends. He went to feed the animals and realized the goose was missing from the yard. He's about ready to go over and accuse Peter Morris of theft."

"Poor Pete. The guy has his hands full being Harrison's neighbor. Send a deputy out. Non-emergency. Have him check the pen in the barn close to Harrison's house. That's where he usually puts the goose before he butchers it for Christmas dinner."

"Maybe we should just leave the poor thing there. Or, better yet, free it. If he thinks it's missing anyway—"

"Emma, you know that wouldn't be the right thing to do."

"It would be right for the poor goose."

"Country living. You should be used to it. You grew up on a chicken farm."

"Why do you think I became a vegetarian?"

Cade laughed and grabbed another cookie, eating it as he walked to Max's office. He knocked once, then opened the door.

Max looked up from his computer screen. "Way to wait for an invitation," he said dryly.

"Am I interrupting something?"

"Just filing a report on the vandalism at the elementary school yesterday afternoon."

"What did the kids' parents say when you brought them home?"

"They were very polite and very sorry. Until the

doors closed. Then I could hear the hollering from the street."

"Good. Maybe they'll put the fear of God into their offspring, and we won't get called out to pick those boys up again."

"Seeing as how both the boys were in hysterics when I put them in the backseat of the cruiser, I think it's safe to say they had plenty of fear put into them," Max said, typing something into the computer. "Plus, they were using washable marker on the windows. I don't think they're hardened criminals just yet. So, what's up?"

"I thought we'd take a ride over to Zim's house. Bring him in and ask him a few questions about that missing angel."

"If we arrest him, we can get his prints while we're at it. I have a feeling we're going to find a matching set on the display case." Max stood and grabbed his coat from the back of his chair.

"If we arrest him, the news will be all over town within an hour. I want to be sure of what he did, before anyone in town gets wind of what we suspect. It will be better for everyone that way. Including us."

"Fine by me, but we'd sure as hell have an easier time of things if we had his fingerprints."

"We'll go by the book and ask if he's willing to be fingerprinted. If he didn't take the angel, he shouldn't protest."

"Zim protests everything. This morning he was at the diner complaining that his coffee was hot."

"It was twenty degrees out this morning."

"He doesn't care what the temperature is, he likes his coffee lukewarm. Now that I and half the town know it, we'll all make sure that's what he gets, just to shut him up." Max grabbed his coat from the back of his chair. "Come on. Let's go pick the old man up. It'll keep me awake."

"Late night?" Cade asked as they walked into the hall.

"Date night. A little honey I met in Spokane." He grinned, leading the way back to the lobby. "I'm seeing her again tomorrow night. Then I'll have to break it off."

"Does she know that?"

"Not yet."

"And you don't feel just a little guilty about that?"

"Why should I? We're having fun together. No promises. No commitment. We both know it, and I'm going to make sure neither of us forgets it."

"By dumping her after the second date?"

"You're a quick study, Cunningham."

"And you're a bastard."

"I know, but at least I won't break her heart."

"Wow! Way to be humble, Max," Emma murmured as they passed her desk.

"You're just bitter because I've never asked you out," he retorted.

"I wouldn't go out with you if you were the last man in the universe, and if you were, I'd probably hunt you down and try to kill you just so I'd know the last son of a b—"

"Okay, you two," Cade cut in. "Enough. I'm not running a high school here, and the people in the lobby don't want to hear you bickering."

"Sure we do," Eli Taverns called, waving a small stack of envelopes as he crossed the lobby, his mailbag slapping against his thigh. Eighty years old with a full head of white hair, he'd been delivering

mail in Apple Valley for longer than Cade had been
alive. In the past decade, his route had shortened to
a mile-long section of Main Street. It took him a
little longer to complete the trek, but he always
managed to deliver every bit of the mail he was
responsible for.

"You're running late today," Emma said, crossing
the lobby and pouring a cup of coffee for him.

"Holiday season. Lots of packages to deliver." He
handed her the mail and took the coffee, a ritual
Cade had witnessed dozens of times.

That was the thing about Apple Valley that had
driven Darla crazy. Everything in town happening
the same way it always did, but it was what Cade
loved most. The familiarity. The routine.

He walked outside, holding the door for Bethany
Sandino and her brood of kids. They lived out on a
farm two miles from town. They didn't have much
money, but he watched as she hung a gift card on
the tree in the lobby.

"Nice lady," Max said as they got into the cruiser.
"She needs to stop having kids, though."

"They're not hers," he said, surprised that Max
hadn't heard the tale.

"Since when?" Max asked, frowning as Bethany
held the door open and seven kids filed out. Short.
Skinny. Chubby. Tall. Brown skin. Fair skin. Dark
hair. White hair.

"Since her parents died and left her responsible for
a boatload of foster kids." Half of them had already
been adopted before the Sandinos died. Rumor had
it, Bethany planned to adopt the others, but the state
was hesitant because she was single and her alpaca

business had taken a hit with the downturn in the economy.

"I've heard them call her Mom, Cade," Max pointed out.

"She's been all they've had for six years. What else would they call her? Now, how about we get back to the business at hand? We're heading to Zim's, remember?"

"Right." Max frowned again, driving away from the station. "Do you really think old Zim took the angel?"

"He's the only suspect we've got."

"So, how are we going to handle this? Good cop–bad cop? Threaten him with jail time? Parade him in front of the town with a sign that says Suspected Thief?"

"Funny, Stanford."

"He's not going to think it's funny when we show up on his doorstep and say we're taking him in for questioning."

"You care?"

"No, but I thought *you* might. You have that small-town sheriff rep to keep."

"I think it'll survive whatever Zim can throw at it."

An hour and a half later, Cade was still sure his reputation would survive, but he wasn't sure *he* would. A couple of minutes of Zim, he could handle. An hour was a little too much. Anything after that, and a sane person was likely to tear every strand of hair from his head.

"What are you accusing me of, Sheriff?" Zim asked for the fiftieth time.

"We're not accusing." Cade repeated his canned answer. "We're questioning."

"Same difference when you drag me out of my house and parade me down the street in your police car."

"Tell you what, Zim," Max drawled. "How about you let us take your fingerprints? We'll compare them to the ones we found on the display case. If they're not a match, we'll stand on Main Street in sackcloth and ashes proclaiming your innocence."

"You think mocking me is going to make you look good in court, when I sue you for defamation of character?" Zim stood, stretching to his full height of five foot six.

"I'm not mocking. I'm offering an option that I thought would appeal to you. If you're innocent—"

"I told you, I did not take that blasted angel!" Zim shouted loudly enough for anyone in the county to hear.

Cade met Max's eyes. The guy was protesting a little too much and completely avoiding the fingerprint request.

"You don't seem very agreeable to having your fingerprints taken," Cade pointed out.

Zim scowled. "I'm not a criminal."

"No one said you are. We're just curious as to why you're so opposed to letting us fingerprint you."

"I'm not opposed. The thing is . . ." Zim's face flushed, his gaze skittering away. Whatever he had to say, it wasn't going to be the truth, but Cade waited him out anyway. "I touched the case. Just like dozens of other people in that room. My fingerprints are probably on it. Circumstantial evidence, but that's how people get convicted all the time, right?"

"Only when they're guilty," Max growled. "And you are, right, Zim? You've been angry with the Rileys for years, and couldn't stand to see the family get so much attention."

Zim went pale, then purple, his eyes bugging out of his wrinkled face. "I don't have to stand around here listening to this. This is an outrage! I'm going to call my lawyer in the morning and sue you both."

"You do that, Zim," Cade said. "Come on, I'll give you a ride home." They'd gotten what they needed. Not a confession, but Cade hadn't expected one. Zim had taken the angel, though. Cade was nearly certain of it.

"I'll get myself home, Sheriff. And don't you be thinking that I'll forget about this. You *will* be hearing from my lawyer. Guaranteed!" Zim stomped out of the office.

"Well." Max leaned against the doorjamb. "I think we have our man."

"I'd say so." Cade grabbed his coat from the hook on the back of the door. "You hit pay dirt with your theory about his motive."

"What other reason would a guy like that have for taking something that's worth maybe a few hundred dollars? Want me to contact the judge and ask for a search warrant?"

"Yes. We probably won't have it in hand until to-morrow, but I can't see Zim as the kind of guy who'd destroy something like that angel. Hopefully, that means it's still in his house. *If* he took it."

"Right. *If*," Max snorted. "What are we going to do to make sure that he doesn't get rid of the angel before we get that search warrant?"

"We'll do a little surveillance. Follow him home. Make sure he goes there and stays there."

"You want to handle that, or do you want me to?"

"I'll handle it. You get the judge working on that warrant. Call me if he's willing to move faster than a snail on it." Cade shrugged into his coat.

"Judge Dennis move fast? Not unless it's life and death, and I don't think he's going to feel like this is worth giving up his evening for. I'll give it my best, though."

Cade hurried outside. He could see Zim heading toward home, the street lights shining on his white hair. He wasn't moving fast. Cade could probably take a few trips around the block and still beat Zim to his house.

He waved to a few people who were window-shopping along Main Street. This time of year, every store had a holiday display, lights and trees, tinsel and gingerbread. The toy store at the corner had an electric train that moved around a track from Thanksgiving until Christmas Eve. The thing seemed to get bigger every year. More little trees, little people, tiny houses and animals.

Cade had watched it for hours when he was a kid, and he'd always imagined that he'd have children one day who would press their faces to the glass the way he had.

Here he was, nearly thirty-two, and all he had was an empty house and a huge yard. Most nights, that didn't bother him much, but he missed having more. Missed going home and knowing someone was waiting for him.

He climbed in his cruiser, trying to forget the way it felt to wrap his arms around warm, silky flesh, to lie in bed at night and listen to the soft breathing of the woman he loved. To wake up in the morning and look into the sleepy face of the person he planned to spend the rest of his life with.

It had gone wrong with Darla. She'd grown impatient with small-town life, and he'd grown impatient with her. They'd stopped looking at each other the way two people who were in love did, and they'd started tiptoeing around the house, avoiding the conflict that always seemed to happen when they were together. He didn't want to go through that again. Feeling like every day was a fight for something he wasn't sure was worth saving. He'd been relieved when Darla had packed her bags and walked out, but that didn't mean he hadn't felt lonely once she was gone.

It was his parents' fault, and his grandparents'. Two couples who were meant for each other, and who'd stuck it out together through good times and tough times. He'd watched them and thought that every love was like that.

He'd learned the hard way that it wasn't. Twice.

He couldn't believe he was even thinking about trying again. But, Tess . . .

She should have been first, and if she had been, there'd never have been any need for a second try.

He drove down Main Street, the ebb and flow of evening traffic as soothing as spring rain. Just a few cars, but people in town called it rush hour. People milled around storefronts, probably discussing holiday plans. It wasn't Norman Rockwell's world, but it was damn close.

He turned onto Fifth, pulling into a cul-de-sac of World War Two—era houses. This was a newer section of town, the houses closer together, the yards smaller. Still nice, though, and attractive to some of the younger families.

He drove around the court, scanning the yards and houses the way he always did when he was working. Nothing out of the ordinary. Just Christmas lights and Christmas trees, smoke puffing from chimneys. A half a dozen families going through their evening rituals.

He pulled back onto Main Street, driving slowly through the town center. It would be a quiet night. No basketball games or soccer matches in town. Most people more worried about finishing up Christmas shopping than causing trouble.

Zim had more than that on his mind, of course. He was probably worried out of his mind that he'd be caught with the angel and thrown in jail. Cade didn't think the theft of a hundred-year-old angel would warrant the guy being tossed behind bars, but Zim was a rule follower rather than a breaker. Whatever had caused him to take that angel, he'd probably regretted it soon after.

If he'd taken it, Cade reminded himself.

Zim was walking up his porch steps as Cade drove by. He looked over his shoulder, the outside light highlighting his deep scowl. Cade smiled and waved, parking at the curb across the street.

"This is harassment!" Zim hollered.

Cade ignored him.

Zim wasn't going to cross the street to confront him. He was too afraid. It didn't give Cade any pleasure to know he was terrifying a seventy-year-old man, but he had a job to do, and if that meant sitting outside Zim's house half the night, so be it.

The lights in Zim's house went on, his Christmas tree showing in the large front window. Zim looked outside, then closed the curtains. They were thick enough to hide whatever he was doing. Probably pacing through his living room worrying that he'd be in jail before morning.

The radio buzzed, the night dispatcher calling for a car to check out a Peeping Tom near Welsely and Ford. Cade knew the person who'd reported it was Eileen McGuire. A fifty-year-old widow, she was notorious for seeing trouble where there wasn't any. Most of the time that was in the form of prowlers or Peeping Toms. A few times, she'd called in to report her neighbors, insisting they were smoking pot in their backyards or selling drugs over the back fence.

Regardless, Cade insisted that her calls be taken seriously. The one time they weren't, would probably be the only time she really needed the police to respond.

Jackson Cramer responded to the call. Younger than Cade by just a few years, Jackson had been injured in Afghanistan before returning to Apple Valley. He was a good police officer, but quiet, doing his job and then going home to a large house he'd inherited from his grandparents.

Like everyone else in town, Jackson knew Eileen's address, and he knew her notoriety. He put the sirens on, anyway. Cade could hear them in the distance.

He caught movement out of the corner of his eye, and his gaze jumped to Zim's house. The curtains were still closed tight. The door shut. Cade had seen something, though.

He got out of the car, searching the area across the street. The Rileys' yard was dark and silent, lights from the porch spilling onto the old swing. It moved slightly, rocking back and forth as if someone had been sitting on it.

No way could anyone have been there. Cade would have noticed when he'd driven up.

Probably the wind. Not that there was any wind to speak of.

The Rileys' door flew open with a bang, and someone tried to push a sofa onto the porch. He crossed the street, grabbing the end of it.

"Hey!" Tess peered out from the darkness beyond the door, her hair in a high ponytail, an oversized sweatshirt falling off her shoulder. "Oh, it's you."

"Don't sound so excited."

"Sorry. I'm just pissed. I thought getting this thing down the stairs was going to be the hard part, but it won't fit through the damn door!"

"It's a two-person job, Tess," he pointed out.

"Unfortunately, the only person around is me."

"Not anymore. Let's lift and turn it sideways. It'll fit better that way."

"I can manage myself, Cade." She grunted, shoving the sofa again.

"I'm sure you can, but why should you, when I've offered to help?"

"Stop being reasonable, okay? I'm tired and grouchy."

"And looking for a fight?"

"Exactly! I also have a splitting headache, and if I don't get this thing reupholstered tonight, I won't get it to James before Christmas."

"James?"

"My boss. *Ex*-boss."

"You're sending this to him as a gift?" He helped

her maneuver it through the door, setting it down at the edge of the porch.

"He wants it for one of his clients. They're moving into their house next week, and they're going to have a huge Christmas party to celebrate. He's paying me a pretty penny for it, too. But, man, getting it down those stairs nearly killed me." She dropped onto the old cushions, shivering and rubbing her arms.

"You should have left it where it was."

"I thought about it, but Gertrude decided to go to bed early, and Alex is sleeping, too. I thought I'd better hammer these in outside." She pulled a plastic bag of rivets from the pocket of her jeans. "I forgot how cold it was, though."

"And how nosy your neighbors are? Weren't you worried about what they'd all think about you hammering on furniture in the middle of the night?"

"It's ten, Cade. That's hardly the middle of the night." She shivered again, and he sat beside her, tugging her to his side and wrapping his arm around her shoulders.

"You'll freeze before you finish, if you don't put a coat on."

"Too difficult to work in. Besides, I'll warm up once I start working." She brushed back thick strands of hair and smiled that easy grin that reminded him of everything that had been great about his childhood. "I thought you were working tonight."

"I am. I'm keeping an eye on Zim, making sure he doesn't destroy evidence before we get a search warrant."

"Poor guy."

"You said that earlier."

"Well, I feel sorry for him. Even if he took the angel, he's not a hardened criminal. He's just an old man who made a mistake." She shivered violently and stood.

"Get up, Cade," she commanded, giving him a gentle shove. "If I don't start this, I really will freeze."

She dragged a large basket from the foyer and rummaged through it, pulling out blue flowery fabric. "Since you're here, maybe you can help me. An extra set of hands is always nice for something like this."

"I did promise to protect and serve when I became sheriff. I suppose this comes under serving."

"Thanks." She chuckled, and if he hadn't been on duty, he'd have done something a lot more interesting than holding fabric.

There'd be time for that later, though. Plenty of it.

That was the thing about Apple Valley. Life would always unwind from sunrise to sunset, lazily and with little rush, people moving through the days the same way they always did. Some called it boring. Cade called it home. Right then, and always, it was really the only place he wanted to be.

He smiled, taking the fabric from Tessa's hands and helping her stretch it across the old Victorian sofa.

Chapter Twenty-One

Finished!

Tess would have done a happy dance if Cade hadn't been standing beside her.

"It looks good," he commented as she smoothed the brocade-covered seat.

She had to admit, it *did* look nice. One of her best projects to date.

"I think James's clients will love it," she responded happily, feeling content in her work and Cade's company.

She hadn't expected to see him again before the party, but she was happy that he was there. She was also happy that he'd helped her finish the project in half the time she'd expected it to take.

As an added bonus, she might actually get to sleep at a decent hour. Something she hadn't done since the funeral.

She tossed the fabric remnant into her work basket, threw the hammer on top of it, and brushed lint from her jeans. "Thanks for your help, Cade."

"I held fabric, Tess. I don't need thanks for that."

"You kept me company, too," she pointed out, shoving the basket back into the foyer.

"I can think of a way you can thank me for *that*, if you're of a mind to do it," he responded, tugging her around so they were face-to-face, his gaze dropping to her lips. Her knees went weak, and it was all she could do not to throw herself into his arms.

"I'm not sure that would be appropriate while you're on duty," she protested halfheartedly, because she really wasn't sure she cared about appropriate.

"A cup of coffee, Red. That's all I was going to ask for." He laughed, and she lightly slapped his arm.

"You're a rat, you know that?"

"But a helpful one." He grinned.

"True. So, I guess I'll get you that coffee as soon as I get this sofa inside."

"*We* get it inside," he corrected her, helping as she maneuvered the sofa into the foyer.

"Good enough," she panted. "I can crate it up tomorrow morning, and the shipper will pick it up before noon. Come on in the kitchen, and I'll get you that coffee."

"Sorry," he said, shaking his head. "I have to wait outside. If Zim slips out of his house under my radar, my deputies will never let me live it down."

He walked down the porch steps, eyeing Zim's house.

From where Tess was standing, it looked silent and dark. Was Zim really biding his time, waiting for an opportunity to rid himself of the evidence?

The *angel*.

It seemed inconceivable, but then, three weeks ago, the idea of returning to Apple Valley had been inconceivable.

And here she was. In Apple Valley.

It wasn't nearly as awful as she'd thought.

As a matter of fact, she might even say the little town was growing on her.

She made Cade a cup of coffee, bringing it out onto the porch and watching as he walked to his cruiser with it. If the wind hadn't picked up and the temperature hadn't been hovering near zero, she probably would have stood there and watched him drink it, too.

She waved good-night, stepping back into the silent house and turning on the alarm. She walked through the lower level, flicking off lights as she went. No more cluttered front room. No more peeling wallpaper. No more piles and piles of junk. After countless hours of work, the place had finally been transformed. Sure, there were things that still needed to be done, but those things didn't distract from the beauty and charm of the Victorian architecture. This-N-That would reopen Monday. Tess could finish up the smaller projects as time permitted.

A posh little antique store in the middle of a picturesque town would be the perfect place for people to shop. She'd used some of her savings to pay the back taxes on the house and had called a dozen creditors to ask for payment plans. She'd been fortunate. Everyone had been understanding, but she still needed to dig out of the debt Emily and Dave had left her.

"I'll make it work, Emily," she whispered to the Christmas tree, because her sister wasn't around to talk to. "Don't worry."

The wind buffeted the windows and made the chimes on the back deck ring. They weren't the answer Tess wanted. What she wanted was to hear Emily say that she never worried, because Tess always made things work.

Even more than that, she wanted to go back in time. She wanted to work a little harder, try a little more to rebuild their broken relationship before it was too late.

"I'm sorry, Em," she whispered to the tree and the silent house, her throat tight, her eyes dry and hot.

She turned off the light and walked up to her room. She didn't bother changing, just pulled off her sweatshirt and dropped onto the bed in her jeans and cami. The old grandmother clock ticked away the seconds, and Tessa closed her eyes. She wanted to sleep. Her body was heavy with fatigue, but all she could hear was the stupid clock.

The windowpane rattled, and Tess gave up sleeping. She didn't turn on the light, just walked across the cold wood floor and pulled back the curtains. Snow fell from the gray-black sky, the flakes fluffy and light.

Across the street, Cade's sheriff's car was dusted with a light layer of snow, the interior light off, exhaust puffing from the back. Behind the car, Charlotte's house was dark. So were the houses on either side of it. Everyone asleep except for Tess and Cade.

She leaned close to the glass, knowing he couldn't see her through the gloom. She was such an idiot to want to go outside and bring him another cup of coffee and maybe one of the cookies a blue-haired lady had dropped by. She knew she'd probably be sorry. She knew that eventually she'd probably get hurt. Cade was a man, after all, and every man she'd ever dated had been a loser.

She couldn't make herself care, though, because when she was with Cade, she felt happier than she had in a long time. When she looked in his eyes, she was pretty damn sure she saw the future.

She turned back to the bed, was halfway there when an earsplitting shriek filled the room. She screamed, the sound swallowed up by the high-pitched alarm.

Alex. He must be trying to get out of the house again!

She ran toward the door, tripping over an ottoman in her haste. She landed hard, her hands and knees sliding across hardwood as the door flew open. Gertrude stood on the threshold, her hair standing up in a thousand different directions, Alex standing near her elbow.

"What the hell is going on?" she screamed as Tessa scrambled to her feet.

"I don't know. Someone must be trying to get in the house." She grabbed a silver mirror from the dresser. Not the best weapon but all she could find. "Stay in my room and lock the door," she hollered.

"You can't go down there alone!"

"Someone needs to stay with Alex, and you have a broken leg. *Stay here*," she repeated, nudging Alex into her room. "Call the police, Gertrude."

She crept through the apartment, replacing the mirror with a butcher knife as she made her way through the kitchen. She approached the stairs, felt a cold draft of air sweep across her feet. The front door was closed tight, but somewhere a door or window was open.

Tess wanted to cower on the landing and wait for help to arrive, but Alex and Gertrude were her responsibility, and she had to take control of the situation. Until she got the alarm turned off, there was no way she could hear trouble coming.

She tiptoed down the stairs, feeling like the dim-witted victim in a horror movie, a monster lurking below while she clutched a puny little knife and pretended she was safe.

She made it down the stairs without anyone or anything attacking and punched in the code to shut down the alarm. The house fell silent, the wind still blustering outside, everything else dead still.

Please, don't let there be anyone here. Please, don't let anyone be here.

Please, don't . . .

The doorbell rang and Tessa screamed, the knife dropping from her hand.

God! She really *was* just like one of those destined-to-die horror-movie ninnies.

She retrieved the knife, looked out the peephole.

Cade. Thank goodness.

And he wasn't alone.

She opened the door and looked into Zimmerman Beck's pale face.

"What's going on?" She stepped back, allowing both men to enter.

"Do you want to tell her, or should I?" Cade asked.

Zim flushed. "Dave's parents gave me keys to the house years ago. I . . . used it to get in your back door."

"Why?" was all she could think to say.

"I was looking for that darn angel," he muttered.

"Who's down there, Tess? What's going on?" Gertrude appeared at the top of the stairs, her housecoat buttoned up to her neck.

Tess wished she had a housecoat. Better that than a lacy camisole and holey jeans.

"Everything is fine, Gertrude. You and Alex can go back to bed," she said, trying to forestall the battle she knew was coming.

"I decide when I go to bed," Gertrude huffed, slowly moving down the stairs, her crutches under her arms. Her gaze was on Zim, her eyes flashing ire. "What are you doing here, old man?"

"Gertrude, don't start." Tess squeezed the bridge of her nose, praying for all she was worth that her aunt would *not* start the war of the century.

"Start what? It's the middle of the night, and he's in my house. I think I have the right to know why."

"You're right. You do." Zim seemed to be growing paler by the minute, all his usual bravado gone. "Like I told the sheriff, I was looking for the angel."

"Why in God's name would you be doing that? It's our angel and not your problem. Unless you think we took it just to get the town's sympathy," Gertrude spat. "It would be just like you to think that, too. You never did like this family, but I can tell you right now, we didn't take—"

"I took it," Zim said quietly.

Gertrude sputtered to a stop, her eyes wide with surprise. "What did you just say?"

"I took the angel."

"You took it, and then came here looking for it?" Tessa cut in, more surprised by that than Zim's confession.

"It's a long story." He ran a hand down his jaw, his face grayish and ancient. He'd aged about a dozen years in the past few minutes, and Tess felt a tug of sympathy for the man.

"Tell you what." Gertrude took his arm. "You come in the kitchen. I'll make some coffee, and you can explain the whole thing."

"Actually, Gertrude," Cade said, cutting in, "I'm going to have to take Zim to the station. I'll interview him there and get back to you in the morning."

"Take him to the station for what?" Gertrude speared Cade with a hard look, acting for all the world like he was the one who'd caused the trouble.

"He stole Miriam's angel. He's going to have to be charged and booked for that."

"He's an old man. You can't tell me that you're going to throw him in jail for this little misstep!"

"I—"

Cade looked as confused as Tess felt. Five seconds ago, Gertrude had looked like she wanted to roast Zim alive. Now she wanted to protect him?

"We won't press charges, will we, Tess?" Gertrude insisted, her hands on her hips, her eyes narrowed.

"He did take the angel, Gertrude," Tess reminded her.

"And I put it back. I really did," Zim blurted out.

"If you put it back, where is it?" Cade asked reasonably.

Zim shrugged, his rheumy eyes nearly dripping tears. "I'll be darned if I know. I put it under the Christmas tree. Wrapped it up in a box and even put a bow on it."

"When? The day of Gertrude's accident?" Cade pressed.

Zim nodded. "Yes. I'm ashamed to say it, Sheriff, but I took advantage of this kind lady's misfortune."

Kind lady?

Tess nearly snorted. He had to be kidding. Surely

he didn't actually think that anyone would think he was sincere. Or that Gertrude actually *was* kind.

"You weren't taking advantage of anything. You were trying to right a wrong. That's pretty damn admirable in my book." Gertrude patted Zim's shoulder, nearly knocking him off his feet.

Tess wanted to press a palm to her head to make sure she wasn't running a fever.

Cade must have been thinking the same.

He smoothed his hair, rubbed his neck, frowned. He finally said, "Tell you what. Let's all go ahead and have some coffee. Zim can tell us exactly what happened, and you and Tess can decide whether or not you want to press charges."

"Coffee would be good," Zim agreed, a little color in his cheeks.

"Let's go, then." Gertrude led the way down the hall, her crutches tapping briskly. She was a woman with a mission, and everyone followed along behind her. Including Tess.

It didn't take long for the coffee to brew. By the time it was done, Zim was halfway through his sordid tale of temptation and criminal activity.

A momentary lapse of judgment during the tea, and he'd slipped the angel from its case because he didn't think a family that had made such a mess of Main Street should be celebrated. He hadn't meant to keep it, he insisted. He'd planned to return it, but doing that had been difficult, what with the entire town whispering about the crime.

Tess sat across from him—Gertrude on one side of her, Cade on the other—and she could barely hold back laughter. Zim had obviously stepped into a lot more trouble than he'd expected to. From the sound of things, he'd been trying to figure out how to return the angel from the moment he took it.

"Sunday, after Gertrude fell, I knew I had an opportunity." He took a deep breath, sipped coffee, grabbed a cookie. Now that it seemed he wouldn't be arrested, he was relishing recounting the details of the story.

"I had the keys to the house," he continued. "Of course, I didn't need to use them. The door was unlocked." Zim shot Tess a reproachful look. "I carried the package under my coat so no one would see it, and once I got inside, I just put it right underneath the Christmas tree. I knew one of you would notice it. I kept waiting for an announcement about the angel being found. Never happened."

"Did you see a present under the tree, Tess?" Cade asked.

"No." She looked at Gertrude. "Did you?"

"I was too hopped up on those painkillers the doc gave me to notice anything. Are you sure you put it there, Zim?"

"I'm old, but I'm not senile! Of course I put it there." He snagged another cookie. "Someone took it. That's what happened. Some miscreant must have seen my misdeed and decided to take the angel himself."

"Why would anyone do that, Zim?" Cade crossed to the coffeemaker and refilled his cup, his five o'clock shadow giving him a rugged outdoorsy look that matched his sheriff uniform perfectly. Tess wanted to rest her hand on his jaw, weave her fingers through his hair.

One thing at a time, she reminded herself. Jaw first. Then hair. Then the buttons on his uniform.

"Pay attention," Gertrude hissed, elbowing Tess in the ribs.

She looked away from Cade, but not before she saw the dimple flash in his cheek.

"Regardless of what happened, you're responsible for the angel's disappearance. You know that, right?" Cade asked once Zim finally wound down.

"My conscience won't let me deny it." Zim moaned, his eyes wet again. "But the angel isn't where I left it, and I don't know how to fix it."

"Let's check the parlor again," Gertrude suggested. "Maybe a customer moved it."

"The store has been closed, and I've redecorated every room in it. If I didn't find the package, it's not here," Tess reminded her aunt, but Gertrude and Zim were already making their way from the kitchen.

"Let them go," Cade said. "It'll make them both feel better. Besides, it's good to see them on the same side for a change."

"Good? More like a miracle. I just wish the angel really was there. Gertrude is still convinced we're cursed because it's not in the house."

"I didn't think Gertrude was the superstitious type."

"I didn't either, but you know Gertrude. She gets an idea in her head, and she can't let it go."

"I'm the same way," he said, snagging her hand and pulling her close. "And I've been having a lot of ideas tonight."

"Have you?" she asked, her heart beating so fast, she thought it would burst from her chest.

"Yes."

He nipped her lower lip, and her breath caught, her entire body wanting to flow right into his.

"You're on duty, remember?"

"Not as of thirty seconds ago," he said, his lips so close to hers that the tiniest breath of movement would have brought them together.

And dear God above, she wanted that! His lips. His chest. His broad, firm back.

"Really?" She sighed.

"Really," he murmured, his hands inching along her sides, his fingers skimming the curve of her breasts.

She was breathless, caught in the moment, and she didn't care. Not one bit.

"You can tell me to stop," he whispered, his gaze dipping to her lips.

"Why would I?" She slid her hands into his hair, loving the thick, silky feel of it.

And his lips!

His lips were like a little taste of heaven.

He groaned, pulling her tight against him. Every hollow, every ridge, every part of him touching every part of her, and she wanted it to last. Not just for that moment: forever.

"We didn't find . . . Whoa!" Gertrude squealed.

Tess jumped back, nearly falling over a chair in her haste.

"Careful!" Cade grabbed her shoulder, his eyes dark with passion, and Tess was seriously ready to fall into his arms all over again.

Gertrude eyed them for a moment, her face set in a deep scowl.

"It's hard to believe, Zim," she finally said. "It really is. After all these years, the hardheaded fool of a boy has finally figured out which one of the Riley girls he's supposed to be with."

"It seems that way." Zim nodded sagely.

"He's not a boy," Tess pointed out.

"I'd like to think that I'm not a hardheaded fool, either," Cade added, flashing a smile that made Tessa's stomach flip and her heart jump and everything inside her shout for joy.

"Right," Tess agreed. "That, either."

Zim cleared his throat and stretched his neck like a rooster ready to crow. "Since Tess does not have a father to look out for her, I think it's best if I step in and ask what your intentions are, Sheriff."

"Yeah. What *are* your intentions, Sheriff?" Gertrude repeated, her eyes narrowing.

"My intentions?" Cade glanced at Tess, his eyes still smoldering, a half smile still curving his lips.

Don't you dare, she tried to say with her eyes, but obviously he wasn't listening.

His gaze dropped to her cream-colored cami and his smile broadened. "Well," he drawled, "if you really want to know, the first thing I plan to do is—"

"You know what?" she interrupted, "I . . . think I'd better check on Alex."

Then she did what any self-respecting woman would do.

She ran.

Chapter Twenty-Two

Ten hours later, Tess wished she had just kept on running.

"You're an idiot," Gertrude said for about the nine-millionth time, her casted leg swinging as she sat on Emily's bed and watched Tessa dress for the dance.

Neither had gotten much sleep after Zim's attempted break-in, and it showed. Gertrude was grumpy, and Tess was about to kill her. Justifiable homicide. That's what she planned to plead.

"An idiot, Tess. There is no doubt about it."

"Takes one to know one," Tess retorted as she slid her arms into the cap sleeves of the velvet ball gown.

"That's the best you can do? What is this, high school?"

"Look, I know you mean well—"

"No, I don't. I mean business. You pined over that boy for years. Don't even try to tell me you didn't. Now he's wanting to be part of your life, and you're not sure it's a good idea?" Gertrude bristled with indignation.

"I didn't say it wasn't a good idea. I just said it wasn't your business."

"Same thing," she huffed.

"No. It's not. As Cade rightfully told you, we have to figure things out ourselves." Tess knew this because she'd stood outside the kitchen and listened, just to make sure Cade's explanation of his intentions didn't give poor old Zim a heart attack.

"I'm as close to a mother as you've ever had, girly. I can't believe that you're trying to cut me out of your life."

"For crying out loud, Gertrude! Do you have to be so melodramatic?"

"Melodramatic? I'll give you melodramatic. I'll melodramatic my way all the way out of this room," Gertrude growled, but she didn't budge from the bed. And to Tessa's surprise, she actually looked hurt.

"Look." She sighed. "I'm not cutting you out of anything, and I'm not saying no to a relationship with Cade. If I were, would I be heading to a dance with him?"

"How should I know, since you're not talking?" Gertrude grunted, but she looked mollified. "I like the velvet. Good choice," she added.

"It *is* pretty, isn't it?" Tess tried to button the dress. Not easy with something so tight fitting. She was breaking a sweat when Gertrude hopped over on her crutches.

"I'll do it," Gertrude offered.

"It's okay. I can manage."

"Just for once, let me do something for you, Tess," Gertrude said softy.

Surprised, Tess looked into her eyes, saw that

same softness reflected in her gaze. "You've done plenty for me."

"I gave you a home and I loved you, but you never let me take care of you. You were always too damn good at taking care of yourself." Gertrude started buttoning the dress. "I always admired your gumption, Tess. But sometimes it's nice to be needed."

She stepped back, done with the buttons, her lined hands hanging loose as she balanced on her one good leg. "There. And you look beautiful."

"So do you," Tess said, hugging her.

"Humph! I'm a lined old hag, but I love you, so I'll accept the compliment. Now, about you and Cade—"

"Gertrude." Tessa sighed again, smoothing gloss onto her lips. "Please, just let it drop for a while."

The floor creaked in the hall, and a shadow passed beneath the closed door. Tess crossed the room, the dress heavy and opulent as it swished the floor.

"You can come in, Alex," she called.

The door cracked open, and Alex stuck his head in, his eyes going wide when he saw Tess.

"What do you think?" she asked, holding out her arms so he could get the full effect of deep purple velvet, layered skirts, and lacy trim. Not that she thought he knew much about 1900s fashion, but they were trying to mesh all their different personalities into that nebulous thing called family, and she knew he wanted to be part of it. Even if he didn't quite know how.

"Pretty," Alex responded, sidling past her and perching on the bed.

"Thanks." Tess touched his shoulder, and he gave

her a rare smile, his eyes meeting hers for a long moment.

"It's amazing what a perfect fit it is, Tess." Gertrude eyed her critically. "You and Miriam must have been around the same size."

"We don't know that it was hers." And it really wasn't a perfect fit. The bodice was a little too snug, and the neckline plunged more than Tess would have liked. The waistline barely left room for her to take a breath.

"Yes," Alex said, sliding off the bed and walking to the dresser. He lifted the mother-of-pearl box that she'd left there. She hadn't tried to find a key, hadn't really thought much about it since Alex had given it to her.

"Open it," he prodded.

"I'm sorry, buddy. I don't have a key."

"Mom has it." He walked to the dresser and reached behind the mirror, his hand gliding up and down for a moment. "See!"

He held up a small key attached to a piece of tape and smiled another one of his rare smiles.

Tessa's heart melted. "You're a smart kid, you know that?"

"Yes. Open the box."

She shoved the little key into the tiny gold lock and the lid popped open. Inside, a black velvet bag lay on top of what looked like a pile of letters.

Tess poured the contents of the bag into her hand, cool white pearls spilling out into her palm. She lifted them. Double strand with a large blue gem hanging from the center. A blue diamond? Tess wasn't an expert, but she thought that the smaller gems that surrounded it were cushion-cut diamonds.

"Wow!" Gertrude breathed. "Is it paste?"

Tess turned the stone over. "It's an awfully nice setting if it is. Was it Emily's?"

"I never saw her wear it. Where did it come from, Alex?"

"Miriam." He sat on the bed again, his hair flopping over his forehead. He needed a haircut. He also needed his parents, but Tess was beginning to think that maybe she could be enough. Not as much, just . . . enough.

"Now, how would you know a thing like that?" Gertrude lifted the necklace from Tessa's hands, the gems sparkling as she held them up to the light.

"Dad told me."

"If they're real, they're worth a fortune. All this time we've been struggling, and we were sitting on a jackpot," Gertrude crowed.

"No." Alex shook his head.

"They're not real?" Gertrude unhooked the clasp and put the necklace around Tessa's neck.

"They can't leave. Just like my angel." Alex stared at the floor, his fingers tapping a rhythm on his thigh.

"Don't worry, Alex. We'll keep them here and take good care of them." Tess touched his soft hair.

"And my angel."

She wasn't sure if he was asking a question or making a statement, so she answered the best way she could. "As soon as we figure out where it is, we'll never let the angel out of our sight again. I promise."

It was all she could say. After Zim's confession, they'd searched every inch of the house, but there'd been no wrapped box, no angel. Nothing.

Alex walked out of the room.

Seconds later, piano music filled the house.

The angel's song, sad and somehow haunting, as if Alex thought he could call Miriam's creation back home.

"Poor kid. That angel should never have left the house. I guess you're not the only idiot, Tess." Gertrude sighed.

"Thanks," Tess said wryly.

Gertrude laughed, cocking her head to the side and walking to the window. "I think I heard a car pulling up outside. Probably your young man."

"He's not mine," she protested automatically, but the little shiver of excitement she felt said something entirely different.

The doorbell rang, and Tessa's stomach filled with butterflies.

"I'll get it. You just take your time in that dress. What with us being cursed, you don't want to risk falling down the stairs and breaking your neck."

"We're not cursed."

Too late. Gertrude was out in the hall, her crutches tapping the floor.

Tess glanced in the mirror before she walked out of the room. The necklace was beautiful, the pendant falling just above her breasts. She touched the center gem, almost afraid to wear it. If she lost it, Alex would be upset, and she'd feel like crap.

"Tessa, Cade is here!" Gertrude called in a sing-song voice that would have made Tessa's hackles rise if she hadn't been so nervous and excited and generally wound up. All because Cade was there, and she wanted to see him again. She thought that no matter how many times she saw him, it would never be enough. She lifted the heavy skirts enough to shove her feet into two-inch heels, then took a deep, steadying breath.

She felt wobbly as she made her way down the hall. Not because of the shoes or the heavy dress. Her insides were fluttering and her nerves were humming, and she nearly tripped when she saw Cade at the bottom of the stairs.

He looked better than good in a black tuxedo, his shoes shined and his tie nearly a perfect match for her dress.

He walked up as she descended, meeting her on the third step, his eyes deep stormy blue. "You look beautiful," he said.

"I was thinking the same about you," she blurted out.

Cade laughed. "Thanks. I think."

"I guess I should have said handsome."

"Might have saved my masculine ego, but a compliment is a compliment, so I guess I'll take it."

"You two going to talk all night, or get out of here?" Gertrude handed Tessa her coat, and Cade helped her into it, his knuckles brushing her jaw as he adjusted the collar.

She shivered, looking into his eyes, losing herself there again.

"Come on, you two! Move it!" Gertrude held the door open and motioned for them both to leave. "Alex and I have a dinner date, and I don't want to be late because of your lollygagging."

That was the first Tess had heard about a date. She stopped short, eyeing Gertrude. She'd been too busy getting ready to notice before, but there was blush on her aunt's cheeks and mascara on her eyelashes. All of it as tasteful and understated as

Gertrude ever managed to be. Even her lipstick looked classy rather than garish. "What date?"

"Nothing for you to worry about. We're just going next door. Zim wanted to cook us dinner. Kind of an apology meal, if you want to call it that."

"*You* called it a date."

"Figure of speech." Gertrude patted her hair and looked smug.

"Then why do you look like the cat who ate the canary?"

"Because a man is cooking dinner for me, kid. That's enough to make any woman swoon. Now, you two get out of here. I have to get Alex moving, and you know how long that can take when the boy is playing piano." She gave Tessa a less than gentle shove out the door.

Cade stepped out behind her and barely missed being crushed by the closing door.

"Man, she's really in a hurry to have dinner with old Zim. Maybe she's had a stroke and isn't in her right mind. Maybe I should go back in and—"

"She's going to be fine, Tess," Cade said, his hand pressed to her lower back as he urged her to his . . . truck?

No. Not a truck. A Model T Ford.

"Is this from 1925?" she asked, touching the glossy black hood.

"Twenty-six, but you were close." He opened the door and lifted her into the seat, folding her gown around her legs so it wouldn't get stuck in the door. Just that easily. Up and in, and she felt giddy with his scent, the cold air, the adventure of going off to a

Christmas party with a man who used to be the boy she loved.

It was a quick ride to town hall, with Cade telling stories about a renegade rooster and a missing Christmas goose. About a hapless blue-haired lady who'd been chased down Main Street by both.

By the time he parked the car, Tess was laughing so hard, she thought she might split the dress. "That poor woman. I'm surprised she didn't have a heart attack."

"Gladys Moran is way too ornery to have a heart attack just because a couple of barn fowl were chasing her."

"Gladys Moran? As in Mrs. Moran the wood-shop teacher?"

"That's the one."

"She's got to be eighty if she's a day."

"Closing in on ninety, but you wouldn't know it from the way she sprinted down the street. It probably helps that she still runs marathons."

"That seals it. I want to be Gladys when I grow up."

"I *have* noticed you running every morning, and you look a heck of a lot better than poor Ms. Gladys did when she was racing past the police station!" He lifted her from the car, taking her hand as they crossed the parking lot.

She felt like a giddy schoolgirl but better, because she wasn't a silly kid with a crush. She was a grown woman who'd had plenty of experience with men. Or at least enough to know how perfectly wonderful it felt to have Cade's warm calloused palm pressed against hers.

Town hall had been decorated with a subtle hand, strings of white Christmas lights twining around the stair railing. A small Christmas tree stood on the landing, decorated with turn-of-the-century ornaments. Dozens of people milled around in period costumes, faces flushed, eyes glowing.

"You made it!" Ida hurried toward Tess and Cade, resplendent in a high-necked ivory gown. "Hang your coats in the closet. There's hot cider in the kitchen and a live pianist in the meeting hall. We've cleared everything out for dancing! I hope you two know how to waltz!"

"Do you?" Cade asked, helping Tessa out of her coat and hanging it up.

"I've gone a few rounds. How about you?"

"I'm not Fred Astaire, but how about we give it a whirl anyway?" He tugged Tess into the meeting hall.

Several couples were already there. Old high school friends that hadn't changed all that much since Tess had last seen them. The Murphys were there, too, Kristen's head resting on Larry's chest as they swayed to the music.

Tessa's throat tightened as she watched. Unlike her parents, the Murphys seemed to know what mattered. They'd been devoted to each other for years and would continue to be forever.

That was what Tess used to dream of. A fantasy. Fairy tale. Happily ever after. It took a lot more than dreams to make something like that work, though. It took two people who were willing to be everything to one another.

"Have I told you," Cade murmured as he led Tess

deeper into the room and began the slow, flowing steps of the waltz, "how beautiful you are?"

"I think you might have," she responded.

"Then I hope you won't mind me saying it again." His lips brushed her forehead. So much more romantic than if he'd simply kissed her lips, because of the sweetness in the gesture. The tenderness of it.

Not that a kiss wouldn't have been nice, too.

Her hands moved of their own accord, sliding under his jacket so that she could feel his warmth through thin cotton.

People were watching, and she didn't care. This was her fantasy, dancing with Cade while soft music played.

"This is nice," she whispered, her fingers trailing along his waistband.

"It is, and I'm wondering why it took us so long to get here."

"You were a little preoccupied when we were kids." Oops! Too much information. Now was not the time for a jaunt down memory lane. Not when she was so cozy and comfortable in Cade's arms.

"Will you ever forgive me for that, Tess?" he asked, touching the pendant, his fingers skimming across flesh as his hand dropped away.

"There's nothing to forgive. I was glad that you and Emily were together," she lied, her skin burning where his fingers had been.

"You really shouldn't make a habit of lying. You're not good at it." He had the nerve to sound amused.

"What do you want me to say, Cade? That I was

crushed? That you broke my heart, and that I never got over you?"

"What I want you to say is that you don't hold my stupidity against me," he replied, and she realized that they weren't dancing anymore, and that half the people in the room were staring at them.

Great.

So much for a beautiful night.

"I'm going to get some cider. Want me to bring you some?" she asked loudly enough for everyone to hear. God forbid, they think she and Cade had broken up before they'd ever really gotten together.

"What I want—"

"Sheriff!" A plump blonde with overflowing breasts and enough Botox in her forehead to para-lyze a dozen faces grabbed Cade's arm. "I was hoping you'd be here."

Tess left the two on the dance floor, her heart galloping so fast she thought it would leap from her chest.

She slipped into the kitchen, smiling at a middle-aged woman who was manning a cider bowl. She took the cup she was handed and walked out the back exit.

Gardens stretched out for several acres, Christmas lights strung from every tree and bush. Piano music drifted from speakers attached to the back porch and lazy flakes of snow drifted through the darkness.

Home, Tessa's heart seemed to say, and she put her hand to her chest, trying to push away the long-ing she felt. For family and love, for a place to settle and grow. Not in business or achievement but in the things that would last when she was old and gray.

She followed the line of hedges, knowing that at the end of it she'd find a bench. There. Just as she'd thought it would be, it sat in the shadow of a large maple, white lights hanging above it.

Footsteps crunched on the grass behind her, but Tess didn't turn. She knew Cade was there. She felt his energy flowing into her, her soul responding with the same deep longing her heart felt when she looked at Christmas lights and snowflakes.

"It's too cold to be out without a coat," Cade said gently, wrapping her in her coat, his knuckles brushing her jaw.

"I thought you were dancing with Boobs and Botox."

He chuckled, pulling her into his arms, moving into the same easy waltz they'd danced before. "I don't want to dance with anyone but you."

"For tonight, I think I like that."

"Just tonight? I was thinking we could repeat this. Many, many times in the future."

She wasn't sure if he meant it. Didn't know if anything said under snowflakes and Christmas lights could last, but maybe she wasn't as much of an idiot as Gertrude said, because Tess just slid her hands beneath Cade's jacket, rested her head on his chest, and picked right up where they'd left off.

And, man, it felt good.

They danced until the snow fell in earnest and Tess was shivering so hard her teeth chattered, and she still didn't want it to end. Not then. Not tomorrow. Not even after fifty years.

"You're cold. We need to go back in." Cade clasped her hand and started walking back, and she thought that if she missed this opportunity there might never be another one.

"I can think of other ways to warm up," she responded.

Cade stopped short, his handed tightening. "I'm not a one-night-stand kind of guy, Tess. Not with you. So if that's what you want, let's skip it."

"Isn't that supposed to be the woman's line?" Her throat was dry and tight, her heart racing, because she wasn't a one-night-stand kind of girl, but she'd have made an exception with Cade. She wanted to tell him that, but he released her hand, his expression hard.

"That's a sexist thing to say. I thought you were better than that," he growled, and she could see in his eyes that she'd hurt him, realized just a little too late that this wasn't a game Cade was playing, a split-second thought that he'd had. All the things he'd said about choosing the wrong sister and being an idiot, he'd meant them.

He disappeared into the house, apparently as disgusted with Tess as she was with herself. Was she so much of a chicken that she couldn't at least try to have the things she wanted?

Even fickle, flighty Emily had done that. Despite all her faults, she'd loved Dave, and she'd stayed in love with him for ten years. Never wavering from it. Even when the two went through tough times.

Funny . . . or not . . . that Tess had had her life together, her career worked out, her finances in order. She'd had her house in the city, her car, everything that anyone standing on the outside and looking in would probably say made her successful.

But she was letting a man she'd loved forever walk away.

Idiot. . . .

She could almost hear Gertrude's voice, hear Emily's laughter floating in the snowy air.

Tess had never been a fool.

Now wasn't the time to start.

She picked up the long, heavy layers of her skirts and hurried across the snow-dusted yard.

Chapter Twenty-Three

Boobs and Botox purred against Cade's chest, and it was all he could do not to politely disengage her arms and tell her the dance was over.

He was at the party. He was going to enjoy himself. With or without Tess. Just thinking about her idiotic comment boiled his blood. He wanted forever. Not a roll in the hay or a couple of nights' fun. If she didn't want the same—

"What do you think, Sheriff?" Botox sighed. "Shall we do this again? Or shall we dance our way out the door and over to my place?"

"Look, B—" He stopped the word just in time. What was her name? Betty? Cathy? She was a transplant to the town, worked in the bank and loved men in uniform. That's all Cade knew about her, because it was all he'd wanted to know. "I'm not interested."

"How do you know unless you give it a try? As a matter of fact, you take me home, and I think we can find out just exactly how interested you might be," she murmured.

Okay. Enough. One dance, because he was pissed off and wanted to make sure Tess knew he wasn't standing around thinking about her. But having an overripe and overeager woman pressing herself against him . . .

Nope.

Done.

He extracted himself from her grasping hands. "Thanks for the dance."

"But the song hasn't even ended," she said, pouting and reaching for him again.

"Can I cut in?" Tess stepped between them, her violet eyes dark, her hair and coat dusted with snow. She was trembling, her teeth chattering, near frozen, and all his anger melted away. He wrapped his jacket around her shoulders, and somehow Botox was gone, and Tess was in his arms again.

"Thanks," he murmured against hair that smelled of winter snow and Tess. God, she smelled good.

"Consider it my way of apologizing."

"Apology accepted." He pulled her closer, his hands resting on her back. "So, what happened? Did you decide it was too cold to hide outside?"

"I wasn't hiding. I was taking some time to think."

"And?"

"I thought I was an idiot. So I came inside to claim my prize for getting the answer correct. You're it." Her palms settled on his chest, and she smiled a Cheshire-cat smile that made Cade's gut tighten.

"I've never been someone's prize before." He spun her around, waltzing her toward the hallway, because there was no way he planned to spend the rest of the night whirling around town hall with Tess.

He had more interesting things in mind. "But I like it," he murmured, brushing his lips over hers.

It wasn't enough. Not even close. "How about we get out of here? Go get some dinner?"

"Dressed like this?" She plucked her velvety skirts.

"I was thinking we could go to my place. I cook."

"Food that's edible?"

"Does it matter?"

She studied him for a moment, then squeezed his hand. "You know what? I don't think it does."

"So, let's—"

The door flew open, crashing into the wall with a bang that was loud enough to silence everyone except the pianist.

Zim ran into the foyer. No coat. His hair standing up around his head.

"He's gone!" he shouted, his eyes wide with fear.

He spotted Cade and Tess, knocked into three blue-haired ladies in his haste to get to them. "Now the old battle-ax is hopping up and down the street on her crutches screaming his name. They're both going to die in this weather! We've got to—"

"Slow down, Zim." Ida stepped through the crowd. "No one can understand when you're sputtering like that."

"The boy is gone! Walked right out of the house while Gertrude and I were playing canasta. Could have been gone more than a half hour before we realized he was missing."

A murmur of concern echoed through the foyer, people pressing in close to hear.

"Did you call it in?" Cade asked, pulling out his cell phone, dialing the office as Zim babbled about a police officer working too slow and Gertrude still out in the snow without a coat.

"I need to go find him." Tess darted for the door, but Cade snagged her arm, holding tight when she tried to pull away.

"Wait," he mouthed as Emma filled him in on what she knew. Max and Jackson were at the scene. So was Doug Fairweather, a nearly retired deputy who'd entered law enforcement before Cade was born. "Tell them I'm on my way, and ask Max to get Gertrude back inside. Forcefully if he has to."

"Will do. You want me to call in anyone else?" Emily asked.

"No." Cade glanced around the crowded foyer. "I think we'll have the manpower we need." He ended the call, finally giving in to Tess's relentless tug.

He didn't know how she managed, but she ran to his car. No worries about snow or heels or long skirts, she sprinted like a woman set to win the hundred-meter dash. He sprinted beside her, pumped up on adrenaline and fear. The temperature had already dipped below freezing, snow falling so thick and heavy visibility was reduced to nearly zero. The wiper on the Ford could barely keep up with the mess.

Idiotic choice for a ride.

"Can't this thing go any faster?" Tessa asked as they got under way, leaning so far forward her head was touching the front window.

"It could, but I don't think that getting into an accident is going to help Alex."

"Sorry." She wiped her palm along her skirts, and Cade grabbed her hand, holding tight as he eased down Main Street. No sign of Alex. Damn it. And the weather was getting worse.

There were three police cars parked in front of the Riley house and several people were standing in the yard when Cade pulled up to the curb. Neighbors, from the look of things. Doug waved Cade over, his bald head gleaming in the street light.

"Glad you're here, Sheriff. Maxwell is heading east on Main. Jackson is going west. So far, no sign of the boy. Fortunately, we have some volunteers who are willing to help." He gestured to the half dozen people huddled nearby. "We need to find Alex ASAP. The weather is only going to get worse."

"Where's Gertrude?" Tess whirled one way and another, her body so tense and tightly wound that Cade thought she might break.

"Looking for your nephew. I tried to get her to go inside and wait, but she wanted none of it. She didn't even have a coat on."

"I need to find them." Tess raced into the house.

Following her wouldn't help Alex, but damn if Cade didn't want to.

"Did you find tracks?" he asked. That would make things a lot easier. Though, with the rate of snowfall, any footprints would be covered quickly.

"None. Makes me think the boy left before the snow started falling."

"We're talking forty-five minutes or more."

"Yes."

"Shit," Cade muttered. "That's a long time. Did Gertrude have any idea where he might have gone?"

"She wasn't here when we arrived. I spoke to Zim. He said that the boy might have gone looking for that angel. He was talking about it all night, asking Gertrude if they could go see it. She finally got fed up and told him to watch some PBS piano concert. No wonder the poor kid ran away."

That was about no help at all, but it was all Cade had. He grabbed his heavy coat and the emergency kit he kept in the backseat of the Ford. Boots. Gloves. Thick socks. Food. Blankets. The kind of thing any Northwesterner packed during the winter.

Took about two minutes to chuck the fancy dress shoes and get into warmer gear. Each minute felt like a lifetime. He walked across Tessa's yard, snow swirling. No wind. Thank God. That might keep Alex alive for a little longer.

"Sheriff?" Matthew Jones called, breaking away from the group still standing in the Rileys' yard. A teacher at the elementary school, he lived a few houses down and had a young son of his own. "My old coon hound, Bailey, might be able to track the boy. Want me to give it a try?"

"It can't hurt. I'm going to start searching. Doug, you organize everything from this end. Radio in if he turns up. I'll do the same."

A wild shriek filled the air, and Cade swung toward the street. A shadowy figure was moving through the snow. Maybe two hundred yards out. No details visible, but Cade recognized the enraged scream.

Gertrude.

Had to be. No other woman could nearly break the sound barrier with her voice.

"Put me down, you bullheaded son of a—"

"Don't insult my mother, or I'll toss your scrawny behind right back into the snow!" Max responded, and from the tone of his voice, Cade would say the guy had lost every bit of patience he had. Cade grabbed a flashlight from the kit.

He didn't have time to deal with Gertrude and Max.

Time was ticking, the temperature was dropping, and Alex's chances of survival were diminishing.

"Let me go, you bastard! I have to find my nephew before the curse takes him from me!"

"What the hell are you talking about, lady?"

"Just put me down and let me do what I have to!"

"On crutches? With a broken leg? Without a coat? Curse or no curse, you have more sense than that, Gertrude." Max's tone had gentled, but Gertrude wasn't placated.

She shouted a string of profanity that would have made a sailor blush.

Cade moved toward the pair, finally seeing them clearly as he drew nearer. Max moved along at a slow jog, Gertrude hanging like a sack of potatoes over his shoulder.

"All you're doing is wasting my time, old lady. If I hadn't had to drag your butt back here, I could be looking for the kid instead of hauling ass back to your place. Hey, boss." He nodded in Cade's direction but didn't stop.

Good.

Gertrude was safe.

Now . . . Alex.

If Zim was right, he'd gone to find the angel, but no one knew where the angel was. So where would a kid like Alex think an angel would be? Where would *any* kid think an angel would be?

Church?

Alex liked to spend time there. Cade knew that for sure. It was a starting point. He turned toward the town center, sounds fading as he hurried up Main Street. A line of cars crept along the icy road, lights splashing on the snow-coated pavement. Looked like most of the town was heading toward him.

The lead car slowed, the driver's window opening. "Any sign of him?" Larry Murphy called.

"Not yet."

"You want us to check in with someone or just split up to search?"

"Doug is at the Riley place. Check in there. He's organizing the search efforts," Cade responded, not slowing his pace. Snow crunched beneath his feet and stuck to the trees and bushes. A heavy, wet snow. Great for building snowmen or for burying a hypothermic child. He kicked at a few piles of snow, uncovering rocks and piles of dirt, but no little boy.

He could see his breath in the air, feel the cold seeping through his thick coat and tuxedo jacket, and he hoped that Alex had bundled up well like he had the last time he'd gone searching for the angel.

"Cade!" Tessa panted up beside him, her head covered by a black knit hat. No hood, and her coat didn't look heavy enough for the weather. She wore gloves at least. And boots. But Cade thought she'd be shivering within thirty minutes.

"You need to go back home, Tess." He kept moving forward, his pace slow enough to search the underbrush and yards. Painfully slow, but there was no other way to be but methodical.

"Not until we find Alex." She wiped her face, and he knew she was crying. Wanted to stop and pull her into his arms, tell her that everything would be okay, but they were short on time, the temperature dropping, and every second counted.

"Go back home, okay? Gertrude needs you with her."

"Gertrude is in Zim's truck, heading toward the edge of town." She swiped at her face again, inhaling a deep, shuddering breath. "God, I hope he didn't head that way. The houses are so far apart, and the Miller farm is there. A hundred acres of nothing before he even gets to the old farmhouse. He could fall and—"

"Don't."

"How can I not?"

"Because you have more important things to do." He kicked snow from a heap near the edge of someone's driveway. A pile of frozen leaves emerged.

"Can we move any faster?" Tess tugged his arm, trying to draw him away from the next pile of snow.

"Not unless we want to miss something important."

"Miss *him*, you mean? Do you think he's already . . . ?" Her voice trailed off. "Gertrude said that he was geared up for the weather when he went to Zim's house. He took all the gear with him when he left. I'm sure he's bundled up. Just like he was last time. He's a smart kid."

Smart wouldn't keep him warm.

Cade didn't say that. No sense in upsetting Tess more than she already was. Besides, she knew. The best cold gear in the world couldn't keep a person warm forever.

Her palm slid from his arm to his hand, her gloved fingers weaving through his. "We have to find him soon, Cade. He's just a little boy, and—"

"We will. If we don't, someone else will. Most of the town is out looking. That's a lot of people."

"But Alex doesn't like strangers. You know that. What if he sees people looking and hides? What if he's afraid to come home because he thinks Gertrude will take away his piano privileges again? What if—"

"Call his name, Tess. He'll answer you if he's nearby," he suggested, because she was going to make herself crazy with conjecture, and because Alex *would* come if he heard Tess call.

"Alex!" she shouted, his name swallowed up by the snow and the darkness. She called again and again and again as they made their way toward the town center. Behind them, other people were calling Alex's name, the muted sounds echoing Tessa's frantic cries. Her voice grew hoarse, but she kept calling as they reached Riley Park.

"You don't think he went to the pond, do you?" Tess asked, her voice brittle with fear.

"He's never shown any interest in it before. The only thing he's ever seemed to be really excited about—"

"The piano!" Tess shouted and took off running.

Chapter Twenty-Four

Tessa raced across the park, the church lights beckoning through the heavy snowfall.

Please, please, please.

Her desperate thoughts matched the pounding of her heart and the slap of her feet on snow-covered grass.

Let him be there.

Just let him.

She stumbled up the steep hill that led to the church, sliding onto her knees in frozen muck. Not realizing Cade was behind her until he grabbed her shoulder, stopping her downward momentum.

"You okay?"

"Fine. But I wish we'd taken the car," she said, panting. She righted herself and headed back up the hill again.

"I was afraid we'd miss him if we were driving. I figured if he was on his way to the church, we'd meet up with him before he made it there."

If.

Such a little word, but it packed a hell of a lot of power. *If* he was there. Good. *If* he wasn't . . .

Where would they look next?

She crested the hill, nearly slipping again as she ran to the church doors. She heard the piano music before she opened the door, and her heart skipped a beat as she rushed into the vestibule.

It could have been anyone playing, but she knew before she saw Alex's red-gold hair and narrow shoulders that it was him.

"Alex!" she called, tumbling all over herself in her hurry to get to him. She didn't care that Cade was behind her or that Alex didn't really like to be hugged. She didn't even care that she was cold and tired and half-near infuriated because Alex had scared a dozen or more years off her life. All she cared about was getting to him, grabbing him up off the piano bench and dragging him into her arms. "You scared me to death!"

He wiggled in her embrace, but she couldn't seem to get her arms to cooperate and let him go.

"Give the kid some air, Tess. You don't want to smother him to death."

Right.

She didn't.

She didn't want to release him, either.

Finally, Alex had had enough. He pushed at her arms, scuffing his feet on the wood floor.

"Are you okay?" She crouched in front of him, touching his cheek. It was warm. He was warm. He'd been there for a while, his hair sticking up but dry, his coat hanging open. His feet were bare, his toes pink. "Where are your shoes?"

"There." He pointed to the vestibule, and she saw his snow boots sitting in a puddle.

Hers were dripping all over the wood.

Smart kid, but he'd nearly gotten himself killed. All for the sake of a porcelain angel.

"You said you were never going to do this again, Alex. You promised, remember?" The words were louder than she'd intended, nearly drowning out Cade's soft murmur. He was on his cell phone, reporting that Alex had been found, and she was glad that he was distracted, because she was crying again, tears just sliding down her cheeks completely unchecked.

She sniffed them back, and Alex looked up, frowning at her through Emily's eyes and his own oddly adult face.

"It's okay," he said, brushing his hands down her cheeks, the gesture awkward and sweet.

"It wouldn't have been if you got hurt, or worse."

"I needed my angel."

"We don't know where it is." She sighed, exasperated and upset, because until the angel was back, she knew Alex would keep wandering.

"*I* know," he responded.

"Oh, Alex." She didn't even know how to respond to that. When he got an idea in his head, it just seemed to never leave. "Get your boots on. Let's go home."

"Max is coming to pick us up. He'll be here in about ten minutes," Cade said. He put his hand on Alex's shoulder, bending down so they would have been eye to eye if Alex hadn't been staring at the floor. "You can't do this again, Alex. You could be hurt. So could any of the people who have to go looking for you when you run off. Do you understand?"

"Yes," Alex mumbled.

"Good, because if this happens again . . ." Cade's voice trailed off. Obviously he was at a loss, too. What kind of threat would be effective for Alex? Was it even fair to make one?

"Go put your boots on, Alex," Tess repeated wearily, dropping into a pew and rubbing the bridge of her nose. This had gone too far. They were going to have to get some professional help. A psychologist or something. Someone who knew a lot more than Tess did about parenting atypical kids. Because obviously *she* had no frigging *clue* what she was doing.

He walked away. Not toward the vestibule and his boots. Toward the piano.

"Alex—"

"He's already here. What can it hurt to let him play until Max shows up?" Cade sat beside her, as weary, it seemed, as she was.

"He needs to be punished. Or . . . something," she said lamely, and he grinned, his hair wet from snow, his cheeks ruddy. So handsome, so wonderfully familiar, so *Cade* that it nearly hurt to look at him.

"It's good that you're clear on your plan," he commented as Alex began to play.

"It's not funny, Cade." To her horror, her voice broke and tears started rolling again, all hot and sticky on top of her already hot and sticky cheeks. Damn! Years of never crying, and now she couldn't seem to do anything *but* cry.

"It's not the end of the world, either," he said gently, pulling her into his arms and pressing her head to his chest.

"But I don't even know what to do with him!" she wailed.

"Sure you do. You love him. Anything else . . . we can figure out together."

Together . . . ?

Oh, man, she liked the sound of that.

Hearing it made the tears fall harder, because she'd returned to Apple Valley looking for nothing, wanting nothing. She'd found home. In the house her sister had left her, the town she'd thought she despised.

In Cade's arms.

"Don't cry, Tess," he murmured. "It breaks my heart when you do."

Not just words, she thought. Truth, and they touched that place in her heart that she tried so hard to hold back from everyone. Filled that spot that had been empty for so long, she'd thought it could never be filled.

"I've always loved you, Cade Cunningham," she whispered, something about the peaceful church and the dim lights and the soft music making the revelation seem just right.

He stilled, and she thought maybe she'd been wrong to say the words, to put it out there between them. She wouldn't take them back, though. Not even if she could.

He tilted her chin, looked into her eyes, studying her face as if all the secrets of the universe were in it. "Have you?"

"Yes." She swallowed down words and explanations and the need to tell him that he didn't have to return the feeling. Yes was enough, because it was the simple truth. And right then, in that place, with Alex's gentle song playing, that was plenty.

"Even when I beat you at street hockey?"

"You never beat me!" she protested, and he chuckled, pulling her back into his arms so that she could feel the rumble of his laughter deep in her soul.

"We'll have to have a rematch to decide who's telling the truth," he finally said.

"Will we?"

"Of course. I can't have the woman I love hanging her supposed victories over my head for the rest of my life."

"Cade, you don't—" *Have to say you love me because I said I love you*, she wanted to say, but he cut her off.

"There's love and there's *love*, Tess. You know that?" He cupped her face, the warmth of his palms searing through her. "The kind that is meant for a season and the kind that is meant for forever. Everyone has a chance at the first, but not everyone gets a chance at the second. I've had two chances. Once when we were kids, and I was too stupid to see what was right in front of my face. I'm not stupid anymore, and I'm not going to pass my chance up this time. You mean too much to me."

He kissed her then, gently, softly. Like the song drifting through the chapel, like the snow falling from the deep gray sky. Like sunrise and sunset. A slow revelation, a sweet unveiling.

And, God, she wanted more. She wanted forever.

The chapel doors flew open and cold air swept in.

Cade eased back, his eyes blazing, his hands gentle as he pulled her to her feet.

Max hurried toward them. He wasn't alone. Dozens

of people spilled into the church behind him. Ida. The Murphys. Charlotte. Jethro and Natalie. People from the party, dressed in Victorian garb, bundled up against the cold, their eyes wide with excitement and relief. Blue-haired ladies and old high school friends, and Alex's music still drifting in the air.

"I tried to tell everyone to go home," Max growled, glancing over his shoulder and scowling. "They wouldn't listen."

"Why should we have?" Ida asked. "The boy has been found, and we've all been out looking. It's good to see that he's fine." She settled into a pew, tucking her big skirts around her legs. Everyone else took her cue, filling the pews, pressing in close to one another.

Alex's music soared, the sweet song he'd been playing changing into a medley of Christmas carols.

"The kid can play," Max conceded. "I'll give him that."

"Shhhhh!" Ida demanded, grabbing his hand and yanking him into the pew beside her, the murmur of the crowd slowly fading.

The chapel door flew open again, and Gertrude hobbled in.

"Alex," she cried, and it was the sound of every parent who'd ever lost a child and found him again. Tess stood, her heart filling for this woman who'd tried her best.

Alex stopped playing, his hands slack on the keys for several seconds as Gertrude made her way down the aisle, Zim close on her heels.

She dropped her crutches beside the piano, falling to her knees and dragging Alex into her arms.

"What were you thinking, boy? What in God's

name were you thinking?" She sobbed, crying like
Tess had never seen her cry before. She reached
blindly, grabbing Tessa's hand and pulling her into
the embrace. Their little family reunited.

Alex wiggled away from Gertrude, patting her old
lined face.

"Look," he said and pulled the piano bench away
from the piano, dropping to his hands and knees
near the foot pedals. He touched one of the swirling
vines that wrapped its way up the piano, his fingers
sliding into the center of one of the flowers. A crack
appeared. Tess could hear people standing and
moving closer, but she didn't look away as Alex slid
his fingers into the crevice and pulled off a panel of
wood. A foot square, it had been carefully crafted
out of thick wood. Alex reached into the hole it
revealed and pulled out a box messily wrapped in
silvery paper.

He handed it to Gertrude.

Someone gasped, and old Zim sputtered, moving
closer, his face ruddy with excitement. "It's the
angel."

"How can it be, you old fool?" Gertrude snapped,
but her hands were trembling as she folded back the
paper.

A shoe box was inside, and she raised the lid, her
face paling as she looked.

"It is," she whispered, carefully lifting the angel.
The box dropped to the floor, something fluttering
out as it landed.

A feather. Snow white and beautiful.

Tess picked it up, held it as the crowd murmured
and old Zim sputtered, and Gertrude asked Alex
how the angel had come to be in the piano.

"I found her under the tree. I put her there," he said simply. "To keep her safe. She's safe now." He put the panel back on the piano, pulled the bench back over and sat. Oblivious to the crowd, to the excitement he'd stirred up. Oblivious to everything but the music that must always be playing in his head and that he poured out onto the keys. The gentle song he'd played before, sweet and beautiful.

People drifted back to the pews.

But Tessa stood rooted in place, listening to Alex's song, the feather silky in her hand.

Cade's arm wrapped around her waist, his fingers splayed across her ribs. He leaned close, his breath warm on her cheek. "We should sit down."

She nodded, letting him lead her to the pew where Gertrude sat, one hand clutching the angel, the other tucked in the crook of Zim's elbow.

She looked dazed but content.

She smiled at Tess, her face caving into dozens of wrinkles. "No more curse," she whispered.

Tess didn't say there had never been one. The song was too beautiful, the night too special to ruin it by arguing. She patted Gertrude's knee and was surprised when Gertrude clung to her hand for a moment, looked straight into her eyes.

"You were always my favorite, Tess. Didn't seem like it, because I had to be hard on you to make sure you didn't turn out like that no-good sister of mine." She swallowed and looked away. "I always felt kind of bad about loving you so much. A mother . . . she shouldn't have favorites, right?"

True? Not?

It didn't matter anymore.

Emily was gone, and Tess was where she'd always belonged.

"It's okay," she said, the feather light and strangely warm in her hand.

"Where'd that come from?" Cade asked, touching its edges, his finger sliding along her palm and then up her wrist. There was a promise in that touch, and she shivered.

"It fell out of the box when Gertrude dropped it. Zim must have put it in there."

"No." Zim shook his head. "The only thing I put in that box was the angel."

"Then Alex must have," she said.

"Where would he get a feather?" Gertrude asked, taking it from Tessa's hand and studying it. "Not any kind of feather I've ever seen. Bet Miriam put it there."

"Oh, come on," Tess said, sighing.

"Sure as I'm sitting right here, that's where it must have come from. This is no ordinary feather. It's from an angel's wing."

If they hadn't been sitting in church, Tess would have laughed out loud. Instead, she snatched the feather back. "Don't start, Gertrude."

"Don't start what? I'm telling you there are things in this world we don't understand. Things a mind too filled up with facts to be reasonable just doesn't comprehend."

"Are you saying—"

"Be quiet. We're in church," Zim growled. "That's no place for arguing. Besides, I want to hear the boy play."

Gertrude scowled but subsided.

"Looks like things are back to normal with old

Gertrude," Cade whispered in Tessa's ear, and she could hear the laughter in his voice.

She smiled into his eyes, felt her heart responding to the warmth she found there.

God, she loved him!

Alex's song slowed, each note sweet and lovely. Feathers on a summer breeze.

Tess frowned, fingering the feather.

From an angel's wing?

Ha!

But she had to admit, it was the prettiest feather she'd ever seen. She tucked it deep into her coat pocket.

Finally, the notes faded into silence. No one moved. No one spoke. Alex stood, shuffling to Tess and Gertrude, his head down, his hair falling over his eyes.

"It's time to go home," he said.

"You're right," Tess responded, taking his hand and holding Cade's and walking down the aisle with both of them. Gertrude and Zim followed.

People sniffed and sobbed, and Tess was pretty sure someone snapped a photo. No doubt they'd be on the front page of the morning newspaper, but she didn't mind. In Apple Valley people cared about the little things, the quiet things, the things that were easy to miss if one didn't look carefully enough.

And, she decided, that's exactly the kind of place she wanted to be.

"You're smiling," Cade said as they stepped outside.

"Because I finally know what it means to be home," she responded simply.

"Took you long enough to figure it out." He

smiled, kissing her forehead, her lips. "What do you say we put Alex in the car with Zim and Gertrude and walk to my place?"

"It's freezing!" she said, but she could see hundreds of Christmas lights sparkling in the park, and the snow was beautiful against the sky, and she thought that maybe a walk wouldn't be so bad. Not if the person she was walking with was Cade.

"True," he whispered against her ear. "But I can think of plenty of ways we can warm each other up once we get there."

"I like the way you think." She laughed, then helped Alex into Zim's car, buckling his seat belt, saying good night to Gertrude.

Then she took Cade's hand and they walked toward town, fat snowflakes drifting like angel feathers on the cold night air.

**Please turn the page
for an exciting sneak peek of
Shirlee McCoy's next Apple Valley romance,**

THE COTTAGE ON THE CORNER,

coming soon from Kensington Publishing!

November 27th.

The worst day of the year.

The worst day of *her* year, anyway.

Usually Charlotte Garrison spent it with a box of tissue and a bagful of mini Reese's. If she were feeling particularly sappy, she'd rent a romantic movie and watch it on her two-decade-old TV.

No need for that today.

She had a real live romance to watch.

Cade Cunningham and Tessa McKenzie's wedding was the most talked about event in Apple Valley, Washington, since Miriam and Daniel Riley had married over a hundred years before. The happy couple had asked Charlotte to make the wedding cake. If she hadn't loved them both so much, she'd have said no. But, she did.

That was Charlotte's problem. One of her *many* problems. She loved the people in her life, and she'd do anything for them. As long as it wasn't illegal or immoral. Which . . . when it had come to her husband . . . had proven to be a problem.

"Do not even go there," she murmured.

The nineteen-year-old kid working salad prep at the counter a few feet away smiled quizzically.

"What?" he asked.

"Nothing." She placed the last sugar flower on the five-tier cake. White on white to go along with the Victorian Christmas theme that Tessa had chosen for the wedding. The cake was beautiful, every flower sparkling with shimmery powder. Anemone for unfading love. Bluebells for constancy. Lavender for devotion. Violet for faithfulness.

Such fanciful Victorian ideas.

She'd have snorted, but town hall's oversized kitchen was nearly bursting at the seams with people preparing Tess and Cade's catered buffet. The last thing she wanted to do was give any of them reason to talk about her.

Not that people weren't *already* talking.

Charlotte and Cade had dated a few weeks after she'd moved to Apple Valley. It had been a moment of weakness on her part. She'd been new to the area and wavering in her conviction that being single was the best thing a woman could ever do for herself. Cade had asked her to dinner. She'd said yes.

Two very nice dates later, they'd decided that they'd be better suited as friends than lovers. That had worked out well, considering that Tessa had returned to Apple Valley to care for her nephew Alex. There'd been no doubt the two were meant to be together. Charlotte had been thrilled when Cade had asked her opinion on the engagement ring he'd bought for Tessa. She'd been overjoyed to hear that that Tessa had said "yes."

That's not what the blue-haired ladies at the diner were saying, though.

According to them, Charlotte was pining with love for the town's handsome sheriff. Half of them probably expected that she'd poisoned the cake. It would be interesting to see how many actually ate a piece of the confection.

Not that Charlotte planned to stick around to find out.

She'd get the scoop from Tessa's aunt Gertrude later in the week.

Tonight, she was going to roll the cake out into the reception hall and hightail it back to her little house. She'd park herself on the loveseat she'd bought from Tessa's antique store, read a book, eat Reese's, and wait for the twenty-seventh to turn into the twenty-eighth.

"That cake about done, doll?" Gertrude McKenzie walked into the kitchen, her bright orange hair curled to within an inch of its life. Forty minutes ago, she'd walked Tessa down the aisle, her sturdy white shoes peeking out from beneath a floor-length pink skirt, her face softer than Charlotte had ever seen it. Now, she looked ready to party, the Victorian-style gown she'd worn to the ceremony exchanged for a short fuchsia dress that hit just above her knobby knees. "'Cause the crowd has eaten every one of those fancy appetizers Rylie made, and we're about ready to move into the reception hall."

"I just finished," Charlotte replied, stepping aside so Gertrude could see the cake.

"Wow!" she said. "Just . . . wow! You've outdone yourself, Charlie."

"Think they'll like it?"

"Like it?" Gertrude exclaimed. "They're going to love it! Come on, let's get it out there. Tessa is insisting on tossing the bouquet before we eat. You don't want to miss that."

Actually, she did.

The last thing she wanted to do was stand in a crowd of clawing jostling women—all of them bent on being the next Mrs. Somebody. Been there. Done that. Had the heartache to prove it.

She rolled the cake into the reception hall. Tables had been set up, a fire stoked in the oversized fireplace. Still a month out from Christmas, but the place had been decorated with white Christmas lights and pine boughs, each of the twenty tables set with ivory linens, white candles, and a single pink rose.

"Right over here, Charlie!" event planner Martha Anderson-Randolph called. Thirty with a fake smile and perfectly highlighted hair, she'd married Henderson Randolph the year she'd turned twenty-five. He'd been ninety and, according to people who'd been in Apple Valley back then, had died trying to keep up with his young bride.

Martha had inherited a million dollars, a house, and forty acres just outside of town. Charlotte could have done a lot with an inheritance like that. Purchased a storefront, bought new baking equipment, put new windows in her house.

Martha had apparently spent her money on clothes, cars, and brand-new double-Ds. Now, she was on the hunt again. The sapphire blue dress she'd squeezed her curves into was designed to let every man in the vicinity know it.

Charlotte pushed the cake to the spot Martha indicated.

"Perfect," Martha cooed. "Just perfect."

"Thank yo—"

"This event will be the talk of the town for generations to come," Martha cut her off. Apparently, it wasn't Charlotte's cake she thought was perfect. "I can't believe that I've pulled it off."

"You're a one-woman marvel, Martha," Charlotte replied without even a hint of sarcasm in her voice.

Martha's eyes narrowed, her Botox-filled forehead nearly rupturing with the need to wrinkle into dozens of frown lines. "What's that supposed to mean?"

"Just that the reception hall looks lovely. The historical society did a great job decorating it last night." Led by Cade's grandmother, Ida Cunningham, the committee had cleaned and polished the tables the local boys' club had brought in, set up the chairs, put out the decorations. They'd been there for hours while Charlotte worked in the kitchen.

As far as Charlotte knew, all Martha had done was stand in the corner barking orders.

She decided against pointing that out.

"Under *my* direction," Martha huffed, her sleek chignon vibrating with the force of her indignation. "My design ideas. My sense of style."

"It's lovely," Charlotte conceded. Mostly because she didn't want to rile the woman up during Tess and Cade's wedding.

"I'm glad we see things the same way." Martha glanced at her gold watch. "I'd better get people moving in this direction. We're on a pretty tight schedule."

Charlotte wasn't sure what schedule that was. Cade and Tessa weren't planning to honeymoon until Tessa's nephew Alex's spring break. The wedding reception would probably go on into the wee hours of the morning.

Charlotte would be sound asleep by then.

Hopefully.

She hadn't been sleeping well the last few weeks. This time of year, she never did. Too many memories. Some of them wonderful. Some of them not. All of them tainted by what Brett had done.

She grabbed her coat from the closet near the front door and slipped outside before any of the wedding guests made it into the reception hall. It was quiet there, everyone who was anyone in the community inside with the bride and groom. She'd parked at the far edge of the lot, her old station wagon squeezed in between a snazzy sports car and a Toyota sedan. She hurried to it, trying to swallow down the hard lump of sadness in her throat. It didn't matter how much she told herself he didn't deserve it, she always spent the anniversary of Brett's death on the verge of tears.

"Charlotte! Hold up!" someone shouted.

She kept right on going, because she knew the voice and had no intention of stopping to chat with Max Stanford. Not when she was so close to tears.

"I know you heard me," he called. "And, since you're not nearly as rude as I am, you may as well stop. If you don't, you'll spend the rest of the night feeling guilty for not doing it."

She hesitated with her hand on the station wagon door.

Darn the man for being right.

She *wasn't* rude, and she didn't make a habit of ignoring people.

There was a first time for everything, though, and this was going to be it.

She unlocked the station wagon and slid behind the wheel.

Max grabbed the door before she could close it, bending down so they were eye to eye. He had midnight blue irises, thick golden lashes, and the kind of movie-star-handsome face that made women swoon.

"Maybe I was wrong about your capacity for rudeness, Charlotte," he said dryly.

"What do you want, Max?" she asked. Not a date. He'd asked her out once. She'd said no. As irreverent as the man could be, he knew how to take no for an answer.

His dark-blue gaze dropped from her face to the front of the dove gray sheath dress she'd bought for the occasion. "You."

"Forget it." She tried to yank the door from his grasp, but the man had more muscle than any human being had a right to.

"For the flower toss," he continued, a smile tugging at the corners of his mouth. He had a nice mouth. Firm full lips with a tiny scar at the left corner.

She looked away. "You mean the bouquet toss?"

"Whatever it is the bride does. Tessa asked me to get you."

"Tell her I went home."

"But you didn't," he said reasonably, snagging her hand and tugging her out of the car. "You went to your car, and now you're going back inside to participate in the festivities."

From the way he said the last word, Charlotte got the distinct impression that Max was as excited about the reception as she was.

"Sorry," she said. "But I'm not. It's been a long day, and I'm ready to go home."

"And disappoint Tessa on her big day? Would you really do that to a friend?" His thumb ran across her wrist as he spoke. An unconscious gesture, Charlotte knew, but it reminded her of things she'd rather forget. Things that could get a woman into a world of trouble if she let them.

She pulled away, wiped her palm on her skirt. "She won't even know I'm missing."

"Then why'd she send me to find you?"

Good question.

She couldn't think of an answer.

No matter how hard she tried.

And, God knew, she was trying.

"Fine," she finally said. "If it means that much to Tessa, I'll go stand in the group of desperate single women and wait for the stupid flowers to be tossed."

"You sound bitter."

She ignored the comment as she walked back across the parking lot. She wasn't bitter, but at some point in her life, she was going to have to learn how to say no. Loudly and with feeling.

Unfortunately, sometime was not *this* time. For Tessa's sake, she was going to squeeze herself into the pack and pretend that she actually wanted to catch the bouquet.

She'd rather catch a basket of vipers.

But, that was just her.

She jogged up the porch stairs, the sound of piano music drifting from inside, the melody light and happy. Alex Riley, she'd bet. Tessa's nephew had a gift for music. After his parents' deaths the year before, he'd struggled to communicate, autism preventing him from connecting in typical ways. Music was his language, and he used it well. From the sound of the music, she'd say the wedding had made him happy.

She was glad, but she still didn't want to go back inside.

"You going to stand there all night?" Max asked, his breath ruffling the hair at her nape as he leaned past and opened the door. He nudged her forward, and half a dozen people swooped in. Martha was in the lead.

"There you are! Tessa is absolutely refusing to toss the bouquet without you. If we don't hurry, the food will get cold. Come on." She snagged her arm and dragged her toward the banquet room.

Tessa was there, resplendent in a vintage lace gown, her red hair pulled back, her face flushed with happiness. She saw Charlotte and smiled. "I see Max completed his mission."

"I never had any doubt that he would," Martha cooed, shooting the man in question what was probably supposed to be a beguiling smile.

"Thanks for your vote of confidence, Marti," Max drawled, giving her a once-over that would have made Charlotte blush.

Martha preened. "How about you thank me with a dance?" she asked. "First, though, the bouquet toss."

A cheer went up, dozens of happy women jockeying for position. Widows. Divorcees. Singles. Teens. Couples crowded around as Tessa positioned herself at the far end of the room, Cade a few feet away. He looked happy and content, his smile broad and relaxed. She wanted so much for this to work for

him and for Tessa. If she could have willed it to be
so, she would have, but all she could do was hope
and pray that they'd make a lifetime of beautiful
memories together.

Cade must have felt Charlotte's gaze. He glanced
her way and winked. She returned the gesture.

"No flirting with the groom," Max murmured near
her ear.

"I'm not—"

"Better get into place." He nudged her into the
crowd of women.

Tess glanced over her shoulder and looked straight
into Charlotte's eyes. Typical of the happily married,
she wanted all her friends to be happily in relationships, too.

Wasn't going to happen.

Ever.

Martha handed Tess a simple bouquet of white
roses wrapped with a hot pink ribbon. One white
feather peeked out from the flowers. Silky and soft
looking, it added a touch of whimsy to the tradi-
tional and suited the bride's taste perfectly.

"One," Tessa said, lifting the bouquet dramatically. "Two."

Charlotte braced herself.

"Three!"

Girls screamed with excitement. Women jumped
and clawed. Charlotte dodged, barely avoiding the
bouquet. It landed in the hands of town librarian
Daisy Forester. She held it up, squealing gleefully
while everyone around her cheered.

Something fluttered near Charlotte's face. No,
not fluttered. *Floated.* The feather, just drifting lazily

in the air. She grabbed it before it could drop to the ground, tucking it into her pocket as Daisy whirled around in circles, clutching the roses like they were a winning lottery ticket.

"There we have it!" Martha announced loudly. "The next Apple Valley bride."

People cheered and laughed, closing in around Daisy and patting her on the back like she'd done something more impressive than snatching a bunch of dying roses from the air.

Careful, Charlotte's better self said. *Your bitter is showing.*

Yep. It sure was.

Time to go.

She sidled to the left, scooted around Lesley Wagner and nearly collided with Rod Lancaster. Tall and lean with a runner's build and a too-confident smile, he taught math at Apple Valley High. "Charlotte!" he said warmly. "I was wondering when I'd see you."

Why? was what she wanted to say, but her mother had raised her with manners. "Hello, Rod. Enjoying the wedding?"

"Yes, and getting ideas for my own. Wink, wink."

"Daisy Forester just caught the bouquet. Maybe you should check in with her and see if she's available."

Rod laughed. "You've got a good sense of humor, Char. I like that in a woman."

"It's Charlotte." She hated being called Char for reasons that she preferred not to think about while she was at her good friends' wedding. "If you'll excuse me, I really need to get going."

"Before you go, I had a question for you."

"What's that?" *Please, don't let him ask me out. Please, please,* please *don't!*

"I thought it might be beneficial for some of my lower-level students to see how math can help them in the real world. Cooking seems like a good way to demonstrate that. I was thinking that we could borrow the home economics room—"

"We?"

"Sure. I don't know anything about cooking, but I know plenty about math."

Next thing Charlotte knew, Rod was explaining exactly what he knew in excruciating detail.

Maxwell Stanford wasn't sure what all the excitement was about. Sure Daisy had caught the bouquet, but he was pretty damn sure that didn't mean her long-time boyfriend was going to propose. From what Max had heard, Jerry Webber had been stringing Daisy along for five years, promising that he'd marry her as soon as he was making enough money to support them. In the meantime, he lived in Daisy's apartment, ate her food, and pretended to be writing the next bestselling murder mystery.

If a few white roses changed that, Max was going to have to reevaluate everything he knew about men.

And roses.

He waded through the throng of people and clapped Cade on the back. "You did good on this one, Cunningham. You and Tessa are going to have a lot of good years together."

"That's an awfully nice thing to say, Stanford. Are you going soft on me?" Cade asked with a cocky grin.

"Just throwing you a bone, since I'm still a better shot than you."

"I think I outmarked you the last three times we went to the gun range," Cade pointed out.

"Only because I didn't want to embarrass you. You're the sheriff, after all. It wouldn't look good for you to keep getting bested by one of your deputies."

"Bull sh—"

"Folks!" Martha Anderson's voice rose above the rumble of the crowd. "The buffet is open. We'll have dancing in the meeting hall in an hour. For now, let's all enjoy the wonderful meal provided by Apple Valley Fritters."

Max didn't have to be told twice. He was a good cop and a descent handyman, but he sucked at cooking. A free meal anywhere was always a good thing.

He hadn't even taken a step toward the buffet tables when Martha approached and dug her too-red and too-shiny nails into his bicep.

"Max," she purred. "How about we get our plates and find a quiet place to talk?"

Not in this lifetime.

Or the next.

He liked women. No. He *loved* them, but Martha had trouble written all over her. "I think I'll have to pass on that, Marti," he said.

She frowned. "You didn't bring a date, did you?"

"No." But, right about then, he was really wishing he had. *Hell hath no fury like a woman scorned.* His grandfather's favorite saying. One that Grandpa James had good reason to know was true. Max had learned a few lessons in that area himself. He had no intention of taking a refresher course.

"Then, what's the problem? You don't think I'm attractive?" She smoothed both hands down her shapely hips and smiled the kind of smile that said she knew that couldn't be the case.

"Your attractiveness has nothing to do with it. I'm just not interested." Short and to the point. That was the only way to deal with women like Martha.

"I bet I could make you change your mind," she purred, running her hand down his bicep.

He took a step away, nearly falling over Charlotte.

He grabbed her elbow, realizing a second too late that Rod Lancaster was holding on to her other arm and staring at her with the starry-eyed gaze of a man in love.

Were the two dating?

If so, he hadn't heard anything about it.

In a town the size of Apple Valley, he should have. Unless, they'd kept it secret. An interesting thought. Charlotte did tend to stay to herself, baking in the kitchen of the little cottage at the corner of Main and Wesley and selling whatever baked good she could to whomever she could.

Not the kind of life Max would have chosen, but he had to respect her for doing things her own way.

"Sorry," he said, holding on to her arm until she regained her balance. "I didn't mean to knock you over."

"You didn't. Much." She laughed lightly, extracting herself from Lancaster's hand in a practiced move that barely seemed to register with the high school teacher. "If you'll all excuse me, I have—"

"To get something to eat?" Max suggested, because she didn't seem any more eager to stick close to Lancaster than he was to be around Martha. "How about we go together?"

"I was planning to—"

"Don't make me beg, sweetheart. Not in front of strangers." He slid his arm around her waist and hurried her toward the buffet table.

"What are you doing?" she hissed, shoving his arm away.

"Just trying to keep you from announcing to my stalker that I'm going to be eating alone."

"Your stalker?"

"Martha. She's got a thing for me."

"She has a thing for any man with two legs, a car, and money."

"You forgot hair. She likes men with hair."

"Her ninety-year-old husband had hair?"

"A full head of glossy white curls," he said, even though he'd never met the man in question.

"Really?" She eyed him from beneath thick black lashes. She'd pulled her glossy brown hair into a high ponytail, and he could see the scar at her temple. He'd wondered a couple of times how she'd gotten it, but since she'd turned down his dinner offer, he hadn't thought it was any of his business.

"You never even met him, did you?" she accused, her dark eyes flashing with indignation and just a hint of humor.

"No, but telling you that I did distracted you long enough to get us into the buffet line."

"That doesn't mean I'm going to stay here."

He glanced at Martha. She was hanging on to Rod's arm and looking at him like he'd hung the moon and the stars just for her. "No need to. We've lost our shadows."

"Hopefully, they'll make each other very happy."

"I'm not sure anyone can do that for Martha." He nudged Charlotte forward, eyeing the food that stretched the length of three tables. Apple Valley Fritters Catering had done itself proud. "Looks good enough to eat," he said, but Charlotte had stepped out of line and was making her escape.

He couldn't say he blamed her.

If he weren't so hungry, he'd have done the same.